MEMORIES LIVE HERE

MEMORIES LIVE HERE

CHERL
BOOK 1

MARC SHEINBAUM

ROUGH
EDGES
PRESS

Memories Live Here
Paperback Edition
Copyright © 2024 (As Revised) Marc Sheinbaum

Rough Edges Press
An Imprint of Wolfpack Publishing
1707 E. Diana Street
Tampa, FL 33610

roughedgespress.com

Paperback ISBN 978-1-68549-414-8
eBook ISBN 978-1-68549-413-1

To Hildy, Noah, and Perri

It's never too late …

MEMORIES LIVE HERE

PROLOGUE

JOSH BRODSKY DROVE through the early morning mist, approaching the La Quinta Inn outside San Francisco International Airport. His brother Donny stood outside, gripping his rolling travel bag.

"Throw your gear in the back," Josh said.

On the drive to Menlo Park, the air was cool, but a row of perspiration formed on Josh's brow. Ten minutes after exiting Highway 101, the car turned down a long gravel driveway leading to a sprawling rustic home.

"Very nice, bro," Donny said. "This is more of what I'd expect from a Silicon Valley big shot. Really freaked me out thinking you were living in a trailer park."

"Let's go in," Josh said as he got out of the car and bounded up the porch steps. "Mom's diaries are inside." Diaries that Donny believed held the truth about how their father died over thirty years ago.

Donny removed his luggage from the trunk and limped up the stairs. He crossed into the living room, admired the surroundings, and said, "I didn't see you as the—"

Before he could finish, he felt a blow below the knees, and his feet slipped out from under him. A flurry of arms and legs pounced on his chest.

Josh shouted out instructions. "Hold him down!"

Donny fought back, swinging his arms wildly, when a second voice called out, "Stop hitting me, you mother-fucker!" The voice of their younger brother, Louie.

Josh and Louie pinned Donny to the ground, securing his legs with zip ties. Josh placed a large piece of duct tape over Donny's mouth. They dragged him to a back room, where the bed and furniture were pushed to one side. Miniature cameras were visible in each corner. A laptop and a speaker sat on a single table surrounded by three chairs.

"Listen to me, Donny," Josh said, after they lowered Donny onto a chair. "I need you to calm down. Every-thing's okay. We're just going to have a nice conversation here—"

Louie pushed his way in, shook his fist, and said, "Unless you want to delete your fuckin' ransomware right *now*!"

"Louie, that wasn't the plan!" Josh shouted.

Donny tried to speak but could only manage a series of muffled groans through the duct tape. Josh sat and flipped open the laptop and started typing. Suddenly, a humming sound came from the speakers, followed by a voice. A distinctive, elderly, female voice, with an unmis-takable Brooklyn accent.

"Hello, boys. It's good to see you all together," said the voice of their mother, who had died and been buried nine days earlier. "But why is Donny tied to that chair?"

CHAPTER ONE

ONE WEEK EARLIER—SUNDAY

"COFFEE, DR. BRODSKY?" Stacy asked, pressing the light switch in the subbasement office.

Josh rolled over on his cot and squinted at his young assistant.

"Sorry," she whispered as she turned the dimmer to the lowest setting. "But you asked me to wake you at seven sharp."

"It's okay, Stacy," he mumbled. "Coffee would be great."

She returned a minute later and placed a steaming mug on the small conference room table and quickly backed away, twisting her nose as if she smelled spoiled milk.

"How many days in a row have you slept in here this time?"

"I've lost track," he said, taking several quick slurps, the caffeine clearing his brain fog. "Is anyone here yet?"

"Dr. Brodsky, it's seven a.m." Stacy had one foot in the hallway.

"Naveen did say he'd have the team here early," Josh said.

"I know, but for Naveen, 'early' could be nine."

"No, no, no," Josh said, standing and making sure the blanket was covering him from the waist down. Naveen understood the gravity of the situation. He had promised Josh that he'd have the entire team at their workstations bright and early. But Stacy was right. His project leader did have his own definition of *early*.

"How many hours did you get last night?" she asked.

"I don't know. I left the team around two. They were still going at it."

"Maybe you should go home and get some real sleep," she said as she stared at his crumpled pants lying by the sofa. "Get a change of clothes. Take a good shower."

Josh picked up the slacks and glanced at his assistant standing in the doorway. Over 50,000 of his fellow employees at Sway Inc. had long ago migrated to fully digitized and robotic support systems, and the capability was finally being installed in his subbasement lab. While there was something quaint about working with the last of the human assistants, Josh was looking forward to the upgrade.

"You can turn that light up. I need to get to the lab."

Stacy dialed up the dimmer, which shed a light on the bare cinder block walls.

"I'll be outside if you need me."

"Just call down to the lab to see if Naveen is here," he shouted as he put on his pants and buckled his belt. "And come find me if Andre calls."

Josh expected the company CEO would burn the

place down if they didn't have a working prototype by the end of the day. He slipped on his loafers. Two more quick sips of coffee and he was out the door.

"Naveen just messaged me," Stacy said as Josh walked by. "He's at his workstation. He said he would have texted you but—"

"If I only kept my cell phone on. I know, I know," he said over his shoulder as he made his way down the hall. Enough about his phone. No matter how many times he explained it, he still took flak. When he entered these demanding periods, he needed to become completely immersed in the task at hand. That's why he slept in his subbasement office, stayed off the internet, and shut out all external distractions, including his cell phone. That's just how he rolled. If he was ever needed, they knew where to find him.

He opened the door and was relieved as he walked onto the observation deck above the lab. The clock on the wall read 7:18, but Naveen had kept his promise. The large room was alive with activity, a bevy of bright and modern workstations, organized in a way that made the room appear like a Ferris wheel lying on its side. Forty artificial intelligence engineers were divided into eight pods lining the circumference, with walkways forming spokes leading to Josh's central control station. Each five-person mini team worked on distinct modules, supposedly to drive team dynamics. But the real goal was to create an intense, competitive tension among the pods—part of the "S" way designed by Sway's CEO, Andre Olaf. There was no denying that in ten short years Andre had built the hardest-charging and fastest-growing tech company in Silicon Valley, specializing in everything from the Internet of Things (IoT) to autonomous passenger drones.

Josh could feel the nervous energy in the room. After countless delays and overruns, every technologist knew it was critical to get to the finish line this time. And now, on this late March Sunday morning, the team was on the cusp.

In the room adjacent to the lab, visible to all if they faced the giant wall-size window, was the center of their universe: hundreds of servers—wall to wall and stacked to the ceiling—enough processing power to crank out over one trillion calculations per second. "The Tower" was the brains of their artificial intelligence universe, physically and virtually separated from the rest of Andre's vast empire.

As Josh walked around the circumference of the lab, the room buzzed with conversations.

"Mr. President, can you repeat that?" asked an engineer in Pod 3.

A husky voice emanated from a speaker mounted on the workstation. "I said that we had no choice but to attack Mexico. They would have been a nuisance to Texas. We just should have been more forceful, taken them out with the first assault…"

Josh continued along, observing the five engineers huddled in the middle of Pod 4, some taking notes, others rapidly changing code during their interaction. He picked up the banter as an engineer listened to a voice booming from a nearby audio device.

"I'm saying that it was inconceivable that we stayed neutral. We should have been preparing for war, I tell you. Thrashed Germany before they had a chance to roll their forces across Europe…"

Josh shook his head. Despite the issues the teams were continually encountering, he was proud of their remarkable progress.

When he was hired earlier the previous year, Andre told him that he was looking for someone who could elevate the level of intensity on the team. And even though Josh had just turned fifty-five, his intensity was never in short supply. He'd been told on more than one occasion it was responsible for the permanent furrow in his brow. It was an intensity that he had developed over his entire life, especially during the twenty-five years he was rising through the ranks at the Department of Defense. Josh's pioneering work with artificial intelligence had created defense systems that recognized enemy attacks before morphing into counterattack mode in real time.

Josh initially struggled with the idea of leaving the DoD, of moving to the private sector and Silicon Valley after a lifetime of government work. But he was mesmerized by Andre's vision, along with the intellectual challenge of leading the most controversial project he could ever imagine.

"History books are worthless," Andre had said during their first recruiting dinner. "Nobody reads them anymore. Especially politicians. Countries and governments continue making the same mistakes. Over and over through the centuries. The same wars, the same stupidity. But what if our leaders could discuss today's challenges with the greatest minds in history. With Churchill. With Roosevelt! What if Lincoln was around to speak to Congress today? You don't think he could talk some sense into these lunatics in Washington? What if Churchill could have strategized with the administration that marched us into the Iraq War? How much would the country have saved in blood and treasure?"

Josh had met many political leaders in his years at the Department of Defense and he knew Andre was right.

Fewer and fewer had any sense of history. Most came out of business or law, or were career politicians, making decisions off sound bites and polling numbers. Very few were students of history or bothered to even read their briefs. Yet these were the men and women making life-and-death decisions.

"Re-creating the great historical figures," Andre had said, "with their vast knowledge and experiences, their thought processes, their personalities, their leadership, and organizational skills. Supercharged with inference engines to fill in what history never recorded. Imagine the possibilities. They could change our destructive pattern. Change the course of history!"

Josh knew from his work at Defense that artificial intelligence and machine learning had advanced exponentially over the past decade, as had the processing power of today's supercomputers, doubling in each of the past three years—a rate of progress seven times faster than that of any previous period. These advancements made it possible to run the complex algorithms and neural networks needed to churn through vast amounts of historical and contemporary data sources, prerequisites to achieving Andre's vision.

So he resigned from Defense, drove across the country, and took over the project, code-named CHERL—Computerized Human Experienced as Real Life. Josh had signed up to raise great historical leaders from the dead.

Now, as he made his way to his own workstation to wait for Naveen, Josh remained as consumed as ever by the prospect, but anxious about his own fate if they missed this latest deadline imposed by Andre. Not to mention the cost overruns, a trend he hadn't reversed since he assumed command. Andre's friendly and warm greetings from the previous year had recently taken on a menacing tone. And then there was the matter of his newly assigned boss, Jenna Turbak, who was always looking for ways to "help."

"Dr. Brodsky," Stacy said, appearing in front of his workstation, waving a piece of paper. "I'm sorry to bother you, but there were a bunch of messages I just picked up on the voice system. Your brother Louie has been trying to reach you. He says it's urgent."

And right behind Stacy, as if on cue, appeared Ms. Turbak.

"Josh!" Jenna called, her head down as if trying to pierce a gust of wind blowing from the hub.

He would call his brother back later.

CHAPTER
TWO

"WHAT CAN I GET YOU, HON?" asked the harried, middle-aged waitress. She flipped her pad and readied her pen. "I'll be right there!" she shouted in response to the elderly woman at the next table, who was lifting her coffee mug with one hand and pointing at it with the other, while chewing a mouthful of who knows what, but enough to render her mute. Luckily the staff didn't need a degree in sign language. They'd seen all methods of getting their attention here at the Manhattan Beach Diner in Brooklyn. A Mexican busboy rushed over and refilled the woman's cup to the brim.

"Let's seeeee," Donny said, squinting and flipping through the plastic-coated menu.

"Come on," Louie said. "The menu hasn't changed in forty years. You've been studying it for ten minutes—it's the same fuckin' food it's always been."

"Chill out," said Donny, smirking. "I can't decide."

"Youse guys need a few more minutes?" The waitress closed her pad and started to walk away.

Louie blurted, "No."

At the same time, Donny said, "Yep."

"Okay." Louie exhaled, his shoulders slumping as he sank into the green vinyl booth. The waitress ran off.

"What a throwback," Donny said. "A real waitress. And I haven't been to a restaurant without a tablet menu in years."

Louie tapped his spoon on the table. "Come on. Decide what you're having already."

Donny rested his head against the back of the booth. He glanced over the top of the tattered and sticky menu that rested on his ample midsection and asked, "Why are you so impatient?"

"Why. Are. We. Here?" Louie asked, not trying to disguise his agitation. "I hate this fucking place."

The smirk below Donny's trim mustache seemed now to be permanently affixed.

"But this is nostalgic," Donny said. He waved his hands around as if showing off a new car on a game show. "This was Mom's favorite diner. This was the high-class establishment we came to for all of our big life events. How could we not come here the day of Mom's funeral?"

His brother was right about that, Louie thought. This was the Brodsky family event hall. Birthday parties, graduation celebrations, Mother's Day, Father's Day. Mom and Dad had done a great job of keeping the rest of the culinary options in Brooklyn a big secret. Okay, truth be told, they did alternate with Moon Gate, the Chinese restaurant on Nostrand Avenue. Until Louie's mother realized that those headaches he'd always complain about after the moo goo gai pan were caused by monosodium glutamate poisoning. After that, the Manhattan Beach Diner it was. Now the smell of the place, the greasy food, the customers right out of central casting, all brought back those memories. Memories that Louie had spent thousands of dollars on therapy trying to forget.

"Youse guys ready?" The harried waitress was back.

"I'll have the tuna melt on whole grain toast, please," Louie said quickly. "And an iced tea, unsweetened."

"White, roll, or bagel, babe?"

"Roll is fine," said Louie, forgetting the lack of healthy choices in the old neighborhood. He was extremely conscious of his food intake, having been lectured by his wife, Vicki, from the first day of their marriage about the hazards of his addiction to pizza, beer, and greasy foods. His conversion to her healthy diet and three-day-a-week boot camp at the Manhattan Athletic Club kept him looking lean and younger than his forty-six years.

"Ahhh, let me see now," said Donny.

The waitress was snapping her gum, impatiently looking around at her other tables.

"Hamburger and fries for me," Donny finally said. "Well done. And lemme have a Miller Lite."

"Ya want cheese?" she asked.

"Sure."

"The deluxe?" she asked, just as a trayful of plates and glasses hit the floor from behind the counter. Neither the waitress nor the customers so much as flinched.

"He's paying—why not?" Donny said as he handed her his menu. He dipped his napkin deeply into a glass of water and wiped something sticky off his hands.

"When are you flying back?" Louie asked.

"Louie, trying to get rid of me already?"

"I don't care," said Louie, knowing his expression was failing to hide his lie. "Stay as long as you want, but what's to do here?"

"You kiddin'? We need to spend time together going

through Mom's estate," Donny said. "Figure out where everything is, get everything appraised."

The busboy brought Donny his beer on his way to clean up the broken plates and glasses behind the counter.

"You know," Donny said after taking a long swig. "How we gonna divide everything up. We may need to bring in a financial forensics team here."

Louie sat up straight in his seat, leaning toward his brother.

"Listen, wiseass," he said. "I spent a lot of time doing *forensics*." He added air quotes around forensics.

"I found her Dime Savings Bank account statement. When we split it up three ways, it means about thirty-two hundred for each of us. But we have to pay the funeral bills first, so don't count on that either. You can have her costume jewelry, if we can find where she hid her shoebox. Jessica just wants one of the cubic zirconia rings." Louie's twelve-year-old daughter had hinted that she thought it would bling up her Halloween witch costume.

"Thirty-two hundred bucks, huh?" Donny's smirk was gone. "Jeez, eighty-three years, and that's what's left."

"You're kidding, right?" Louie asked.

The waitress dropped off his iced tea and tossed a straw on the table.

"What do you think she was living on, her pension from the thirty odd jobs she kept getting herself fired from?"

Donny didn't answer. He sipped his beer, staring out the window at the fishing boats lining the pier across Emmons Avenue. Louie stared out too. It was sunny and cool, and the street was busy. An older couple, bundled up, arm in arm, bent into the unseasonably strong wind. A pack of giggling teenage girls flirted with a larger band of cigarette-smoking, buzz-cut boys on the promenade across the street. The group passed by the dozen or so piers and slips, with their ninety-foot vessels docked and displaying their spoils of battle on the open seas—row upon row of beautiful flounder. Shoppers and the curious crowded in to watch the expert filleting technique, which, Mom never failed to tell them, was handed down for generations.

Louie looked back at his brother.

"As soon as we're done, we should get started on her apartment," he said.

With or without Donny, Louie had to finish cleaning things out tonight so he could be at his office in the morning. The huge fee he was about to earn on the Virtual Bank deal would be his first real payday in over three years. Nothing would get in the way of his getting that agreement signed this week.

"Okay," Donny said as the waitress brought their food. Then, shaking his head, he said, "I still can't believe Josh didn't come to Mom's funeral."

CHAPTER
THREE

JOSH WATCHED Jenna coming and rubbed his eyes. Turbak—or Turbo, as she was known throughout the Sway complex—was a bulldog within the company. Andre had assured him that Jenna was "there to help," but to Josh, his new boss was just a pain in the ass. And he had been around long enough to know an implicit threat when he saw one. His team needed to deliver, or Turbak was ready to move in. To take over. He steadied himself as she approached his workstation.

"Hi, Jenna. What's up?" he mumbled.

"What's up? Exactly! What's up?" she spat out. "I thought you were sending me an email last night on status? It's almost seven thirty. Andre's gonna be all over me for an update. We've promised him a demo today."

"Sorry, it was late last night when we finished up."

She brightened. "Finished? Did you say finished?"

"No, no," Josh said. "I just meant it was late when we finished for the night. I'm waiting to get an update from Naveen."

Jenna stood back, crinkling her nose.

"You look like hell," she said.

He took a drink from his mug. The coffee was cold.

"Yeah, well. It was a late night," he said. "We ran into some complications."

"Complications?" Jenna's face and shoulders slumped in unison. "What kind of complications?"

Josh glanced at the engineers surrounding him, working feverishly with their respective teams.

"Pod 8 was working on the final testing of the inference engine," he said.

"I know, I know," she said. "You told me that was going on three days ago. I thought the test was going well."

Josh swiveled away from his screen and faced her. He noticed her foot tapping up and down rapidly, giving the impression that her whole body was about to launch up to the ceiling.

"It was," he said. "Until we added adjustments to the final two cognitive functions—the ones dealing with empathy and behavior. Each worked fine on its own, but not together."

"Okay, okay, okay." Her leg action was picking up. "Are they still testing it now?" she asked, motioning with her right hand toward the lower pods.

"We needed to give them back to Pods 6 and 8," Josh said. "Make further adjustments before we can retest."

Josh's workstation dinged with an instant message.

NAVEEN:
Getting strange output. When can we talk?

"How long?" Jenna asked, but Josh was distracted by Naveen's message and typed back his answer:

Thought you were coming here.

"Dr. Brodsky, I need to know how long!" Jenna said. "I have a meeting with Andre today at noon. He's expecting that demo."

Naveen texted back:

Meet me in rm 5.

Josh looked up at Jenna. He could see in her eyes a combination of frustration and insecurity. She was still learning how to flex her authority.

"I'll come find you after I meet with the team," Josh said, rubbing the eight-inch scar behind his right ear. "Give me an hour."

She straightened up, then slowly backed away.

"Text me in thirty minutes," she demanded, a slight quiver in her voice. "I need an ETA." After a several-second pause, she said, "Andre will not be happy if we miss another deadline." Before turning away, she added, "And have that assistant of yours order you some fresh clothes."

Josh watched Jenna storm from the hub toward the exit, thinking how absurd it was to have to answer to her. He hurried to the conference room to find Naveen, trying to shake off the unsettled feeling he always had after an encounter with Jenna. Naveen and his team were huddled around the conference table.

"What's the latest?" Josh asked.

"Hey, mon, what's going on?"

Naveen's cheerfulness surprised Josh, given the urgency and tone of his text. But then Josh remembered who he was dealing with.

"Naveen, you called me up here. You said you were getting strange results."

"I know, mon," said Naveen, grinning broadly. "But we saw the dragon lady coming for you. Had to get you away from her."

Josh exhaled, relieved but annoyed. "You scared the hell out of me. I thought we had another glitch."

"No, mon, just helping out my partner in crime. No way we'd leave you down there on your own."

Naveen Gupta was a practical joker with a Princeton-minted master's in computer science and machine learning. After graduate school, Naveen spent two years decompressing in Jamaica. He wore his hair in dreadlocks and spoke with an affect that made him sound like a Rastafarian after too many nights listening to Bob Marley, with a healthy dose of ganja by his bedside.

"What did Turbo Taxidermy want from you this time?" Naveen asked, while the six engineers banged away at their respective laptops. Two were biting their lips to suppress giggles. The team shared Naveen's passion for sophomoric behavior—dressing like slobs, engaging in spitball fights, and playing incessant practical jokes. Josh rarely appreciated the humor, but he did appreciate the intellect and, most of all, the loyalty. After only one year at Sway, Josh had no doubt that Naveen and team had his back.

"Cut it out, Naveen," Josh said. He motioned for Naveen to follow him into the hallway, out of earshot of the engineers. "Where are we?"

"We made some breakthroughs after you left last night, mon," Naveen said, his demeanor shifting into his professional mode. "I guess it was actually this morning, around two-thirty or three a.m. We're running tests now."

Josh put his hand on Naveen's shoulder. "You guys pulled an all-nighter again?"

"We're all under the gun," Naveen said, still smiling.

Throughout Josh's career, he made it a point to shelter his teams from any pressure from the senior ranks. It was his job to take the flak. But rumors were everywhere that Andre's patience was running thin. If Naveen's team didn't deliver soon, they could all be working directly for Turbak.

"Thanks, Naveen," Josh said.

"Thank me after we've got it right, mon. The empathy engine is humming, but we still need to dial down her aggression."

"Just don't dial it down too much," Josh said. "CHERL won't be much use to anyone that way either."

"We got it, mon. I should have something by the end of the day. Can you hold off the Turbo lady?"

"Don't worry about her. She just wants to keep Andre up to date, so I'll tell her where we are. Maybe she can help us put him off until Wednesday." What's another couple of days? Josh thought. They were so close.

Naveen smiled. "Just be careful, mon. I don't want to be stuck working for her."

"Well, then, I guess you better go in there and get me a convincing prototype." Josh gently squeezed Naveen on the shoulder and took off to find Jenna.

CHAPTER
FOUR

THEIR MOTHER HAD BEEN GONE for two days, but Donny could smell the residue of Marlboro smoke that hung in the air of their family apartment as if she had just lit up this morning. The yellow-green carpet, a thick shag when she had it installed twenty years ago, was matted down, especially on the well-worn path from the flower-print sofa to the kitchen. With its peeling linoleum floor, the kitchen had just enough space to fit the fridge, stove, and sink. Their father had removed a cabinet to fit the GE dishwasher of Mom's dreams, so her pots and pans were relegated to the hallway coat closet. This was the two-bedroom, one-bathroom, 900-square-foot theater where the Brodsky family drama played out. The home was quiet now, but it wasn't at peace.

Donny opened a box of black garbage bags. "You want to do this together, or should we divide and conquer?" he asked.

"Let's do it together," Louie said. "Shouldn't take us too long."

They entered their mother's bedroom, which had an

even stronger cigarette aroma. Here was the same bed and bedroom set she had shared with their father for the twenty years of their marriage, and the place she slept alone for the thirty-three years since he'd been gone. The few pieces of artwork on the wall were paintings done by her friend Maggie—scenes of flowers, fruit bowls, and sailboats. Their mother had loved Maggie, whom she'd known from her childhood growing up on the Lower East Side. It wasn't anything you couldn't find coming out of a basic high school art class. But no matter—anything Maggie did was a masterpiece in their mother's eyes.

"Seriously, what should we do with this furniture?" Donny asked as he opened the bottom dresser drawer. He flinched at the sight of her familiar shirts and sweaters.

"I already asked the super if he knows anyone who wants it," Louie said, packing slacks and dresses from the bedroom closet. "He said he knows a lady in building two that could use the sofa. I told him to just take everything out of here for us and he could give it all to anyone he wants."

Donny looked up and paused, holding an armful of sweaters, which still held a strong odor from their mother's stale perfume. "What do you mean, *give*? Why'd you do that? This stuff's gotta be worth something."

Louie dropped the bag and turned toward him.

"Who's going to work on that—*you*? You posting a letter on the bulletin board downstairs? You gonna handle all the calls? How about Josh? No, probably not, right? If he couldn't get his ass to Mom's funeral, I don't think he'll be posting this stuff online in his spare time. And I don't have time to do it either. I'm telling you, it's old and it'll cost us more to get it out of here than it's worth."

Donny shook his head and used a twist tie to close the

first garbage bag of clothing. It was easy for his big-shot younger brother to walk away from making some money; a few hundred was pocket change to an investment banker. He had to be rolling in dough, Donny thought. He guessed it would be easy for Louie to lend him the money he needed. No big deal to a master of the universe. But Donny would save that conversation for later. Even so, he wasn't walking away from a few bucks for the furniture. He went to the bedroom window and gazed out into the parking lot.

"I just think we should see what we could get," Donny said. "I'll go down and see the super. I'll offer him twenty percent of anything that sells. I know it doesn't mean much to you, bro, but I could sure use the extra cash."

"Suit yourself," Louie said as he resumed emptying their mother's clothing from the dresser drawers. "But let's finish this first."

Donny grabbed a fresh garbage bag and opened the small drawer on the nightstand next to their mother's bed. After throwing out the clutter from the top section—half-empty packs of Marlboros, two cigarette lighters, a few old *Cosmopolitan* magazines, a leaking Bic pen—he discovered a deep pile of old photographs. Dozens and dozens of faded snapshots. Almost all the photos were of him and his brothers when they were boys.

"Check this out."

Louie tied the bag and tossed it into the corner. He sat on the edge of the bed next to his brother.

"Holy shit," Louie said. "Look at all this."

They sifted through the piles. Shots of Donny and Louie running in the park, riding bikes. Of their older brother, Josh, in cap and gown at his MIT graduation. Another of Louie in his crew cut, a wide grin revealing missing incisors, a small trout dangling from the end of a fishing line.

"I remember that fish," Louie said. "My first one."

A few shots of the three of them standing next to each other, expressionless, like they were waiting to be identified in a police lineup, Josh and Donny always towering over Louie. Poses in front of the apartment building, in front of their father's old lime-green Buick. Donny stopped and stared at one taken on the apartment terrace. He turned the photo over and read the writing on the back: "Josh, twelve. Donny, nine. Louie, three."

"Forty-three years ago," Donny said, handing the picture to Louie.

Louie let out a slight laugh and said, "Man, we were a motley crew."

Donny picked out another picture of himself. He was in his high school football uniform, big and broad shoul-dered, standing with his father, who had one arm around his son. His father held a football, his expression filled with pride. Donny glanced down at his ever-expanding midsection. Nobody who saw him today would connect him with the athletic figure who filled out the uniform in this photo. Standing next to the father who nurtured his natural talent from the time Donny could hold a ball. Showing him how to hit a baseball, how to dribble and shoot a basketball, and how to throw the perfect spiral even when his hands were too small to grip a football.

By age ten, Donny's skills and ability were far above his peers'. While all the neighborhood kids fancied them-selves ballplayers, imitating their favorite sports heroes, regaling the crowd in the play-by-play during their exploits, Donny stood alone. Football eventually became his favorite sport, but when he was young, he played them all. For Donny, the playground and the ball field were his escape from the chaos in the apartment. The constant fighting. His mother yelling and screaming. It would get so loud the neighbors would bang on the walls. He tuned it out as best as he could. And the football field became his sanctuary. His arm was strong and accurate, and by his junior year of high school, he was the star quarterback of the varsity team. He and his father both dreamed of a college scholarship. Maybe even turning professional.

But the summer after his junior year, the world as he knew it came crashing down. Donny blew out his knee sliding into second base during a baseball game, requiring career-ending surgery. His father had spent time with Donny in the recovery room, both of them crying, consoling each other over what could have been.

And it was the last time Donny saw his father alive.

"Let's keep going," Donny said. He stuffed the picture into his back pocket and grabbed another garbage bag. "I wanna catch that flight tonight."

Louie's phone rang. He lifted it from his pocket, glanced at the caller ID, and answered.

"What the fuck, Josh? Where have you been?"

CHAPTER
FIVE

JOSH HAD NEVER WORKED for anyone twenty years his junior, had had only one female boss in all his years at Defense, and had never worked for anyone who had ADD or sprinkled speed on her morning granola. High-energy and high-strung, Jenna Turbak raced around the office wearing the company uniform for young female executives—black skinny jeans, simple blouse, black rectangle glasses, and flats. Josh had absolutely no idea what Executive Director Turbak really did for a living other than asking for updates. A fairly simple job that shouldn't require a degree from Caltech. But if nothing else, he needed to buy Naveen the rest of the day. So he spent the better part of two hours walking her through the work plan and status of each workstream. Especially that of Pod 8, which dealt with empathy and aggression.

"We're close, Jenna," he said, "very close. To be safe, if we could have until Tuesday, I think we'll have a great prototype. We both need to be careful not to show anything to Andre before we've nailed the inference engine down."

"I'll do what I can," she said. "We could always do a demo for him and avoid parts using the inference engine."

Not very feasible, Josh thought. How would they limit Andre's questions and interactions? CHERL's whole purpose was to insert the greatest political and military minds from the past into today's volatile world, to infer their thoughts and actions.

"It would be better if you could buy us one more day," Josh said.

"I'll let you know what he says."

Josh left Jenna's workspace on the executive floor, uncertain if his candor was a bonehead move. In her three weeks on the job, Turbak had done little to help. When she stuck her head in his team meetings, her only contribution was creating a distraction, not just with her naive questions, but also with the fact of being young and attractive in a room full of sequestered and overworked male engineers. At the very least, he figured, she should be able to manage the company CEO.

Stacy was waiting for him when he returned to his workstation.

"You called your brother, didn't you?" she asked. "He said it was urgent."

"Forgot all about it."

Stacy looked at him disapprovingly.

"Okay, okay. I'll call him now." He sat at his workstation, put on his headset, and dialed Louie. His brother answered before the first ring.

"What the fuck, Josh?" Louie said. "Where have you been?"

"What's up, Louie?" Josh asked.

"What's up?" Louie said. "You ignore my messages for four days!"

"Calm down," Josh said, swiveling his chair around to avoid being overheard, but the engineers were on all sides. "I didn't ignore you. I didn't even know you were trying to reach me."

"I left you tons of messages. Tried your home, your cell."

"I haven't been home," Josh said, cupping his hand over the mouthpiece. "And my cell—"

"Let me guess. You went off the grid again for some fucking work thing. For four fucking days? That's long even for you."

If Josh had known his brother was calling to give him hell, he would have made the call from one of the conference rooms. But, for now, he just wanted him off the phone.

"What is it, Louie? I have a lot going on at work."

"I do too," Louie snapped. "I'm busy too. Somehow I still manage to stay connected to the real world, especially when I have an eighty-three-year-old mother. Or at least *had* one."

"What?" Josh said, loud enough that several engineers looked up.

"Mom's gone," Louie said, calmly.

"When?" Josh suddenly felt light-headed. He leaned forward, his head below the workstation. "What happened?"

"They said it was a heart attack. She went in her sleep."

"I can't believe it," Josh said. "She was healthy as an ox!"

"She was eighty-three, Josh. She smoked like a chimney. It shouldn't be that shocking. When was the last time you saw her?"

"I don't know," Josh said, trying to recall the last time he had been in New York. He thought he'd spoken to her two weeks back. Maybe it was three.

"Well, that's it," Louie said. "It's too late now. She's gone."

Josh took a long deep breath and slowly exhaled, trying to regain his focus. But his mind was a jumble of thoughts. He had intended to visit her the next time he was back east. Intended to finally clear the air. He had always wanted to, but it was never the right time.

"You there?" Louie asked.

"Yeah, I'm here," he said, struggling with what to say. "I…I didn't even know she was sick."

"She wasn't," Louie said. "Not that she told me. Like I said, she just didn't wake up."

Okay, she passed on her own, Josh told himself. He didn't miss any deathbed vigils. No need to feel guilty about not being by her side. He lifted his head and sat up. The sight of the engineers surrounding him snapped his mind back. It was always the work that helped him regain control. Numb the emotions. Focus on the work—a skill he had learned and perfected as far back as grade school.

"Louie, I—" Josh said.

"You missed the funeral," Louie said. "We couldn't wait to hear from you. Buried her this morning. And she didn't want a shiva. She made it very clear in her will. Her lawyer highlighted that part in bold. She probably didn't think anyone would come."

Josh exhaled again, relieved that he wouldn't have to fly east, but trying to suppress the bile he felt coursing up from his stomach.

"Where's Donny?" he asked.

"Right here," Louie said. "Here, Donny, talk to—"

"Wait. Not now—"

"Hey Josh, where the hell have you been?" Donny asked.

"It's a long story. I'm sorry I wasn't there."

"Yeah, well, probably never knew what hit her."

Josh and Donny were both silent for a few seconds.

"Funeral was this morning," Donny said. "You missed Mom's funeral."

Josh pinched the bridge of his nose, taking more deep breaths, starting to feel somewhat relieved that he hadn't known what was happening. He couldn't have managed to be in New York with everything going on out here.

"Which cemetery?" was all Josh could ask.

"Where else?" Donny said. "Next to Dad."

Too bad for Mom, Josh thought, running his fingers behind his ear.

"He was expecting her," Donny said. "Double head-stone and an empty plot next door. Plenty of room."

Josh glanced at the clock hanging over the entryway. It was almost noon. He wondered how Naveen was doing.

"Listen," Josh said, "I really have to go. If there's anything else I can do…"

"Anything you can do?" Donny said. "Er, well, I thought you'd be here. I wanted to ask you in person. I have a bit of a favor. But can I call you later?"

"Things are really…"

Josh heard a commotion on the line and then Louie's voice.

"You want to know what you can do?" Louie asked. "I have an idea. Mom's buried. That's all done. But we're here in her apartment, clearing everything out. Donny's flying home tonight, and I have to get to work too.

Maybe it'd be nice if you came to New York and finished this up. You know. Help us out a little bit. What do you think about that?"

Stacy was back in front of his desk. Josh covered the mouthpiece and whispered to her, "What now?"

"Andre wants you to call him," she said. "Right away."

Josh removed his hand.

"I can't get there now," Josh said to Louie. "I'm really sorry. I screwed up."

"Fuck you."

"I'll come to New York as soon as I can. I promise I'll make it up to you. But I gotta go. I'll call you later."

"Wait, you motherf—"

Josh hung up and motioned to Stacy to connect him with Andre.

"Hello?" Josh said.

"Identify yourself, please," said an automated, genderless voice.

"Josh Brodsky," he said.

A moment later, he heard the unmistakable high-pitched voice of the CEO.

"Brodsky?"

"Hi, Andre," Josh said. "How are you?"

"How we doing down there?"

"We're making good progress," Josh said, shifting in his chair. "Didn't Jenna speak with you?"

"She did. But I'm not around Tuesday," Andre said. "I have to be in LA. I want to see CHERL in action first thing tomorrow."

"But Andre—"

"I know you're still having issues. I want to see for myself."

They had run out of time.

"I understand, Andre. Naveen should be ready by then."

"Fine," Andre said. "I'll have Jenna join us. And Brodsky…"

"Yes, sir?"

"Load up someone big. I want to see what she can do."

The line went dead.

"Shit," Josh muttered.

CHAPTER
SIX

TRAFFIC WAS HORRENDOUS. Louie's head was throbbing as he snaked his BMW along the Belt Parkway, heading back to Brooklyn to finish up at his mother's apartment. He had wasted a half hour looping around JFK, first crawling along to Terminal 4, before Donny belatedly realized that his Delta flight departed from Terminal 2. After two hours of bottlenecks on the road, Louie regretted not putting his brother in one of the new air taxis that flew from Coney Island in under ten minutes. But Louie hoped the drive would give them time to clear the air. They rode with their respective windows down to take in the breeze, as if trying to strip away the layers of tension created over the past few days. Today was considerably warmer and less windy than the past week, and the thaw was obvious as the piles of emission-stained snow dampened the pavement on the side roads along the Parkway. But there was no thaw in the mood that had descended upon the car. There was little conversation along the way.

Their curbside goodbye at Terminal 2 was quick, the customary man hug, a double pat on the back.

"Safe flight." Louie waved as Donny pulled his roller bag toward the terminal.

Donny turned and said, "Take care, Louie. Say hi to Vicki and Jessica."

Louie stood for a few moments, watching his brother favor his bad leg as he dragged his oversize bag through the revolving doors and out of sight. A horn blared, startling Louie, and he turned quickly, accidentally banging his knee against the car bumper.

"Hey, buddy!" screamed an approaching airport traffic cop. "Let's move it outta here, come on!"

Louie limped into his car and drove to a side street just outside the airport terminal and double-parked. He removed his phone and opened the ClubTrack app, checking the results of the fifth race at Sam Houston Race Park. Lucky Strikes, his latest big wager, finished seventh, way out of the money. Another ten grand drained from his home equity credit line. Fuck it. He'd try to recoup his losses as soon as he got back to his mother's apartment, before the later races got underway at Santa Anita. This losing streak had to end soon.

He drove back to Brooklyn, keeping the windows up and the radio off, trying to cope with the dizzying emotions of the past few days. His mom's death and funeral. The no-show by Josh. The day spent in his dusty childhood apartment going through their mother's possessions. The track losses were already buried in the recesses of his mind. But looking at the Band-Aids on his bloody fingers atop the steering wheel, his mind kept replaying the argument he'd had with Donny as they were clearing out the apartment.

"Amazing she never left this place," Donny had said

while stuffing socks and shirts into one of the last bags being prepared for drop-off at the local Goodwill.

"She never wanted to, right?" Louie said as he applied twist ties to each of the black garbage bags. "She always said this was home. She was comfortable here. Just wanted to do her thing."

"I mean, she did talk about getting out of here," Donny said. "A few times, at least."

"That was years ago, before Dad…"

"You mean, before the accident," Donny said, his fingers indicating air quotes as he said the word *accident*.

"You're never letting go of that, are you?" Louie asked, sitting back against the bedroom wall, wrapping his arms around his legs.

Donny got up and grabbed some more sweaters. "She told us what she wanted us to believe," he said. "It never made sense."

"It was an accident."

"All I know is, one minute Dad's with me in the hospital. We're both crying about my knee. About my career—"

"I know what happened, Donny."

But Donny paced the room, clutching a sweater in each hand. Nothing Louie said could stop his brother from reciting his recollections, just as he'd done a thousand times over the past thirty-five years.

"Next thing I know," Donny continues, "the doctor asks to speak with him. In private. When Dad comes back, I can tell he's upset. He was completely white. I assume they told him more bad news about me, but he says he needed to step out. That he would be right back."

"Donny, you—"

"He said he'd be right back, Louie!"

"I know, Donny. I've heard this—"

"Two hours later, Mom comes to the hospital to tell me he's dead."

Louie stands and starts emptying another set of drawers when Donny turns on him. "You and Josh always accepted her bullshit story about a blue Chevy swerving into her lane."

"Because the cops said that's what happened."

Donny shoved the sweaters into a garbage bag and pulled another drawer open so hard it slid off the tracks and fell to the floor, underwear and socks pouring out. He bent over and tossed the drawer against the wall.

"Then why weren't there any witnesses that saw a blue Chevy?" Donny asked. "Why did the one witness say that he watched her car suddenly accelerate and smash the passenger side into that lamppost?"

"Come on, Donny. Your witness was a street bum. Cops said it was an accident."

Donny kneeled down, gathered the loose socks, and said, "Why was Dad in that car with her, Louie? What was so urgent that he had to leave the hospital with Mom?"

"What's the difference?"

"Come on, we just found out my football career was finished. I know you can't imagine how that felt, Louie, but trust me, Dad was as upset as I was. He wouldn't have left me like that. He said he'd be right back."

Donny tied another bag closed and mumbled, "And nobody saw a blue Chevy either."

Louie shook his head. Thirty-five years had passed since their father's death. Louie was only eleven at the time—but he remembered when the director pulled him from swim instruction at Brighton Beach day camp. Then his mother came. Louie never had any reason to question her explanation. Everyone accepted that it was nothing more than a tragic car crash. Everyone except Donny.

As they worked in silence, the room took on a growing echo from the opening and closing of each drawer, and from the sound of a basketball pounding on the blacktop in the park outside. Empty plastic garbage bags snapped open as full ones were thrown into a pile against the wall.

After another hour, Donny finally spoke, asking, "So why didn't you help her more?"

"What?"

"I was just saying, if she wanted to move, you could've helped her. With the money, I mean."

"We're back to that?" Louie asked. "Didn't we just say that she didn't want to move?"

Donny stood up and put his palms up. "I didn't mean nothing," he said. "I'm just saying. You have the money. If she told you she wanted to move, you would've helped her."

Louie stood and dropped the garbage bag. "What are you getting at?"

"Nothing," Donny said. "I just mean if one of us needed something, you'd try to be there. That's all I'm saying. If Mom really wanted to move out of here, you would have helped her. If me or Josh needed anything, you'd help us too, right?"

"Don't play fuckin' games with me."

"I'm not playing games, Louie."

"Mom never asked me to move her out of here," Louie said.

"I didn't say she did."

"She never asked anything from any of us," Louie said. "She never asked for any money from me."

"Louie, calm down," Donny said, walking to the

window and staring down at the parking lot. "I'm just saying, if one of us needed money, you'd be there for us. Wouldn't you?"

That's where this is going, Louie thought. His brother was maneuvering back to the topic of money. That explained the fixation on the size of their mother's bank account, and her worthless furniture. Let's get this over with, he thought, approaching Donny at the window.

"What do you need this time?" Louie asked.

Donny looked down, shuffling his feet.

"That's it, right?" Louie asked, leaning against the wall. "You need money again?"

Donny's head stayed down, but his eyes looked up. "I have a chance to start a new business."

"Again?" Louie shouted.

Donny moved toward his younger brother with a pleading look and his arms extended. "This time will be different, man. It can't miss."

Louie snickered and shook his head. "Just like the last time?"

"That wasn't my fault," Donny said. "Those franchise guys stole my money too."

Louie wanted to laugh but held it in. Donny was either incompetent or a thief, given how quickly the plumbing supply company he'd bought went out of business, taking Louie's and several other people's money down with him. Not to mention the dance studio fiasco. And of course, it was never Donny's fault. Always someone else to blame. How could Donny be so stupid to think Louie would invest again? How could he be so stupid to give up his steady work as a programmer? But that was his brother. Never could stay focused on any one thing. Against his better judgment, Louie asked how much Donny wanted to throw in a sinkhole this time.

"Not much," Donny said. "A hundred, maybe a hundred fifty grand."

A few years back, Louie wouldn't have blinked at that number, even if he knew he'd never see the money again once it went into Donny's pockets. But until Louie could look at his own bank account and see something other than zeros, he would need to blow Donny off.

"You're out of your fuckin' mind," Louie said, turning away. "Stick with the programming jobs."

"What's the big deal?" Donny asked, shaking his head. "That's chump change for you. I'll pay it back to you, with interest."

"Just like you paid me back from the last failed business. And how about the one before that?"

"It'll be different this time. It's all new tech. All artificial intelligence."

"What the fuck do you know about AI?"

"I have a partner—"

"Great," Louie said. "At least this time you won't have yourself to blame when you fuck it up!"

As soon as the words left his mouth, Louie wished he could have pulled them back. But what else could he do? Tell Donny he didn't have the money? That he hadn't earned any real money in over three years, and between his wife's spending and his own penchant for gambling on the horses, he had burned through their life savings? Donny would never believe him. But Louie knew it was too late to fix when he looked up to see Donny's eyes narrow and his expression grow darker as he came closer to Louie.

"So that's what you think of your brother, huh?" Donny asked. "You think I'm a fuckup?"

Louie didn't respond, busying himself with packing, but he could feel Donny standing over him. Looking up, he saw Donny point at him and say, "Well, at least I didn't sell my soul to line my pockets!"

Louie got up and stood face-to-face with his brother, feeling rage rising within him.

"That's what you call it?" he snapped. "You think I sold my soul? That's what being successful is to you? Let me tell you—it's called doing what you need to do."

"Anything for the mighty buck."

"Oh, and you think you're above it all?" Louie said, his voice rising, the blood rushing to his temples. "Then don't come to me looking for handouts if you don't like it."

They heard banging on the walls, coming from the apartment next door.

"Hey, keep it down in there!" came the muffled plea from behind the notoriously thin wall.

"I had to fight my way through plenty," Louie whispered, seething through clenched teeth. "Plenty of times it could have been all over for me."

"I know," whispered Donny with a sarcastic smirk. "You did what you had to do. You always did what needed to be done. At least when it came to work. You and Josh. It's all about the work."

"That's right, that's right, it is," Louie said, sticking his finger into Donny's chest. "You do the work, you get paid. I know it sounds complicated, but it's really an easy concept. Trust me. I'm told that all the time. No deals, no payday. They don't care how hard I work. I have to deliver. It's the only way money flows into my bank account. Unless I have a big day at the…"

Louie stopped himself, not wanting to give Donny any more ammunition.

"A big day at the what?" Donny asked.

"Nothing," Louie said as he turned back toward the closet and grabbed more blouses.

"Problems?"

"No, fuck it," Louie said. "And fuck you too."

Louie bent down, grabbing a handful of twist ties. He lifted the bag to shift the clothing to the bottom, stirring a large plume of dust into the air. Finish the job here and get the hell out of this place, he thought. And away from this asshole. He started cinching the top of the last bag.

"You agree with me," Donny muttered.

"Excuse me?"

"About Dad. About what Mom did. That's why you didn't help her more."

Louie could feel the anger coursing through him, not wanting to react again to Donny's verbal flailing. He kept his head down, tying up the last three garbage bags. As he finished the last one, he sensed his brother standing over him.

"You better wash those hands off, Louie."

Louie looked up and saw that Donny was staring at the garbage bag, wincing. Louie followed Donny's eyes down to his own hands as he continued twisting the ties, over and over. The metal edges of the ties had dug into his fingers, causing them to bleed.

CHAPTER
SEVEN

A RIDE SHARE service picked Donny up in front of Terminal 2 at O'Hare, dropping him thirty minutes later in front of his second-story walk-up in the Wrigleyville section of Chicago. The midnight streets were quiet. As he slowly climbed the two flights, dragging his bag and bad leg up to his one-bedroom apartment, he had almost put Louie out of his mind. Before unpacking, he sat in front of his computer and sent out some nasty messages to the star players on the Bulls. Donny had watched the entire game on the flight from JFK. His team had blown another last-minute lead.

"Unconscionable!" he started one post on the social media site of the Bulls' star player. "You really should just retire," began another. "Everyone can see you suck!"

Finally, to the power forward, "Your four-year-old daughter has a bigger set of balls than you!" The player hadn't fought hard enough for a crucial rebound.

Donny took a deep breath and leaned back, feeling refreshed for the first time in days. It wasn't too late to sign in to OneNiteFrenz and arrange a rendezvous with some lonely heart. He decided to take a quick shower first, since the last time, his date showed up faster than the pizza delivery guy.

It pleased him that he could send these missives and arrange his social life, all from the sanctuary of his apartment, his home since the breakup of his second marriage several years ago. He'd originally lived in Wrigleyville back in the eighties when he worked as a computer programmer for a hotel chain. The neighborhood hadn't changed much over the years. Row houses and low-rise apartment buildings, none taller than six stories, defined the neighborhood. The occasional McMansion had sprung up, crammed into tenth-of-an-acre lots. Moving close to Wrigley Field after his second marriage disintegrated added a measure of comfort. Maybe had he and Angela moved here instead of the suburbs of Arlington Heights, things would have worked out differently. But she insisted on living in the neighborhood where she had grown up, close to her mother and childhood friends. Donny hated the suburbs. Mostly, he hated the seventy-minute commute on the crappy trains to his downtown job.

Angela convinced him to quit and buy a business close to home. So he sank his life savings, plus $50,000 he borrowed from Louie, into buying a plumbing supply franchise in nearby Rolling Meadows.

He loved everything about it, at least at first. The shop was ten minutes from home. He didn't have to answer to any dickhead bosses. But the reality of running a business on his own hit him harder than a middle linebacker. The hours were brutal, as was the grind of finding qualified people who were willing to put in a full day of work.

Then the financial pressure started. The cash short-falls, the inability to meet payroll, insurance, and rising lease costs, not to mention the franchise fees—eventually, it all wore him out and did nothing for his marriage. Subconsciously, he probably thought managing his own business would help save what was already a cratering situation at home, but that didn't lessen the shock when he came home unexpectedly one midafternoon to find Angela in bed with the Andersen Windows sales rep. At least he finally understood why she'd insisted on upgrading their perfectly fine windows.

He and Angela divorced. She moved in with Mr. Andersen and didn't really fight Donny for alimony. She knew the well was dry. Donny sold the plumbing shop six months later for a fraction of what he'd paid going in, gave Angela $10,000 in a onetime settlement, and moved back to Wrigleyville.

He bought a new computer, dusted off his program-ming manuals, and set up a consulting business, calling it Wildcat Associates, of which he would be the only associate. None of his clients seemed to care that he worked out of his apartment. They'd email him a project, organize conference calls to discuss its status, provide secure access from his home laptop, and away he'd go. He sat at his desk, working mostly in his underwear, at least until late fall, when the frosty Chicago days would kick into gear. Shaving wasn't necessary, except every now and then for the occasional videoconference. Enough days passed between events that his stubble quickly turned mangy, but his clients were none the wiser.

The isolation that came with coding in his bedroom didn't bother him at all. He did his best work when he was on his own. And besides, he had the companionship of the entire World Wide Web at his fingertips.

He appreciated the diversion, especially when it was too cold for his midday walk to the luncheonette on Dearborn Street. He spent hours checking box scores, the latest headlines from DC, or the gossip columns. He was particularly fond of the "Where are they now?" and "What they look like—then and now" features. Those were the first sites he started trolling. It was innocent enough at first, posting messages to movie stars' social media videos, like "What did you do to yourself?" and "Get a life," all using the anonymous name Foul Baller. He knew enough about disguising IP addresses that no one ever traced these missives back to him, his confidence in his anonymity making him bolder. Over time, his posts took on a considerably darker edge.

"You low-life piece of shit," he posted to the mayor's social media account, for no particular reason, other than he didn't like the tone the mayor had struck at a benign news conference.

"Get the hell off the show, you fat pig, you no-talented perv," he posted to a late-night talk show host who performed a sketch Donny found irritating.

As the months moved on, Donny found himself spending less and less time going out and more and more time surfing the web, posting snarky comments, and enjoying no-commitment encounters. Who needed a social life when you had social media and an endless supply of willing females who shared a similar perspective on needless dating rituals? He was perfectly content to hang out in the comfort of his apartment. In his underwear. His two divorces were expensive lessons he was not eager to repeat.

So why was he nervous to tell Ana he didn't have the money to invest in her business?

Louie had shut him down, but he would reach out to Josh in the morning. For now, the buzzer told him he had a guest waiting for him at the front door.

CHAPTER
EIGHT

MONDAY

JOSH CONVENED his team in the conference room next to the subbasement lab. Standing by the doorway, he could feel the tension rise when Andre entered, with Jenna a few steps behind. Naveen sat looking nervous, his eyes darting everywhere except in Andre's direction.

"I hear you have something to show me," Andre said, positioning himself at the head of the table.

Josh and Jenna took seats on opposite sides of Andre. In the center of the table rested a large device that looked like a speaker. A laptop sat open on the far end. Josh's eight team leaders stood in the back, leaning against the cinder block wall, ignoring the dozen empty chairs.

Jenna walked to a large whiteboard, grabbed a green marker, and held it out in Naveen's direction. "Before we start the demo, let's show Andre the basic structure of CHERL—how she's designed and the tools we used to build her."

Josh could see that Naveen was hesitant. They both knew that CHERL would perform well if they could limit the system to a demonstration of historical recitations. They were less certain of the inference engine. And as confident an engineer as Naveen was, he hated presentations, especially in front of senior management. Josh also worried about Jenna's penchant for trying to exert her authority, anything to demonstrate to Andre that she was in charge. Josh would need to help Naveen navigate through some choppy waters.

"It's okay, Naveen," Josh said. "Take Andre through the design elements."

Naveen walked slowly to the whiteboard and took the marker from Jenna's hand. He began drawing a series of circles, eight large ones surrounding a smaller one in the center. He wrote the word *interconnectivity* in the central circle. Within each of the outer circles, he placed a component name: emotional expression, language processing, social behavior, organization, attention span, imagination and creativity, reasoning, and knowledge and memory.

"Naveen is drawing the various processes of the human mind," Josh said as Naveen completed the last circle.

"Um, yes," Naveen started. "Yes, that's true. Each of these processes has its own set of neural networks. Massive neural networks, actually."

Josh was relieved that Naveen had only a slight remnant of his Rasta dialect. He prodded Naveen forward, saying, "We built them within CHERL using something called deep learning. It creates——"

"It creates the cognitive functions," Jenna interrupted.

"I know that," Andre grunted, keeping his attention

on the whiteboard and Naveen. "But what's inside? What makes it work?"

"Um," Naveen said. "Well, deep learning is the most advanced machine learning tool we have at our disposal. It drives our neural networks to find complex patterns in large amounts of data."

"Neural networks have been around for decades," Andre said. "CHERL has to be more than a bunch of neural networks."

Naveen smiled. "That's true. Neural networks are just a set of algorithms, and they have been used since the 1950s. But they were limited to single applications, like finding credit card fraud. Now that we have almost infinite processing power, we can layer hundreds of massive neural networks, each with thousands of algorithms, into a single model. All running simultaneously, relaying information in nanoseconds."

"That's the training process, right?" Andre asked. "How we teach CHERL everything we know about Lincoln? About Churchill?"

"Exactly," Josh said. "There's practically no limit to how much data each CHERL model can absorb. But it's the processing capacity and speed that allows CHERL to recreate cognitive functions. That's how—"

Jenna cut in. "That's how we create her humanlike behavior. They're the same processes we use for the inference engine."

Josh glared at her. She kept her eyes on the whiteboard and continued. "That's how CHERL knows the decisions these leaders would make today."

"That's what I want to see," Andre said, grinning, his attention still locked on Naveen. "How do you communicate with it?"

"We key our questions into the system," Naveen said.

"Some test knowledge of facts, knowledge only the person would have had. Other questions target memories of events, both personal and historic. These tests have been flawless. We step up the interactions, moving on to feelings—feelings about people, favorite places, things that happened in the subject's life. Again, flawless."

Andre's brows furrowed. "If I want to talk to it, I have to key in my questions?"

"Of course not," Jenna said, her foot tapping sending a rhythmic vibration through the conference table.

"We just use written questions for fact-checking, Andre," Josh said. "After that, CHERL is running the latest in speech synthesis and natural language processing. We can have a very normal conversation."

"That's right, boss," Naveen said. "We can put CHERL through a variety of interactions. Fewer questions and answers and more conversation, two-way dialogue. Simple at first. We talked about favorite subjects, careful in offering up our own opinions. But over time, we inject opinions into the conversation. Simple debates. Then we step it up, introducing, you know, arguments. Mostly the same arguments that people were having at the time our subjects lived."

Andre glanced at his watch. "I mean, enough with the dissertation," he said. "Boot this thing up, for Chrissake."

Josh nodded toward the team leaders standing against the wall, and introduced Dennis Habib, leader of Pod 2, an expert in natural language processing.

"Bring up XLT 36," Josh said. Dennis sat in front of the laptop, running his fingers rapidly across the keyboard. Josh still hoped they could bypass or explain away any issues that might arise from the inference engine.

"XLT is Ulysses S. Grant," Josh said.

Andre leaned forward and clasped his hands on the conference table. He had told Josh that he had several historical figures in mind when he funded CHERL. While Churchill and Lincoln were high on his list, Andre had a passion for great military minds, especially those who navigated complex political issues that accompanied a war. And Andre wanted to talk to people who knew how to win. Who better to strategize with today's leaders than the man considered by many historians to be the greatest commander in American history? A man who possessed skills that Andre believed were sorely lacking in modern times.

"Grant turned out to be a perfect subject for CHERL," Josh continued. "His life was well chronicled. We have a vast library of material written on him, including a very reflective memoir and over three hundred letters."

"This really allowed us to triangulate the subject," Jenna said. By now, everyone was ignoring her.

"Ready to go," Dennis said.

"Okay," Josh said. He exchanged glances with Naveen.

Dennis punched the keys, and background static started coming through the speaker.

"This is Dennis Habib, running XLT 36, test scenario fifteen."

"We record all of our interactions," Josh whispered to Andre.

"Hello," Dennis said. "Who am I speaking with?"

The static faded. A clear but low voice came from the speaker. "Good day, sir. My name is Ulysses S. Grant."

Andre said, "I can barely hear him."

"We pulled soundalike voices from our library," Josh said. "Grant was known to speak softly."

"We can turn up the volume," Jenna said.

"Shhhh!" Andre snapped.

"Hello, Mr. President," Dennis continued.

"You do not need to call me that, sir."

"I'm just trying to establish who we are speaking with," Dennis said.

"You can call me General."

Andre looked up at Josh and smiled.

"Hello, General," Dennis said. "We'd like to ask you a few questions."

Over the next hour, Dennis probed the subject, delving deeper and deeper into Grant's history. The CHERL version of Grant described for Dennis his time at West Point and his early battles in the Mexican–American War, as well as his appointment to lead the Union army and his relationship with Lincoln. Throughout the conversation, what came through was not just CHERL's ability to state facts, but to convey everything Josh had learned about Grant's personality. CHERL presented Grant as quiet and shy, while also dignified and confident.

"Lincoln was a marvelous leader. Not another man could have won the war and kept the country together."

Josh could feel Andre's excitement building with each passing minute as the CEO sat at the edge of his seat, rubbing his hands together like a hungry kid about to attack the buffet line.

"Let's move on to the time of your presidency," Dennis said.

"Enough of the history lesson," Andre interrupted, standing and thumping Josh enthusiastically on the arm. "This is absolutely tremendous!"

Josh motioned for Dennis to press the mute button,

while flexing his right arm to make sure Andre hadn't broken anything.

"Let's get to the point," Andre said. "You've proven you can create a terrific portrayal—a fantastic portrayal. Truly amazing. You've all done a fine job."

Josh and Naveen sat stone-faced. The rest of their team, including Jenna, were smiling.

"But that's not why I invested all of this money," Andre said, returning to his chair. "The game changer is, how can he help us—today! How he can help our leaders *today*!"

The demo had gone extremely well. Not a single behavioral irregularity. Josh had hoped the demonstration could end there, but Andre was having none of it.

"Have the interfaces been completed?" Andre asked.

The interfaces were those connecting CHERL's neural networks to the unsecured databases from the Defense and State Departments. XLT 36, and all the other CHERL subjects, would have access to a complete history of every battle and every war that the United States had entered over the past one hundred and fifty years, from the Civil War through Afghanistan. She also had access to every digitized article from top political and military magazines and newspapers throughout the world, going back fifty years. This version of Grant was up to speed on the state of the country and the military, as well as that of allies and adversaries. CHERL's Grant model was optimized with all the information needed to formulate opinions on current affairs of state.

Josh nodded, thinking this was only an internal demo. They should be able to explain away any abnormalities in CHERL's thinking.

"What are we waiting for?" asked Andre, holding his hands out.

"I agree," Jenna said.

Josh nodded to Dennis, who started eagerly banging on his laptop. In less than a minute, he gave Josh a thumbs-up.

Andre stood and moved around the conference table, leaning closer to the speaker.

"General Grant," Andre said. "I just have one question for you, sir. What country would you say is the greatest threat to America's national security today?"

CHERL was silent, the tension permeating the room.

"General Grant?" Andre repeated.

Dennis ran his fingers across the keyboard. Finally, the voice returned, speaking slowly. Almost deliberately.

"There is only one country I fear today, sir. A country that has been lying in wait for the past fifty years. Reconstituting itself, economically. Appearing to be a good neighbor in the region. But, sir, I tell you, they are lying in wait. You can see the factions within pushing for the country to reconstruct itself militarily. They say it's to better protect themselves. But I don't see it that way at all, sir. I can clearly see the path they are on if America lets it happen again. We must coalesce all our efforts, all our energies, to contain Japan before it is too late."

CHAPTER
NINE

"WILL you be going out again, Mr. Brodsky?" the parking attendant asked with a trace of a Spanish accent. He opened the door of the BMW 740i, allowing Louie to stand and stretch his back, aching from the long ride home from Brooklyn, where he had spent the previous night at a hotel near his mother's place. At least he'd finished with the apartment.

"In a little while, José," responded Louie, handing the attendant the valet key. "Just dropping some things off and changing."

"Okay, sir," José said. "I'll have it ready."

Louie waved as he grabbed the black garbage bag out of the back seat and made his way to the lobby of the historic Art Deco apartment building across from Central Park. The building, dating from the 1930s, was considered second-tier by the socialite New Yorkers of the first half of the twentieth century. By the time Louie and his wife moved in, seven years ago, it was prominently known as the Ghostbusters Building, having been used as "Spook Central" in the 1984 movie. That's all the movie-crazed

Louie needed to know before mortgaging himself to the hilt.

After entering the foyer, Louie dropped the black bag and emptied his pockets—keys, cell phone, Prozac—onto the dish he kept on the oak cabinet by the entryway. He heard the familiar hum and whoosh sounds echoing throughout the four-thousand-square-foot penthouse and saw a pair of petite feet hanging over the side of the Biedermeier sofa. Vicki sat up, phone to her ear, and held her index finger up.

"No, no, no, Mom, he's right here," she said. "He just walked in. Let me call you back later, promise. Love you too. Okay, bye."

"Oh, babe," Vicki said, walking toward Louie and putting her slender arms around him, hugging him closely, silently.

He buried his head in her shoulders, his deep breath taking in the scent of her hair, the light perfume on her neck. After what seemed like several minutes, she lifted her head back to look at his face.

"Jeez, you look awful," she finally said.

"Thanks." He laughed. "Good to know."

He let go and started toward the kitchen.

"What's in the bag?" Vicki asked.

"Just stuff from her apartment. Papers, some trinkets for Jess. I'll go through it next weekend."

"Well, can you put it in your closet? I don't want it sitting there all day," she said.

"I will. I gotta get something to eat first."

Louie rounded the corner of the living room and entered the large center-island kitchen, where the hum and whoosh noises grew as the automated floor scrubbers did their business.

"I'll make you something," she said, entering the kitchen.

"Coffee," Louie said, and the Presto coffee maker light illuminated, proceeding to grind and brew a perfect blend of his favorite, dark roast, topped off with just the right amount of low-fat milk. He opened the stainless-steel door to the oversize Viking refrigerator and grabbed a leftover bowl of linguine in meat sauce.

"Louie, that's a lot of carbs for seven o'clock in the morning!"

He removed the cellophane wrap from the bowl, sat at the counter, and sipped from the steaming mug. "How's Jess?"

"She's fine. She misses you," Vicki said. "She had dinner at Rachel's last night, working on a big class project."

Louie stuffed his mouth with a large forkful of pasta.

"Come on, put the linguine away. Let me make you some breakfast." She turned toward the refrigerator and bumped into the floor scrubber, which was hovering over a tiny stain. Louie wished Vicki would give these devices a rest when he was in the house, but unless they had company, his wife had them marching up and down the floors, curtains, and windows like a small army on maneuvers.

"Don't bother. I just wanted to shower and change clothes. I have to get to the office."

"Why don't you at least work from home today? You must be exhausted."

"I can't, Vic. My deal's closing this week. I can't fuck around with this one."

Vicki sat beside him at the counter and slipped a coaster under his coffee mug. "I wish you had let me come to your mother's apartment after the funeral," she said. "It was ridiculous—Just the two of you doing that alone."

"It's done," Louie said. "Brooklyn's done."

"You don't have to go back?"

"Nope," he said. "I turned in her keys."

"Was Donny at least helpful?"

Louie walked over to the kitchen window and stared out at Central Park, the apartment brightened by the large southern exposure.

"He stuffed his share of bags," Louie said. "Helped me carry them to the dumpster." Louie paused. "I guess he was helpful."

"Did something happen with Donny?" she asked.

"Let's just say he had his needle sharpened. And he was poking it pretty good."

"About what?"

"What's the difference?" Louie said, not wanting to rehash the entire day. "Just family crap."

"What did he say?" Vicki asked. "Tell me."

Louie exhaled and returned to the counter to polish off the linguine, trying to ignore the question. He was used to Vicki's persistence. She carried herself with class and elegance at all the corporate and social functions. She was polite, poised, engaged. But underneath it all, she was still a Jersey girl, raised in a household where everything in life was on the table. No holds barred. All emotions, both good and bad, laid bare for everyone in her family to see and share. It was the polar opposite of the Brodsky household. He'd grown up burying all feelings, all emotions, running from personal confrontation. He saved his confrontations for the deal room, not for here at home. His shrink said having a dissimilar partner was a way to compensate for one's own short-comings, or some crap like that. All he wanted was to take a shower and get to the office. But Vicki was having none of it.

"What did he say?" she asked again.

Louie looked up at his wife. "For starters, he asked for money."

Vicki sat up in her chair.

"Again?" she said. "How much does he want to steal from us this time?"

"One hundred fifty thousand. An investment in another business," Louie said, his eyes locked on the pasta.

Vicki left her chair, turned on the faucet, and grabbed a sponge. "What's he doing now?" she asked. Louie knew he had to get through this part of the story quickly before she scrubbed a hole in the sink.

"Who knows?" he said.

"We're not doing that again," she said as she dried the sink with a paper towel. "What else?"

Louie looked up at his wife. "I don't know. Oh yeah. He's still harping on Dad's accident."

Vicki began cleaning the countertop with a paper towel. "Always looking to blame some tragedy for his own fuckups," she said.

"But he also thinks we should've done more for her."

Vicki looked up.

"Thinks we should've moved her out of Brooklyn," Louie said.

Vicki nodded slowly, staring at Louie. "He's got balls," she said.

Louie looked up quizzically. Not the reaction he expected. "What do you mean? You've been hounding me for years. 'Get her outta there. Move her to Florida. Put her someplace nicer, safer.' Right?"

"I know," she said, her voice rising. "But he still has

balls throwing that at you. You did plenty for her. And she never wanted to go to fuckin' Florida."

"He's in his own world." He lifted the bowl to scrape out the last strands of linguine.

"Lays this all out on you?" Vicki grabbed Louie's empty dish and clanked it into the sparkling sink. "You did more than either of your fuckin' brothers."

Louie started walking toward the bedroom as Vicki turned on the faucet to clean the splattered sauce. If he told her any more, she would be on her hands and knees, competing for space with the scrubbers for the rest of the day. He would leave the part about his selling his soul for another time.

"I have to get to the office."

"Let him lay that on Josh," Vicki said. "Let him ask Josh for money."

"Vic—enough. I'm fried with this shit."

"Did Josh call you?" she asked.

"We talked," he said. Now was not the time.

"Why didn't he have the decency to come to his mother's funeral? Why didn't he move his mother to DC when he lived there? Did you ask him?"

Louie looked at his wife.

"Vicki, please," he said. "We'll talk when I get home later. Enough, please."

She took a deep breath. "Okay," she said, her expression slowly morphing back to that of the Manhattan socialite. She stood up tall and straight, shaking off the Jersey girl. "Okay, I'm sorry."

He headed down the hallway leading to the master bedroom.

"I'll be out in a minute," he said without looking back.

"Louie?"

He stopped and turned.

"He's a thief. Don't give him any more money."

He gave her a slight smile and headed back toward the bedroom. Vicki called out to him.

"Louie?"

He looked back.

"The garbage bag, please!"

CHAPTER
TEN

DONNY HAD MET Ana three weeks before his mother's funeral, on the day he enrolled in the Horizon Programming Boot Camp, where experienced coders learned skills that would land them jobs in the expanding world of artificial intelligence. Several of the assignments Donny was bidding on required AI experience. He hoped Horizon would teach him enough to be coherent on his proposals and, more importantly, to fake his way through some well-paying projects.

Most of the coding classes Donny had attended over the years were male-only workshops, so he noticed Ana as soon as he walked into the classroom that first day. She had long blond hair that flowed over her shoulders and a shapely but athletic figure, and she was smiling and laughing with three male students near the coffee machine. Donny pegged her as mid to late thirties. She walked down the aisle and took the seat to his right.

After class, a group would gather for drinks across the street at McGee's Tavern, Donny always sliding over to wherever Ana was hanging out. While usually surrounded by other classmates vying for her attention, one night he managed to elbow his way close enough to overhear parts of the group's conversation.

"Companies are getting rid of more and more people," a guy with sandy hair said. "Even programming jobs are gonna be hard to find. Now they've got software that writes its own code."

"Isn't that why we're all here?" asked an Asian student wearing pink eyeglass frames. "To get AI skills so we'll be the ones that are left standing?"

"How will we find those kinds of jobs?" Ana asked. "Do you think Horizon will make connections for us when this is all over?"

The sandy-haired one said, "I hope so."

"Well, if they don't," she said, smiling, "we can help each other, right? Sharing connections and contacts." Donny saw her take a sip from her martini and glance at the cluster of students who were eagerly nodding their agreement.

As luck would have it, the next day the instructor divided the class into teams, and Donny found himself sitting next to Ana in a small breakout room, where he had difficulty keeping his eyes off her slender legs. His thoughts drifted in and out of fantasies that involved the two of them late into the evening. She was serious eye candy, but it turned out that she was also very smart. Even when she wasn't contributing to the group, her expression suggested she knew the solution to whatever the task at hand. During one of their breaks, he decided to approach her by the coffee machine.

"You know, I couldn't help overhearing you at McGee's last night," he said. "I agree with what you were saying—about us all helping each other with job contacts."

She pressed the cappuccino button on the machine and said, "That's good to know."

"No, really," he said, moving closer. "We should share contact information when this is all over."

"That would be great," she said and turned to head back to the classroom.

"I know some very powerful people," Donny said. "In big jobs."

Ana stopped and looked back at Donny. "Really?"

Locking in on her alluring green eyes made his mind freeze, his heart rate accelerate. Then he blurted out, "Sure, er…like my brothers. That's right. My brothers. They're both big shots. They both have very big jobs."

"That's very interesting," she said. The corners of her mouth turned up slightly.

Donny cleared his throat. "Yeah. One was a very senior AI guy at the Defense Department. Now he's in Silicon Valley. He has a really big job at Sway. They're always hiring."

"Wow, he's at Sway?" Donny had her attention. "Does he like working there?"

"He loves it," Donny said. The truth was he knew nothing about Josh's job other than he moved out West about a year ago, but that didn't matter right now. Donny was dancing, anything to keep her engaged. "Except everything's top secret with him. But he knows a lot of people in the AI world. I'm sure he'd help us."

"Are the two of you close?"

"Of course. Very close." Donny's heart rate settled down. "With my other brother too. He's an investment banker. He works on deals with big companies all the time. Tons of contacts for jobs."

"Is he in Silicon Valley too?"

"Louie? Not him. He has this monster penthouse on Central Park West. He'll never leave New York."

"That sounds amazing," she said as the instructor called everyone back to class. "I'd love to hear more about them."

Over the next few days, Donny and Ana continued their casual conversations around the coffee machine during morning and afternoon breaks. Mostly they compared notes on the class, the teachers they liked or thought were idiots. Slowly, they revealed more about themselves, Donny careful to embellish anything about his successful brothers and their close relationship. He hoped he could keep all his new details straight in his head. Ana seemed similarly guarded, sharing only that she'd grown up in Oregon, studied business at Portland State, and moved to Texas when she was twenty-five, after marrying an oil executive. Donny noted with particular interest that her husband had been twenty years her senior, and they'd divorced three years later.

She told him she spent her career jumping around various technology companies as a trainer, including a short stint with a company called Digital that moved her to Chicago last year. She had quit two months before to retool her skills, hoping to break into artificial intelligence.

The day before his mother died, Donny found himself working with Ana and two other students late into the evening, when she suggested the team continue their session at Gibson's Bar and Steakhouse. The other team members peeled off after two drinks, leaving Donny and Ana alone in a corner booth. After the waiter brought their third vodka martinis, Ana slid over to Donny's side, startling him. Sitting this close to her in the dim light of the bar, he found himself mesmerized by her alluring green eyes.

"I'm glad they left," she said. "They weren't helping much."

"I'm not sure I am either," he said, uncertain if he was slurring his words. "You've got this stuff down cold. I mean, you could teach this class. What are you doing here?"

"You're perceptive," she said, laughing before taking another sip. Her green eyes stayed locked on Donny. "Let's just say it's an investment of my time."

Donny leaned back. "What kind of investment?"

"Well," she said, removing the swizzle stick and picking off an olive with her teeth, chewing slowly. "I'm doing reconnaissance. Seeing what I'm up against." She leaned in closer and whispered, "And lining up some partners."

"What kind of partners?" he asked, hearing his own voice crack. With an erection slowly forming in his jeans, he nonchalantly shifted in his seat and took a gulp of martini.

"Well," she said. "I know a lot about technology. I'm not seeing anything in this class that would be so difficult to teach. I'm already a pretty good trainer."

"You're a great trainer," Donny blurted, realizing he sounded like an overzealous teenager.

Ana giggled. Then her expression changed into a fake pout. "But I don't know much about raising money to do it."

Donny took three quick sips of his drink, then said, "What are we talking about here? I mean, what kind of business?"

Ana's facial expression became businesslike. She pushed her chest forward and her head back.

"I want to open up my own programming boot camp. Only AI languages—Java, Python, C++. These Horizon guys are doing a terrible job. My students would come out so much better prepared and qualified than anyone who's finishing our class here."

Donny stirred his martini, thinking of the possibilities. Maybe he could be a partner…a partner with benefits.

"I've put a plan together," she continued. "But I need investors to get it off the ground." Ana sipped her martini, then asked, "Do you think your brothers would be interested?"

"My brothers?"

"Yes," she said. "I need funding to get it off the ground. Do you think they would invest?"

So that was her angle. She had latched on to his comments about his brothers being connected, about being big shots. Instead of helping with a job search, what she really wanted was money connections. Investors. But he was intrigued by the potential of a partnership. Maybe he could keep the possibilities going, at least until he could reap some of her side benefits.

"I don't know, Ana," he said. "I guess if they thought they were investing in me, that would be one thing. But…"

Ana smiled slightly. "Well, I do need someone with a good business sense. I don't really know much about running a business. But I do know technology. And I'm a good teacher."

He slid the drink away and folded his hands on the table, trying to stay cool. Stay calm.

"Well, Ana," he said. "It just so happens that I have run and sold several companies, so I know a little bit about what it takes to manage a successful business."

"Really?" Ana said, her face brightening.

Donny turned up the embellishment again. In his telling, both the dance studio and the plumbing supply company were wildly successful, multi-state enterprises, attracting buyers who paid him ten times his initial investment.

"I'm just doing these programming gigs until I can find my next big idea," he said. "Something I can sink my teeth into."

"You never told me. That's all so impressive." She slid closer. "Do you think you could help me?"

Donny drained what was left of his martini, hoping he could gain control of the movement between his legs before he had to stand up. Ana removed a thumb drive from her purse and slid it in front of Donny.

"Would you and your brothers take a look at my business plan?"

He stared at the small drive. This woman was serious if she went to the trouble of developing a real business plan. Maybe his brothers would kick in some funds. It couldn't hurt to ask, if only to further the possibility of an encounter with Ana.

"I'm sure they would," he said. This could be very interesting. What was also interesting was that her hand was now sliding over the top of his leg. He tried to speak.

"Maybe we..." The words got stuck in his suddenly dry throat.

"Yes?" she said, looking away nonchalantly.

He tried again. "Maybe...we should go...look at it together."

Ana finished her drink and pushed the glass away, her hand still resting on his thigh.

"I guess we'll just have to see what you can bring to the partnership first," she said, slowly sliding away and gathering her bag and coat. She stood and smiled, saying,

"Maybe we can pick this up next week. You can let me know what your brothers say."

———

NOW HE WAS COMING BACK to class on Monday morning, fresh from his mother's funeral, empty-handed. He had loaded the contents of the thumb drive onto his laptop. He had read the business plan on the plane to New York and found it surprisingly good, even compelling. Ana had done her homework, including an analysis of the size of the market in Chicago, weaknesses of the competitors—including Horizon—capital requirement for equipment and facilities, and, most interesting, financial projections that showed they could make a ton of money. He wondered if she had help pulling the document together, as it was more sophisticated than he expected from someone who had only worked in training and education.

She was looking for one hundred and fifty thousand dollars of seed capital—not a lot of money, but he knew he had no Rolodex of investors, no vast business contacts. Truth was, Louie and Josh were the only people he knew with that kind of money. But he got struck down without so much as a hearing from his younger brother. And Josh wouldn't stay on the phone long enough to even consider it. Donny would have to find another way to keep this idea alive with Ana.

"I thought maybe you'd left town for good," Ana said when he entered the classroom.

"How'd you know I was out of town?" he asked.

"Well, er, you missed two days of class last week. I just assumed..."

"Got a little sidetracked," he said. "My mom died. I was in New York taking care of her affairs."

"Did you share my business plan with your brothers?" she said, looking firm.

"Not exactly, Ana," he said. "I did look at it. But did you hear what I said? I was at my mother's funeral."

Ana's expression quickly changed. "Oh, no, I didn't hear you say that. Oh, I'm sorry to hear that."

"Well, I did speak to my brothers about it while I was there. Well, at least with one of them."

"And?"

"Not a good time for him to make investments."

"He didn't like my business plan?"

"I didn't get a chance to show it to him."

"Why not? You didn't like it?" she asked, pouting and turning away.

"That's not it at all," he said, holding her arm. "Your plan was terrific. I'd really be very interested in doing this with you. I think it has huge potential."

"Just not enough potential to show it to your brothers." She pulled her arm away.

"That's not it. They're just very busy, but don't worry. I have plenty of other people to reach out to." Fabricating a few names would be easy and would buy him some time to figure out his next move. "I do have some questions about the business. If we could talk through them, I'd be a lot smarter when speaking to investors. How about going over it over dinner? Are you free tonight?"

"I could understand if they saw the plan and didn't like it. But I don't understand why you didn't send it to them. Especially if you're really interested in working with me."

One thing was for sure, Ana would be an assertive partner. If only Donny had had a partner like her when he owned the plumbing supply company, he might still be in business. Louie could have a change of heart about investing if he read Ana's business plan and believed that Donny had developed a well-thought-out strategy. And Josh knew all about AI. If he wouldn't invest, perhaps he'd be an adviser.

"I'll send it to them tonight," Donny said. "I'm sure they'll reconsider."

She leaned closer and whispered, "Why don't you send it now?"

"Now?"

"Aren't you a man of action?" she asked, playfully punching his arm. "Isn't that what businesspeople do?"

Donny smiled and removed his laptop from his backpack.

"I'll send it to them both, right now," he said.

"Excellent," she said, beaming.

CHAPTER
ELEVEN

LATER THAT EVENING, hours after the demo with Andre had ended, Josh drove his ten-year-old Ford Taurus down a gravel road leading to Sequoia Mobile Homes and parked in front of Unit 12. As he walked toward his trailer, he nodded at the park manager—an older woman with a constant cloud of cigarette smoke billowing from her mouth—staring out her window. Josh was happy he wasn't around enough to be ingesting her secondhand fumes and having to answer her nosy questions, especially why he was now on his thirteenth month-to-month lease. He wasn't about to explain to her that what started out as a two-week stint while he searched for more permanent housing turned into a series of short-term extensions. He spent most nights sleeping at the office anyway, so why bother finding something more permanent, even if the trailer had a perpetually musty odor? While things were looking up at Sway, he wasn't a Silicon Valley millionaire yet, and he wasn't going to waste his savings on an apartment that was half the size of his comfortable place in DC, for three times the money. Most of his possessions were sitting in a seven-teen-by-twelve temperature-controlled unit at Storage Land USA and could be packed and loaded on a truck in a matter of hours. But maybe he'd be confident enough to find a more suitable living arrangement soon. He had to admit, CHERL's inference engine had performed better than expected. Andre had been spellbound by XLT 36's comments about the Land of the Rising Sun and the depth of Grant's understanding of the geopolit-ical and economic position of modern-day Japan.

Andre was ecstatic, ready to reveal his creation to his contacts in Washington. But first he wanted Josh to present CHERL to Sway's board of directors. That gave Josh a chance to take a nice hot shower, get a good night's sleep, and clear his mind. Tomorrow, much to his colleagues' happiness, he would finally don fresh clothes.

Work had pushed all thoughts of his mother's death into the deepest recesses of his mind, but he finally let it seep in. Sadness that she was gone. That, in all the years of their lives, he hadn't been able to confront her. To clear the air between them. Guilty that he was always off the grid, especially over the past few days. Unaware of her death and funeral. And sorry about not being there for his brothers. Letting these emotions wash over him left him tired and depressed, making it impossible to sleep.

After tossing in bed for an hour, he turned on the lamp and padded into the kitchenette. He would do what he always did when these feelings surfaced: he would get back to work.

Josh booted up his home computer. He could at least start developing the presentation for the board. That should be enough to allow him to refocus. But not before handling one last personal task that was gnawing at him.

Perhaps it was the lingering guilt, but something told him to make sure that some other calamity hadn't befallen his family in the past few hours. He decided to check his personal emails.

He reached for a wide-open bag of stale pretzels and a bottle of flat club soda, and quickly scrolled through the two-week backlog. Scattered among the junk mail were several messages from Louie and Donny from the previous week, urging him to respond. Pleading with him to come to New York. Information about the funeral that had already taken place. His forefinger hovered and continuously depressed the delete key until he came to one last message from Donny with the telltale paper clip indicating an attachment.

"Would be great to get your thoughts on attached. Could be great opportunity for me to get into the AI training business. Just need some money to get started, and maybe your help as adviser to me and partner? A chance for you to get in on the ground floor. Could you review and let me know what you think?"

Over the years, Josh had avoided investing any of his time or money in Donny. All those years on a government salary didn't exactly leave him flush with cash. But he was in Silicon Valley now, and the demo had gone well. Perhaps Josh did have a future at Sway. Maybe he would be around to see some of those options vest, after all, so he could finally be in a position to help his brother and make room in his life for his family. Besides, Donny was only asking for his thoughts, his advice. Josh could certainly afford to do that. It wasn't much, but it could be a start. When he clicked on Donny's document, the title page appeared: "Building an Artificial Intelligence Boot Camp."

Before he could scroll down Josh's cell rang.

"Naveen, it's two a.m. Why are you still awake?"

"Where are you, mon? I've something to show you."

"Came home for a shower and some real sleep, although not working out so far. Thought you did the same."

"Can't, mon. We just finished with XLT 64!"

While XLT 64 didn't fit neatly in Andre's mold of great political and military leaders, he was Naveen's personal hero, so he had lobbied hard to have him included him in the initial pilot group.

"You have to sign into CHERL so I can show you." Naveen was gushing.

Josh knew he should tell Naveen to go home. Tell him he left his work computer at the office and this could all wait until morning. But Naveen's passion was contagious, leaving Josh with the realization that his quest for a good night's sleep was over. He minimized Donny's document on his screen, pulled up the URL that provided access to the Tower at Sway, and signed into CHERL.

"I'm in, Naveen."

"Okay, mon. Go ahead. Ask him anything you want."

For the next hour, though exhausted, Josh engaged in a fascinating, far-reaching conversation about poverty, freedom and oppression, racial discrimination, and income inequality. A conversation that Josh started as he had every CHERL test dialogue since he moved to California.

"Hello. Who am I speaking with?"

"Hello, sir. My name is Gandhi. Mohandas Karamchand Gandhi."

CHAPTER
TWELVE

LOUIE EXITED the elevator on the top floor of the fifty-story skyscraper on Fifth Avenue. Inside the investment banking offices of Peabody & Munson, he found the plush hallway corridors teeming with activity. He entered his corner office overlooking the Plaza Hotel and Central Park South, and before he could set his briefcase down, a female voice said, "Mr. Peabody was here to see you."

"I'll walk down there in a minute," Louie responded.

"He asked that you come see him as soon as you arrived."

"Off," Louie said, deactivating his personal assistant, knowing it would hound him endlessly until he crossed the threshold of his boss's office. He closed his door and signed in to the ClubTrack app, the red arrow flashing news of yet another loss, this time $50,000 on the trifecta at Santa Rosa. That's it, he told himself, feeling his pulse quicken. No more betting the horses until his bank account was replenished with his share of the Virtual Bank–Peachtree merger fees. The deal was set to close in just two days. Three days, maximum. He could hold off placing any more bets for seventy-two hours, right? In fact, he could stop whenever he wanted, cold turkey, just as he did when he kicked the gambling habit ten years back.

For almost a decade, he never came close to a race-track or a casino, focusing his energies on helping Peabody & Munson build an important, midsize invest-ment bank, all while generating massive revenue on a slew of mergers and acquisitions. The firm was started by former partners at Goldman Sachs, Jonathan Peabody and Dale Munson, who hustled business away from the white-shoe firms, leveraging their reputation and low-fee model. They had also built a reputation for extracting top dollar for investors and shareholders in the rough-and-tumble world of mergers and acquisitions. Munson, with his big personality, was the relationship guy. While at Goldman, he cut his teeth on several big mergers in the early 2000s, and now led the sales and client manage-ment side at P&M. He had recruited several rising stars from Goldman, including Louie. Peabody, dubbed the Iceman for his cold stares, managed day-to-day opera-tions, including training the staff in "the Peabody & Munson way." Peabody showed them the ropes, and the firm paid top dollar in exchange for a twenty-four-seven, three-sixty-five work ethic and every ounce of their energy. A hungry boutique firm like P&M was more aligned with Louie's personality, and he initially thrived in the aggressive deal culture, rising to become the number one producer five years in a row.

A financial whiz kid, Louie had brought his specialty: bank mergers. He competed with Keefe, Bruyette & Woods on the smaller deals and with his former Goldman colleagues on the larger ones, always winning by knowing his clients' numbers better than their own CFOs. His secret was simple. He immersed himself in the data, requiring—no, insisting—on creating his own financial models, using unvarnished information that he and his team garnered directly from clients' accounting and financial systems.

But after fifteen stellar years of existence, the firm, and most notably Louie, had hit a wall. Over the past three years, all the big deals were happening in Silicon Valley, as fintech, machine learning, SaaS platforms, and artificial intelligence were exploding. Each deal required deep knowledge of these technologies. Even his competitors were using AI, developing financial algorithms that neutered P&M's analytic advantages. They were outmaneuvered by other hotshot boutique firms with far greater knowledge of these disruptive technologies, firms willing to cut fees and corners to win business away from P&M, and the other big dogs on the street. Peabody & Munson were desperate for a win. They had yet to bag a deal with a big Silicon Valley company.

He'd better get down to see Peabody. The old man didn't like to be kept waiting.

"Hi, Jon," said Louie, knocking and entering Peabody's corner suite. Peabody, now in his fifties, tall and fit, his neatly cropped hair more salt than pepper, was sitting in his leather swivel chair with his back to the door. Louie knew that his boss was checking his large computer screen for the latest on premarket conditions before heading to the trading desk. Peabody swung his chair around and stood to greet his onetime star talent. "Louie, welcome back. Come in, come in."

Louie shook Peabody's extended hand and dropped himself into the straight-backed wooden chair on the opposite side of the desk. Peabody pulled up a chair and sat beside him.

"Are you doing okay?" he asked matter-of-factly.

"I'm fine, Jon. Thanks for asking."

"Sorry I couldn't get to the funeral. It's been crazy around here."

"No issue," Louie said. "It was a small service. And thanks for the flowers. They were really nice."

"Well, I'm sorry for your loss," Peabody said uncomfortably. Not much for small talk, he glanced out his office door at the activity in the corridors. His eyes turned back to Louie. "You sure you're ready to get back in the saddle?"

"Ready to go."

"Great." Peabody slapped Louie on his knee as he bounded out of his chair. "It's a big week for you. For us. We really need your A game on this Virtual Bank deal."

"You've been getting it, Jon."

"No, I'm serious, Louie." Peabody glanced at his trading screen. "We're getting crushed out there. There are no big deals left in financial services. This is our chance for a win in the tech space. A big win."

Louie took a deep breath, blowing out slowly. He knew Peabody was right. The firm specialized in traditional bank mergers, which had completely dried up. But Virtual Bank, a powerful and rising online bank in Silicon Valley, was about to merge with one of the largest regional brick-and-mortar banks in the country, Peachtree Commerce. The combined entity would dominate the banking industry, distributing Peachtree's suite of lending and investment products through VB's world-class e-commerce sites. Louie had shepherded the deal through due diligence, months of negotiations, and countless delays. And it was all about to pay off. The deal would establish P&M as the go-to investment bank in the emerging cross section of technology and banking and would replenish the firm's coffers with the significant fees worthy of a $50 billion merger. Most important to Louie, his share would pour much-needed cash into his own bank account. Because after three straight years of earning zero bonuses, his lifestyle and gambling losses cleaned him out. Louie was flat broke.

"You eat what you kill," Dale Munson had told everyone when they joined the firm. "No deals, no bonuses."

That was the contract everyone signed in the investment banking world. And Louie lived by that dogma throughout his career, riding the wave as transactions grew larger and larger, with paydays to match. But the money flowed out of his household faster than it came in. In hindsight, stretching with a large mortgage on the Central Park West apartment wasn't the best idea in the world, but Vicki loved the place, and when they bought it, he assumed his paycheck would grow faster than his lifestyle. But too many dry years had left their personal finances in a precarious position. With his career on the decline and his cash reserves depleted, Louie reached for the only thing that made him feel better, his new Club-Track app, where he could conveniently bet on the horses twenty-four-seven. After depleting their savings accounts with one losing bet after another, he moved on to their home equity line of credit. As long as Louie's shrink kept the Prozac flowing, Louie felt he could hang on until he landed a big deal.

"This deal is in the bag, Jon," Louie reassured his boss.

Peabody, smiling, swiveled his chair to face Louie. Louie had seen that practiced smile before. It was the same smile Peabody had on his face when he'd addressed the staff last December, announcing the elimination of bonuses for the year.

"We haven't brought in enough revenue to justify a payout," he told the employees gathered for an impromptu meeting, one week shy of the holiday party.

It was the same smile Peabody displayed when laying off the entire oil and gas industry team after they lost out on a huge Eastern European merger. The third straight oil and gas deal the firm had been passed over for.

"We're obviously not a player in oil and gas," he'd said while human resources passed out the severance agreements.

Yes, Louie knew that smile all too well.

"You let me know if I can help," Peabody said, turning back to face his computer screen.

Louie let himself out of Peabody's office, marched down the long corridor, and closed his office door behind him. "What a fuckin' asshole," he muttered.

"Calpers is looking for you," his assistant said.

"Who turned you back on?" he asked, adding, "Get him in here."

Louie planned to update the financial models, dig out any last positive pieces of information, so the CEOs of Peachtree and Virtual Bank would practically beg him to close the deal. While waiting for Calpers, Louie turned on his laptop and scanned through emails from the past few days, mostly condolence notes from associates and clients. He deleted them all, except those from potential clients. In the middle of the long list of condolences, he came across an email with an attachment from Donny. What now? Louie thought, clicking on the email.

"Hi Louie. Sorry things got a little sideways at Mom's. I didn't mean anything by it. But didn't really get

a chance to show you my business plan. Please take a look
and let's talk. I think you'll see it's a great opportunity.
And a great potential investment."

Donny was like a dog with a bone when he got something in his head. Just delete it and get back to work,
Louie thought. But something stopped him. Maybe it was
morbid curiosity to see what his lunatic brother was up to
this time. Whatever the reason, Louie wasn't sure why, he
double-clicked on Donny's attachment. It took several
seconds, but the document finally opened to the cover
page: "Building an Artificial Intelligence Boot Camp."

"What the fu—"

Two knocks on the door and Phil Calpers appeared.

"You ready, boss?"

Louie minimized Donny's document and motioned
his associate to join him at his desk, where they signed in
to Virtual Bank's system to extract and analyze the latest
financial results. Maybe he'd look at Donny's stupidity
later if he had the time.

CHAPTER
THIRTEEN

DARK GRAY CLOUDS floated menacingly over the western coastline of Lake Michigan. A storm was about to dump a late spring snowfall on much of Lake Shore Drive. The southbound lanes restricted to human drivers had ground to a halt. Donny fumed watching cars in the lanes reserved for autonomous vehicles whisk along at the posted speed limit. He leaned on his horn, earning several middle-finger salutes.

Donny despised driving downtown in his low-tech piece of junk, and he normally avoided being on the road during rush hour in either direction. But his Horizon class hadn't ended until midafternoon, and a new client, a failing clothing retailer, wanted him to attend a late afternoon brainstorming session about back-to-school marketing programs. *Back-to-school marketing programs being developed in March?* These idiots would be lucky to still be operating by summer. Better get the business from them while he could—and make sure he got paid before the creditors swarmed in and grabbed all their cash. He would spend a few hours with the client, take copious notes, and commit to coding a prototype for their campaign tracker by month's end. No matter how complicated, it wouldn't take him long to develop, but why not stretch it out and get a couple of extra weeks of billings?

The radio droned on with sports fans calling in their ideas about the upcoming NFL draft pick for the Bears.

"Ehhh, da Bears need to take dat wide receiver from Montana," said a caller, identifying himself as Jim from Winnetka. "Dey got nobody fur Jake to trow to."

"Well, defense wins championships," said Deveon James, the former Chicago Bull, now a radio sportscaster.

"What the fuck do you know about football anyway?" shouted Donny. "And you couldn't guard your mother, so what do you know about defense winning championships?"

Donny made up his mind that as soon as he got home, he'd post some blistering messages on the Chicago-area sports blogs that would make this former jock's head spin. All unattributed, of course, as was his MO.

As Lake Shore Drive came to a complete stop, Donny glanced to see if any messages were flashing on his phone. Again. Still nothing from Louie or Josh. It had only been a few hours since he emailed Ana's business plan, but he hoped for some type of confirmation—a message saying that they'd consider it, that they'd get back to him. But nothing. At least Ana couldn't have been expecting a quick answer. She never returned to class after lunch.

Donny inched the car forward and clicked on OneN-iteFrenz to see who was around for tonight, scrolling through several willing ladies until he found a forty-some-thing brunette with an adventurous smile that had "admired" his profile. He accepted her invitation for nine o'clock at her apartment on the Gold Coast, then tossed the phone back onto the passenger seat.

His phone immediately started buzzing, interrupting Harry from Hyde Park, who was mouthing off about the Northwestern Wildcats on the radio. Looking down, he saw the screen flash "Unknown Caller."

"Donny here."

A raspy but barely audible female voice said, "You should be ashamed of yourself!"

Donny pressed the disconnect button, reconnecting his radio in the middle of Harry's opinion about the Wildcats. His eyes darted back and forth, probing the faces of the drivers crawling along next to him. He pulled off Lake Shore Drive at the next exit, stopped his car, and checked OneNiteFrenz, thinking his Gold Coast date had made the call. Maybe she was one of those religious nutjobs who threatened to release names and information on the johns who frequented these hookup sites. Even though tonight's date had a dozen "authentication stars" next to her name, he couldn't be sure. But when he replayed her voice in his head, he thought the caller sounded more like an older woman. Somewhat gravelly. Or was it just static for the three seconds she was on the line? He wasn't completely sure of anything.

He searched his mind for traces of mistakes he might have made in his trolling endeavors. Maybe he'd left clues behind—a handle that had given him away. An IP address he had failed to reroute. Donny was trying to calm himself when the phone rang again, with the "Unknown Caller" showing.

Donny hit the ignore button on his console and waited. Waited to see if she'd call again. Minutes passed.

Maybe she had dialed the wrong number, or her call wasn't for him in the first place.

Donny pulled the car back onto Lake Shore Drive, rejoining the traffic crawl, finally reaching Michigan Avenue. After another twenty minutes of meandering through side streets, he arrived at his client's building on LaSalle. He decided to check his voice messages before heading upstairs.

"You have one unheard message." He hoped it was Louie or Josh.

Donny clicked the number 1.

"First unheard message…"

"Hello," said the gravelly voice. "I'm not sure I have the right number. But this is your mother's friend Maggie. I need you to call me. I need to give you a piece of my mind. What you did—it's shameful. It's just shameful."

———

LATER THAT NIGHT, after canceling his "date" with the Gold Coast lady, Donny returned to his apartment and resumed his favorite position—at his desk, in front of his laptop. He responded to a couple of business emails—nothing from his brothers—and tried to get some work done, but he was too distracted. The call from Maggie had jarred him.

What did she mean? Had he inadvertently sent her one of his nasty troll-a-grams about some bitch actress? He couldn't have been that careless. He didn't even have Maggie's contact information. Then why would she call him now? He'd seen her at his mother's funeral, hunched and moving slowly, with the aid of a cane. She hardly looked the part of an internet sleuth.

"She couldn't speak a lick of English," Mom always

told them about the language barrier her best friend faced when their family emigrated from Poland. "There were no bilingual teachers, no hand-holding—she and her sister had to learn on their own. If you couldn't speak the language, you couldn't go to school. It was that simple."

Maggie Berman's father worked long hours on the loading docks at the Brooklyn Navy Yard, and her mother helped out by teaching Hebrew at a Jewish day school. Money was always in short supply, so at the age of fourteen, Maggie took a job at a textile factory to help make ends meet. It was there that she met Donny's mom, doing her own part to earn extra cash. They became life-long friends.

But how could Maggie really know anything about what Donny was doing? He decided to find out. He dialed Maggie's phone number but hung up before the connection was made. Maybe this wasn't smart; he should just ignore her message. He paced the room, looking at his phone, out the window, back at his phone.

"Oh, fuck it." He dialed again.

The phone rang three times. On the fourth ring, he heard a click, followed by a muffled thud, as if the phone on the other side had been dropped. Then, after more muffled sounds, a weak voice said, "Hello?"

Donny listened but could not respond.

"Hello?" Her voice was clearer now.

Donny cleared his throat. "Hi," he managed to mumble. "Uh…is this, um…"

"Joshie? Joshie, is that you?" she asked.

"No," he said, his voice firming. "Maggie?"

"Yes," she said. "Who is this?"

"It's Donny," he said. "Ruth's other son."

"Donny, sweetie," she said. "Oh, I thought it was your brother calling me back."

"Did you call him too?" Donny asked.

"I did call him," Maggie said. "I wanted to give him a piece of my mind."

Donny leaned back in his chair and exhaled slowly.

"Er, Maggie. I think you called me."

"No. I don't think so. I don't think I called you, honey. I want to talk to your brother. He should be ashamed of himself. Your mother was no angel, but how could he not show up at her funeral? Why wasn't he there?"

Maggie hadn't meant to call him after all. She knew nothing of his extracurricular activities. His mind was starting to play tricks. There was no need for him to be fearful. He had, in fact, taken all necessary precautions. He chuckled. Who really cared that he sent nasty messages to celebrity idiots?

"I dunno," he finally said. "Josh is in his own world, I guess."

"Well, he should get himself some help," Maggie said. "I know you all had problems with your mom. I had plenty too. But at least you and Louie had the decency to have a funeral."

Donny squirmed in his chair. Only about a dozen people had shown up to the funeral. That's probably why his mother didn't want a weeklong shiva for mourners to gather and pay their respects. Guess she knew it would be a low turnout.

"Well, if you want to call him, I'll give you the right number," Donny said. "Good luck getting through to him."

"I know your mother was a piece of work," Maggie rasped. "We were totally different people, that we were. She was angry half the time, and the other half she was sad. But she could always make me laugh. I had a hard time listening to her ranting and raving. Oh, I stopped talking to her for the longest time too. But she still wanted to tell me what was going on, so I'd give in. She'd call and I'd listen."

"Maggie," Donny tried to interrupt, now that his business with her was done.

"I don't think she knew or gave a hoot about what was going on in my world, in my family," Maggie said. "But she wanted to tell me everything, like I was some type of confessional. Especially when your father died. So I listened. It wasn't easy."

Donny sat up in his leather chair. "She talked to you about that?"

"Do you think I wanted to hear all the details of what went on?" Maggie continued, oblivious to Donny's query. "No. I certainly didn't but listen I did. She never should have married your father in the first place. They had no business together. But her father pushed her into it. She fought it and fought it hard. But you just didn't have many choices back in those days. What could she do? She couldn't live at home any longer. None of us went to college. She couldn't make enough money to live on her own. What was she going to do? What did any of us do?"

"Maggie, Maggie!" Donny practically shouted at the phone. "Please, Maggie, what did she tell you about what happened with my father?"

"Oh, and then she sent me all her diaries. Afraid that you kids would find them in her apartment. I just stored them away. I didn't want to know any more."

"Diaries? She kept diaries?"

CHAPTER
FOURTEEN

WEDNESDAY

JOSH KEPT EYEING HIS WATCH, wondering if he'd misunderstood the start time. Now eight minutes past the hour, he sat alone in the oak-paneled boardroom and stared out the windows overlooking the picturesque, perfectly manicured thirty-acre grounds that surrounded the headquarters complex. A lone runner made his way around a two-mile jogging path that circled a large, man-made lake. Finally, members of Sway's board of directors leisurely entered the room, grabbed coffee, and engaged in idle chitchat. Josh had spent several hours the previous evening studying the background of each director, and his or her role on the board. He made it a point to always know his audience.

It was twelve minutes past the hour when Andre finally arrived with Jenna in tow. As everyone took their seats, the sidebar conversations died down, although Tom Brennan, chief financial officer, and Hector Torres, chief operating officer, strolled in two minutes after Andre, each wearing the company uniform of tan khakis and an open-collared golf shirt adorned with the Sway logo, an aqua colored "S."

"You all know Jenna Turbak, our newest executive director," Andre began. "And this," he said, pointing at Josh, "is Dr. Joshua Brodsky. Dr. Brodsky came to us from the Department of Defense—he was in charge of artificial intelligence weapon systems. He runs day-to-day on the CHERL project. I thought it was time to bring everyone up to speed."

"Did I miss the deck on this?" asked the lead board member, Michael Yellen, former CEO of the nation's largest car manufacturer. A research report speculated that Yellen was released by his own board for being late to embrace the demand for electric vehicles back in the early part of the century. The company simply announced he was "retiring to spend more time with his family."

"I have it here," Josh said, as he passed out the presentation he had spent the past two days developing. Jenna had waited until an hour before the meeting to text Josh that the board required all materials at least twenty-four hours in advance, giving everyone time to read and prepare questions. "I assumed you knew," she texted, but of course Josh didn't. He was about to apologize to the board for the oversight when Andre cut him off.

"Skip the paper," Andre said. "Just talk us through the project."

Josh had spent the better part of the previous evening practicing his presentation in front of a mirror, scribbling copious notes to himself in the margins. But now, without the crutch of his presentation, he hesitated, and Jenna pounced, saying, "Why don't I start, Josh, and you can fill in where needed?"

Without waiting for him to respond, she launched into an explanation of the project. "We call it CHERL," she said. "It's an acronym for Computerized Human Experienced as Real Life. It's the most ambitious artificial intelligence initiative the company has ever attempted. But it builds on technology we've already perfected."

Seemingly without taking a breath, Jenna went on to describe the history and the recent advances in AI that had made CHERL possible.

"Analyzing thirty years of flight paths, along with weather patterns by time of day to better guide autonomous personal aircraft. Medical diagnosis tools that process millions of patterns extracted from medical journals, textbooks, and the greatest minds in medicine, with our AI team accelerating the development of vaccines for intractable diseases."

Josh seethed as her explanation stretched past the ten-minute mark. Jenna was crisp, she was coherent, and she was definitely rehearsed, leaving little doubt she expected Josh to falter. Another demonstration of her brand of "leadership." If he didn't speak up soon, she'd plow through until there was nothing left for him to add. But Andre may have concluded the same when he raised his hand and said, "All true, Jenna. But no one, and I mean no one, has pushed the envelope with AI like the US Department of Defense. So when I wanted something bigger, something bolder than has ever been done before, there was only one place to turn."

All heads finally swiveled toward Josh. He glanced at Jenna, and while her mouth was open, no words came out. She seemed to understand the signal coming from the CEO, as did the directors.

"Is CHERL like IBM's Watson?" David Paulson asked. Paulson was a former senator from California, who had served in Congress for over twenty years, including eight as head of the Armed Services Committee.

"CHERL is vastly more powerful than Watson," Josh said. "Watson's a good data cruncher, a great analyzer—really good at solving big quantitative-type problems. That's not what we're after."

"So Andre, what do you mean, 'bigger and bolder'?" asked Jeffrey Allen, who led the venture capital fund that provided Andre with the initial seed money to build Sway.

"It's simple," Andre said, smiling. "I want people to be able to speak to history."

Yellen shifted in his seat, but Andre was beaming.

"We're bringing people back from the past," Andre said.

"What?" asked Yellen.

Andre smiled and said, "Not *what*, Michael—*who*?" He then waved his hand toward Josh, prodding him to take control of the discussion.

Josh cleared his throat. "Well, it needs to be someone with an extensive written record. And I don't mean someone who's been written about by others."

"Someone with an autobiography?" asked Allen.

"An autobiography can be a starting place," Josh said. "But in truth, autobiographies have some built-in bias."

Allen squinted, looking confused.

"An autobiography is your own story," Josh continued, "told from your own point of view. It's your own spin on who you are, what you did, why you did it. But when we've only used autobiographies, the results are somewhat limited."

"He means one-dimensional," Jenna added awkwardly. Everyone's focus remained on Josh.

"That was our early experience," Josh added. "Turns out, no one truly sees themselves."

"Isn't that why we rely on biographers?" asked Gary Elliot, a recently appointed director from the packaged goods industry. "For objectivity?"

"Biographies aren't much better," Josh said. "They have biases too—either for the subject, if done cooperatively, or against the subject. Perspectives are often politically motivated."

"So what do you use that doesn't have bias?" Allen asked.

"Everything has some degree of bias," Josh said. "But we've tried many different subjects: politicians, generals, humanitarians. The more prolific, the better the results. Those writings, even when about subject matters other than their own personal history, tell CHERL a lot about the deep psyche, the essence of the personality of the author."

"If they're historical figures, how do you know if your model works?" Paulson asked.

"It's difficult," Josh said. "To some extent, we're relying on comparing the output against the same data that CHERL uses to recreate the persona. It's inexact. But we are now using more recent historical figures, so we can test the responses against a living review panel."

"He means bring in people who knew the person well," Jenna said.

Josh felt his jaw clench every time she interjected.

"Why don't we just read about them in history books?" Yellen asked, his eyes piercing. "Bias and all. Why go through all of this?"

"Come on, Michael," Andre said. "Who reads books anymore? Do you think any of our politicians read anything other than their own poll numbers?" Andre eyed the former senator and shrugged. "No offense, David. But you know I'm right. Name me the last president who was a student of history."

Paulson stared back blankly.

"This will give us so much more than we could ever learn from history books," Josh said. "And by adding recent history to their knowledge base, these great historical figures know so much more today than they ever understood when they lived, even their own impact on the world—ten, twenty, one hundred years after they lived. We can bring them into dialogue with today's leaders."

Andre interjected, "Dialogues where CHERL infers how the greatest leaders from the past would tackle today's challenges!"

The board was silent for a few seconds, until Allen said, "Andre, if your team can pull this off, it would be incredible! I can't imagine it."

"We have pulled it off, Jeffrey," Andre beamed. "I just had my own conversation with General Grant."

"Ulysses S. Grant?" Elliot asked.

"Yes, it was as if he was right there in the room with me," Andre said. "And his insights were outstanding."

"Remarkable," Allen said. "Who else have you built?"

"We've been working on Churchill," Josh said. "I think he's close to being ready. And we're a little farther behind on Napoleon. FDR is in the queue for next month."

Josh thought it best to keep Gandhi to himself for now, at least until his team had more political and military leaders completed.

"How far are you going to take this?" Paulson asked, leaning across the table. "I mean, would you bring back Stalin? Or Hitler?"

The room was silent again, everyone looking to Andre. From Josh's very first day at Sway, he and Andre had discussed the type of projects CHERL would undertake. Stalin and Hitler did not fit their agreed-upon profile of "great leaders"—those who had a "positive long-term impact on mankind."

But Paulson continued, "You don't only learn about leadership from the heroes of history. Maybe a few rogues would help us head off some of the darker trends we're seeing around the world today."

"Technically," Jenna said, "there are no limits if we have rich data to—"

"Maybe down the road, David," Andre interrupted. "That wouldn't be my top priority right now." Paulson shrugged his shoulders.

Yellen spoke up. "Andre, this is all very interesting. But I still think the whole endeavor is off strategy."

Allen pushed back from the table and said, "You can't be serious, Michael. This is right in our wheelhouse—"

"Our wheelhouse is making money," Yellen said. "Lots of money. That's what our shareholders expect us to do."

"We work on things to advance society," Allen said. "Space tourism, medical robotics. Things that make life better."

Yellen looked directly at Tom Brennan, the CFO. "How many millions have we sunk into this, Tom?"

When Brennan responded that Sway had already spent several hundred million dollars on CHERL, the directors launched into a series of side arguments, for and against the project. Josh was stunned at the level of disagreement this far into Andre's major initiative. He heard Yellen continue making his case about financial payback; Allen was passionate about CHERL's positive impact on the Sway brand; Elliot worried that "the ethicists will have a field day when they find out about this." Throughout, the CEO leaned back, seemingly unconcerned, disinterested. Josh tried to keep a mental scorecard of each director's position, feeling the entire project slipping away. He could no longer keep quiet.

"Aren't we supposed to be the visionaries?" he said, loudly enough that the banter ceased.

"Excuse me?" said Yellen. "What did you say?"

"Josh, don't," Jenna said, placing her hand on his arm. Josh pulled away.

"I said, aren't we supposed to be the visionaries?"

"Listen, Dr. Brodsky," Yellen said, "when we want your—"

"No, he's right," Jenna said, this time placing her arm in front of Josh, as if holding him back. "I've been with the company for ten years. We have never been afraid to take big swings."

In all the time they had been working together, Josh could not remember a single moment Jenna took his side. Until now. The directors sat silently for a few moments when Allen, pointing toward Jenna and Josh, spoke up. "They're right. Since the day Andre started the firm, we've led the world into the future."

Andre stood and slowly walked to the boardroom door. He turned back and said, ominously, "Well, this has been a very revealing conversation."

Yellen rubbed his jaw and said, "Look, Andre. You're chairman and CEO. This is your call. I just think the board has a right to understand how we'll monetize this. Maybe we should take a pause until—"

"It's too late for a pause, Michael." Andre held on to the doorknob. "I had a call with the Secretary of State last night. I told him all about CHERL. He understood the ramifications instantly. He's coming to have his own discussion with our General Grant next week."

Josh scrutinized the faces in the room for reaction. The directors sat silently, eyes downcast. Yellen was rubbing the back of his neck. Finally, Allen said, "I think CHERL will be historic."

Paulson looked up and added, "This is going to be transformational for the company. I want to see a demo with FDR when you're ready." Each director started nodding in agreement—all except Yellen, who was scribbling on his notepad.

Andre scanned the room. He opened the door and addressed Josh. "Dr. Brodsky, I need you and your team ready for the Secretary next week."

Josh's mind was swirling, thankful that Andre had closed down the debate, at least for the time being. But his relief was short-lived. A conversation with the Secretary of State was practically a full-scale launch of CHERL. One wrong recommendation from CHERL's inference engine—or one flaw in Grant's thought process —could have a massive impact on US policy toward Japan and elsewhere. Josh had to be sure CHERL was truly ready for such a discussion. He was about to ask Andre for two weeks instead of one, when Jenna spoke up, "We'll be ready."

Andre turned and left. Meeting adjourned.

CHAPTER
FIFTEEN

LOUIE COULD SEE through the glass wall of his office that the two young bankers from his inner circle were heading his way, and he was excited. The day of the merger consummation had finally arrived, and Louie felt positively giddy. Virtual Bank's team was already in the building, awaiting the arrival of Peachtree's CEO, Darrell Evans, who was flying up from Atlanta. It was eight a.m. Louie calculated that all the agreements would be signed and the deal would close by noon. Peabody & Munson fees would be deducted from funds changing hands, Louie's multimillion-dollar share deposited in his bank account first thing tomorrow. Feeling confident, Louie had his team wait in the hallway while he opened ClubTrack. He smiled while placing a small bet on Paco Bell, a three-year-old filly running the third race at Gulfstream Park. It was just a harmless, pre-deal celebration of his coming financial restoration. He had plenty of capacity in his home equity line to float the $25,000 wager. Besides, all his loans would soon be paid off in full.

"Come in, guys," Louie said, taking a long, deep breath as his team entered.

Phil Calpers was tall and athletic, in his early thirties, with dark, slicked-back hair. Susan Bossard, a recent Harvard grad, sat next to Calpers at the conference table, pen at the ready for any last-minute instructions. The pained look on Calpers' face telegraphed his worry.

"The Peachtree guys are in the building," he said.

"Evans is here?" Louie asked, standing. "Great, come on. Let's do this early."

"Not yet," Bossard said. "He's on his plane, but the rest of the team is down the hall."

"But Louie," Calpers said, "they're in a panic." Calpers was Louie's right-hand man, with a sharp, analytical mind. He wasn't easily ruffled.

"About what?" Louie asked as he joined them at the conference table. "You sent them the updated financials, right? The numbers look better than ever."

"It's not about the numbers, Louie. Officially, they want Evans to handle it with you when he gets here."

"It could be about the share price," Bossard said.

"Bullshit," Louie snapped. "We've been through this with them. That's the price. What else?"

"It's not about price," Calpers said. "At least, I don't think so. The CFO said they were looking into a security breach."

"You mean leaks?" Louie asked. "What do they think this is, amateur hour? Nobody's leaking anything to the press before the deal's announced."

"Not leaks—IT security. They've had an outside consultant monitoring Virtual Bank's systems for weeks. Same guy they use at Peachtree."

"Due diligence was over weeks ago," Louie said. "What now?"

"The consultant told them Virtual Bank may have had some type of cyberbreach over the past day."

"That's bullshit too. Everything checked out. Whatever they don't like after the merger, they can fix it."

"Well, that's all I know," Calpers said. "Like I said, they want Evans to handle it when he gets here."

"This is crazy." Louie was trying to maintain his calm exterior, but he felt a bead of sweat roll down his face. He shouted out to get Darrell Evans, the CEO of Peachtree Commerce, on his airphone.

Moments later, his assistant said, "Mr. Evans is on."

"Darrell." Louie greeted the CEO with a feigned, matter-of-fact enthusiasm. "How are you?"

"Good, Louis," replied Evans with his unmistakable Southern drawl. He always preferred to address people by their more formal name, in sharp contrast to an accent that made him sound like a hillbilly. But Louie knew that Evans was one of the sharper CEOs in the banking business. "Glad you're back in the office. Say, very sorry to hear about your mama."

"Oh, thanks, Darrell. Very kind of you."

"Was she ill for long?" Evans asked.

"On and off for a few years," Louie said. "But she went quickly at the end."

"Well, I'm sure she had a good life."

"Ah, yeah. A good life. Hey, Darrell, where are you now?"

"I don't know," Evans said. "Somewhere over Virginia, I think. I believe I can see the coastline. It's a bit foggy out there. I land in New York…let me see…"

"Okay, okay," said Louie. So much for the small talk. "What's going on with your team? My guys said some new issues came up. Something about an IT consultant."

"Yes, well, I was planning to discuss that with you

when I arrived. My guys are really nervous about a potential cyberbreach. They say it may have happened over the past twenty-four hours."

"Hold on, Darrell," Louie said, pacing behind his desk. He felt himself hyperventilating but kept taking low, deep breaths so Evans wouldn't hear his panic. "There's been no breach. You guys have been all over the company for three months. You've scrubbed through every system. You've seen the security they have." He paused, trying to catch his breath. "And if there had been a breach, you know they would have heard from customers. Denied credit card charges, false credit bureau reports, falsified tax returns. Not one complaint."

"I know," drawled Evans. "That's what I told them. But they're insistent that it's a fresh breach. I don't understand either, but my guys are afraid of the financial and reputational cost of proceeding."

Louie stopped pacing behind his desk, the phone pressed to his ear. Gathering his thoughts. But here it was, the eleventh-hour grenade about "higher costs than expected," meaning that Evans was fishing for better terms. Louie had worked in investment banking for over twenty years. Almost every deal had some type of last-minute crisis, each involving an unknown risk rising to the surface, always right as documents were being readied for signature and public relations was ready to announce. Pure negotiating tactics, rarely legitimate concerns. Bald attempts to squeeze better terms or demand better jobs post close for senior executives. Louie learned very early on in his career, there was only one way to deal with these tactics.

"Darrell," Louie said, trying to sound calm, but feeling like a vise was squeezing his chest. "Listen, the Virtual team is sitting in their offices with all the documents, pens in hand. You guys had an exclusive on this deal—but that runs out tomorrow. I understand your concern. But I think you should talk your team off the ledge."

"I don't know, Louis," Evans said. "They seem pretty lathered up about this. A breach could add a bundle of expenses."

"I understand, Darrell," said Louie, feeling his heartbeat slow and his breathing become more normal. "Look, you can talk to your team when you get here. We're finishing up some last-minute changes to the docs, and we'll get them out to everybody." Louie looked over at Bossard and Calpers. He saw Calpers mouth, "What changes?"

Louie winked. "But Darrell, I hope you'll be ready to close the deal when you get here. Virtual Bank has negotiated in good faith for the past two months. But if not, that's okay. I'll walk down the hall and let VB know there's been a change in plans, and we have to go to your competitors and see if we can get them to beat each other up on who's going to step in. Everyone wants to merge with VB."

"Hold on, Louie," Evans said, the friendliness leaving his Southern drawl. "We've spent a lot of time and money on this deal."

"I know, I know," Louie said, taking a gulp of his coffee, looking over at his team. "That's why it would really be too bad to lose it when we're all so close."

Louie could hear nothing but the churning engines of the corporate Cessna in the background. Finally, Evans said, "My team is very concerned. A breach could be catastrophic for the value of the merger."

"I'm sure it would be, Darrell," said Louie. "But there's been no breach at the company, I can assure you.

Again, talk to your team, and let me know what you decide to do."

"Right," Evans said. And with that, the line went dead.

Louie held the phone, gathering his composure.

"What'd he say?" Calpers asked.

"Just all bullshit," Louie said. "Get the closing documents into those conference rooms. No more delays."

Louie could see that Calpers still looked concerned. "What's the story, Phil?"

"You know the other regional banks were way behind on price," Calpers said. "They'll never close the gap if Evans drops out."

"I know," said Louie. "But look, Evans gives you all that sweet Southern yukkity-yuk. But he's just a bully. He's got to know he can't come in here thinking he has us by the balls and squeeze for better terms."

"Is it possible there's been a breach?" Bossard asked meekly. Louie had forgotten she was even in the room.

"What?" snapped Louie, startling her.

She cleared her throat. "Is it possible?" she repeated.

"Who gives a shit?" Louie said. "It's too late! This deal has to close. Now get the fuck out of here and get the docs ready for those signatures!"

Bossard gathered her papers and quickly exited Louie's office. Calpers moved a little slower, staying back. "Should we let the guys over at VB know what's going on?" he asked.

"No way!" said Louie. "Come on, Phil. You know this is bullshit."

"What if it's not?" Calpers asked, hanging in Louie's doorway. Louie knew it was a good thing he had returned to the office before this deal blew up. Calpers wouldn't be able to handle this situation without him, always wrapped up worrying about everything; the liability, the ethics, trying to make all sides happy, having a good outcome for all parties. Louie had saved Calpers's career more times than he could remember. Maybe Munson was right. "Calpers is too nice for this business," he had told Louie on more than one occasion.

Louie walked up close to his associate. "It's bullshit, Phil," he said, jabbing his index finger at Calpers's chest. "Let's go close this fucking deal!"

CHAPTER SIXTEEN

THE LINE at the Budget Rent-a-Car counter at LaGuardia Airport stretched around the roped-off lanes. Based on the pace, Donny estimated he'd be at the counter in another thirty minutes. One clerk manned the desk serving both the preferred customers and the nonpreferred customers, working first to clear the preferred lane before serving those on the lower rung of the food chain. Eventually, Donny was sitting in the back seat of a driverless electric car, programmed with Maggie's address in Floral Park. While the car made its way through New York traffic, Donny checked for text messages and emails. No messages from his brothers. More concerning, he hadn't heard from Ana in over two days. She had missed last night's Horizon coding class. Again. How could she just drop out of sight?

After a thirty-minute drive, Donny had the car park itself one block from Maggie's house, as he wanted to walk the rest of the way to get his bearings. He had no familiarity with the neighborhood. If his mother ever visited the Berman household when they were growing up, she must have come alone.

It was a pleasant, tree-lined street, with an array of two-story brick houses. At Maggie's address, he walked up a wheelchair ramp zigzagging from the walkway to the front door. Before he could ring the doorbell, a voice came from a small speaker perched above the transom.

"Can I help you?"

The voice was formal, female but too young to be Maggie's. Donny thought it sounded like the same woman who made public address announcements at O'Hare.

"Sorry, lady," Donny said. "Must have the wrong house. Do you know where Maggie Berman lives?"

"This is Mrs. Berman's residence," the voice came back. "What is your business?"

"Oh, it is?" Maggie hadn't mentioned live-in help. "I'm Donny Brodsky, Ruth's son. I told Maggie I was coming to visit her today. She's expecting me."

"Please face the door," the voice requested.

Donny did as he was told, not sure what he was looking at. Or who was looking at him. But less than ten seconds later, the door opened and the voice was back.

"Welcome, Mr. Brodsky. Please come in. Maggie is waiting for you in the first room to your left."

Donny entered, seeing no one on the other side of the door. He looked around the foyer, in which a dark oak grandfather clock ticked away next to three small tables filled with bric-a-brac.

"Donny?" called a voice, this time a much older woman's. "I'm in here, sweetie."

Donny followed the sound toward the living room, careful not to bang his leg into the tables. Maggie was sitting in a chair at the end of the room, close to the kitchen.

"Sweetie, it's so good to see you," she said, waving him over. "Come in. Come sit down."

He had just seen Maggie at his mother's funeral, but he was startled to see how feeble she appeared now. At the funeral, her hair had been puffed up, and the complement of makeup must have added to a more youthful appearance. Today she looked at least ten years older.

"Hi, Maggie," he said. "It's good to see you too. But where'd your aide disappear to?"

"Aide?"

"Yeah. The woman who answered the front door?"

"Oh, that," Maggie said, laughing softly. "There's no aide. Well, not every day, at least. Today I'm on my own. I saw you on the TV monitor, so I told Wilma to let you in."

Donny peered around the room, confused. If Maggie was on her own, who was Wilma?

"Oh, I could have come to the door on my own," Maggie continued. "I get around the house fine. But people are always trying to sell me something, so it's easier letting Wilma chase them away. I call her Wilma, but sometimes, when I get bored, I change the voice to a him and call him Fred."

"Huh?"

"My Richie's got the whole place computerized. It's like having a full-time staff around here. Sometimes it makes me crazy."

"Oh, I got it," Donny said, chuckling. "I've been hearing about these home assistance programs. It must be very helpful."

Maggie leaned over and whispered. "She really gives

me a headache, and I have to turn her off. But don't tell Richie."

"It can be turned off?"

"Right there on the wall." She pointed at a screen mounted next to the kitchen light switch. "But I can only shut her down for fifteen minutes. Richie doesn't want her off longer than that. I'll hit it two times, but she still comes back on in fifteen minutes."

"It'll be our secret," Donny said, making a mental note of Wilma's cutoff switch. The computerized aide must not be programmed for housework, Donny thought. The air was warm and musty, with a medicinal smell that reminded him of the Bengay he used to slather on after a particularly rough workout. The curtains were drawn, except at a lone window, where dust particles floated through the sunlight.

"I can't believe you came all this way from Manhattan," Maggie said.

"I don't live in New York, Maggie. I flew in from Chicago."

"Oh my, you flew? That's a long way. Did they feed you on that plane? My Richie says he brings his own food. He says they never feed him anymore."

"Nah, it was a short flight. Just a bag of pretzels."

"I remember when we flew to California to take my grandkids to Disneyland. Oh, the meal they gave us! A beautiful piece of chicken, and vegetables, and a roll. Everyone thought the chicken was like rubber, but I thought it was delicious. Do you believe they didn't charge us? Not even for the drinks. It was wonderful."

"Airlines don't give you much anymore."

"Did you eat anything?" she asked.

"I'm good, Maggie. I'm really not hungry."

"I could put up some soup. I don't have much in the

house. Wilma is ordering groceries for delivery tomorrow. But I don't really need anything. Just some soup and a few bananas. I try to eat one every day. I'm not sure what they do, but Richie says they're good for me. He's a podiatrist in the Bronx. You want a banana?"

"I'll get something later."

The living room walls were covered with Maggie's paintings: bowls of fruit, flowers, and scenes of floating sailboats. At least twenty, all with some variation of these three scenes. His mother's walls were covered with these same paintings. No family pictures on the Brodsky walls. Their mother just wanted Maggie's paintings. The muscles in Donny's neck tightened.

"Did you study art?" he asked.

"Oh, no. Well, I took some art classes before the kids were born."

"You're very talented," Donny mumbled.

Maggie cupped her right ear and tilted toward Donny. "What's that?"

"I said you're very talented," Donny said louder, pointing at the paintings.

"Oh, those things? I haven't painted in years. Can't hold the brush steady. They're not really very good. I'd take them down, but I don't have anything else to put up. Richie's kids like them. I don't really have many left. I gave a lot away."

"I know—Mom had a bunch," Donny said, straining to smile. "She thought they were great."

Maggie laughed. "Your mom didn't have much taste. I think she just wanted something to put on the walls that didn't cost her anything."

The mantel over the fireplace was cluttered with dozens of family photographs. He walked over to get a closer look.

"You have a big family," Donny said, picking up a picture of a large family on a beach. "These your grandchildren?"

"They're all mine," Maggie said. "I lost count. I think I have ten. It might be eleven. I don't see them very much these days. But we always get together for the holidays. The kids are very close."

Close family, Donny thought, looking at the photos. Everybody's laughing, hugging, enjoying each other. Probably support each other too. If one asked the other for a favor, help with a project. Help mow the lawn. Fix a roof. Fix a business. Lend them money. Bet they're right there for each other. That's what families do for each other, right?

"How old are your kids?" Maggie asked.

"No kids," he said, returning the frame to the mantel.

"Oh my, well. That's right. Richie tells me how successful you are, working in Washington, DC, in that big job. It's nice that the two of you stayed in touch. But it must be hard to have a job like that and raise a family."

"That's Josh, not me," he said, sitting back on the chair. Enough of this chitchat. "Maggie, why do you think my mom gave you her diaries?"

Maggie rubbed her hands together, staring at her slippers.

"She didn't want you boys to see them."

"Why not?" he asked. "What was she hiding?"

Maggie hesitated, looking at her hands. "I don't know," she said. "There were a lot of things."

Donny came to find the truth about the accident that killed his father. About why his dad left the hospital just as Donny learned the extent of the damage to his knee and to his career. Was Maggie implying that his mother had other secrets too?

"When did she give them to you?" he asked.

"It was probably a few years ago. I don't really remember time anymore. The days just float by. I don't think she could bring herself to throw them away. In some ways, they were nothing. In other ways, they were everything to her. Like I said, I don't think she knew what to do with them. But she didn't want you boys to have them."

"Have you ever read them?"

"I read some of the earlier ones. Not from when she was a child. Mostly from when she first got married and when she first had you boys. Getting married wasn't a very happy time for your mother. But she liked to write about it, for whatever reason. I guess that was her therapy. When things happened with your father, I couldn't read them anymore."

Donny leaned forward.

"What did she write about that time?" he asked.

Maggie took a deep breath, staring out the window.

"I don't know. We all have our dark days. You're the youngest one, right?"

"No, Maggie. That's Louie. I'm Donny—the middle son."

"Oh, that's right. Joshie was the oldest. I think she protected him from your father. Your dad was one of those sports dads."

"I know," said Donny, a small smile coming to his face.

"But he was hard on Joshie," she continued. "Joshie never wanted anything to do with a ball. Josh was quiet. He just stayed by his mother's side. Always with a book. That made your dad even madder. They tried having another child, but that took a lot longer than they both wanted. What's the age difference between you and Joshie?"

"Three years," Donny said.

"Three years, that's right. By the time they had you, I think things were pretty bad. I know their marriage wasn't great from the beginning, but it certainly wasn't great by the time you were born. Even though your dad got what he wanted—another boy."

Donny didn't remember seeing much of Maggie. He remembered his mom visiting her a lot, but mostly for lunch or an afternoon of shopping. He was amazed at how much detail Maggie knew about their lives. How much more did she know?

"What did she tell you about what happened with Dad?" he asked.

She kept staring out the lone window. She cocked her head when two birds landed on the branch of a tree in her front yard. "It looks like a beautiful day," she said.

"Maggie, I—"

"I'm feeling kind of tired," Maggie said. "I think I'm going to take a nap."

Donny glanced at his watch. He had been there only twenty minutes. He needed more time, but she was fading. He had to get what he'd come for. "It's okay. Why don't I let you rest? I'm gonna find a hotel close by. Can I come back tomorrow?"

"Tomorrow?" she asked. "I think my Richie's coming in the morning. We're going to lunch before he goes to work. I think he wants to clean some things out of my house. He's always cleaning and throwing things away."

"Well, how about later in the day?" he asked. "I can hang around town until then."

"Oh yes." She beamed. "I'd like that. I don't get much company."

"Sure. Say, do you think it would be okay if I took my mom's diaries with me?"

"Oh, no," Maggie said, her back straightening. "I don't know about that. She never wanted you boys to see all that."

"But she's gone now. And I'd really like to learn about her life, her life with Dad, and what really happened."

Maggie was silent again for a long while. A voice spoke, seemingly coming out of the living room walls.

"Miss Maggie," said Wilma. "It is time for your afternoon nap."

"You don't need to see all that," Maggie said, putting her hand on Donny's. Her voice was firm. "It wasn't meant for you boys." She paused, then muttered, "I should have thrown them away like she wanted me to."

"What?" Donny asked. "She wanted you to get rid of them?"

Maggie looked up, a confused expression on her face.

"I'm really feeling fuzzy right now. I…"

"Mr. Brodsky." Wilma again. "Visiting time is over. It's time for Maggie's afternoon nap."

A quiet hum started up and gradually grew louder. Donny turned toward the noise and saw a low, motorized device making its way toward where they were seated. When it reached Maggie, a drawer came out and presented a tray of pills and a glass of water.

"I need to take my medicine," Maggie said.

"Can I at least see them?" Donny asked.

She held a handful of pills out for him to examine.

"No, no, not the pills—the diaries."

Maggie swallowed each pill and drank some water, seeming to be lost in thought.

"I don't think that's a good idea," she said.

"I won't take them with me—I'd just like to see them."

Maggie sat quietly drinking. Her eyes seemed distant. But after another sip, she looked up and said, "Oh, I guess there's no harm in that." She used her arms to push herself out of the chair. She grabbed the cane propped on the coffee table and started shuffling down the hall. Donny followed close by her side. When she approached the den, she pointed to the closet door. Donny moved over and opened the louvered doors, assaulted by the strong camphor odor coming from within. On the floor were four boxes marked "R.B."

"Those are them," she said.

Donny kneeled and took the lid off the top box, amazed by what he was seeing. There had to be twenty booklets, neatly aligned, with years clearly marked on the spines. The first box was from the 1940s and '50s.

"This is unbelievable," he said. "How many are in here?"

"I don't know—every box is full. Like I said, she sent me everything."

"Wow," said Donny, running his hand over the spines. "Okay, well, look. I don't want to overstay. Can I just use your bathroom before I leave?"

"It's that door over there," she said.

Donny placed the lid on the box, closed the closet door, and followed Maggie out of the den.

"I'll just be a minute."

Donny went into the bathroom, closed the door, and listened to Maggie's cane knock on the floor as she slowly made her way into the kitchen. He quietly turned the handle on the bathroom door and tiptoed back into the den. He gently opened the louvered doors, bent down, lifted the lid. He heard the clump of Maggie's cane. No time to find the diary from 1988—the year his father died —so he randomly grabbed one and stuffed it inside the liner of his jacket. Moments later, he was back in the bathroom, flushing the toilet and washing his hands. She stood outside the bathroom as he opened the door.

"Are you coming back tomorrow?" Maggie asked as Donny walked to the front door.

"Yes, Maggie. In the afternoon, remember? Richie's coming for lunch."

"Of course," she said as the front door automatically opened. "The afternoon's good. I can make us some soup."

CHAPTER
SEVENTEEN

THREE COMPUTERS LINED the conference table, each running multiple diagnostics as Josh powered through the afternoon, digging into CHERL's inference engine. A large steaming cup of coffee and a half-eaten bag of chocolate Munchkins were at his side. Naveen had his team gathered in the adjacent room, executing every conceivable test on the neural networks. By the time Andre hosted the Secretary of State next week, CHERL better be operating at peak performance. The repercussions of incorrect insights from Grant could be devastating to the country, not to mention the future of the project. Josh's concentration was broken by Jenna's soft rap on the door.

"They told me you were in here," she said. "Mind if I come in?"

"Sure, what's up?"

"You're here late." She closed the door behind her.

"Yeah, well, lost track of time."

"Me too. I just checked on the team. They're still in there. So's the Chinese food from last night."

Josh saw Jenna stare at the bag of Munchkins.

"Better get in there if you're hungry," she said.

"I'll pass, thanks."

"Guess we should have brought them some breakfast," she said. "They're like a bunch of vultures."

"Can be."

"What's all this?" she asked, waving at the computers.

"Just running my own diagnostics on the inference engine. Been going through as much of the code as I can."

"On your own?"

"Yeah, well, my team is pretty much heads down on the neural nets. I wanted to do my own digging."

Jenna crossed her arms and leaned back against the wall and said, with a biting tone, "You like going your own way, don't you?"

Josh tossed his pen onto the table. "What's that supposed to mean?"

"Just what I said. You like doing your own thing. It's pretty obvious."

Josh had too much to do. This wasn't the time to engage in a showdown. Try to defuse, if he could. "Jenna, what I'm doing is not a group activity. My team knows what they have to do."

"That's the second time you've said that," she said.

"Said what? That my team is—"

"Make that three times," she said. "I didn't realize they were your team."

"They *are* my team," Josh said. "I hired them, I direct them. I've been with them since the beginning. Yeah, they're my team."

"Look, Dr. Brodsky," she said, narrowing her eyes, "I know you think this is your personal project. You've operated that way since the day I showed up. Let me ask you, have you always been an asshole to your bosses?"

Josh glared at Jenna, incredulous that she was picking this time to have a confrontation. When she added, "You've been dismissive of me since day one, and I want to know why," Josh couldn't hold back.

"I don't think I've been the asshole," he started. "But let me ask you this. You see, Andre hired me. He asked me to move my butt all the way to the West Coast to lead this project. He knew my credentials, and he knew my track record in artificial intelligence. I assume that's why he hired me to lead CHERL." He paused, then added, "Why did he hire you?"

Jenna moved around and sat down. She leaned forward and clasped her hands.

"Dr. Brodsky, I've been here for ten years. So you're right. He didn't hire me for this project. I've worked my way up from the bottom. I've coded, I've done design work, I've led important initiatives. And, unlike you, I've delivered for this company. I've delivered for Andre, time and time again. That's why I'm here. That's why I've been promoted into this position. Not hired—promoted. Now, if you're asking why I'm your boss—is that what you're asking?"

Josh sat back and folded his arms.

"Andre trusted me," Jenna said. "He trusted that I would help you get CHERL to the finish line."

"How? By withholding information?"

"When did I withhold information?" she asked, leaning onto the table.

"Why didn't you tell me the board wanted to get my presentation ahead of time?"

"I thought you knew that."

"How would I know? I've never been to any of

Andre's board meetings. And you were sure ready to jump in and take my place."

"I'm always ready!" Jenna's face turned red. "But I wasn't trying to get in your way. I was trying to help you."

"Helping? You took over the whole damn meeting!"

Jenna sat back. She appeared surprised by the accusation. "Just until you got your footing," she said. "You seemed rattled when the meeting started."

"I was rattled because I spent hours on that presentation and then Andre didn't want to use it."

"What should I say?" she asked. "That's Andre. You have to be ready for anything."

He nodded. "I thought the board was about to kill the project."

"Look, I knew Andre was just letting the board blow off steam," she said. "They have to feel like they have a say. But when things got ugly, I didn't let you hang out there on your own, did I?"

He put his hands up to acknowledge her point. "I appreciate it."

"Look, my being your manager," she said calmly, "maybe that's not what you had in mind, but I'm sure it's also a test for me."

"What kind of test?"

"To see if I could move from being a doer to being a manager. But you see, it wasn't a fair test. Because if I was really your manager, I would have fired your ass. Stiff-arming me at every turn. Lack of transparency. Lack of communication. What boss would put up with that garbage? It's like you're hiding some big secrets." She paused, then added, "You're like a wall."

You're like a wall. Those simple words cracked a lightning bolt to Josh's central nervous system. He wanted to explode. But he conjured up the tools he had learned during all those years in group therapy. Breathe in, breathe out. De-escalate the situation. Lower the temperature. Remember the mission. If that didn't work, fake it. Like the rest of the world. Josh slowly rubbed the scar behind his ear.

"So why didn't you just fire me?" he asked calmly.

"Because you are Andre's guy. He wants it to work. How would it have looked if I went to him and said I was firing his handpicked expert on his most important initiative? I don't think that would have been a feather in my cap."

"I guess we're stuck with each other," Josh said, exhaling.

Jenna stood and moved to the door. She held on to the handle and looked back.

"Why'd you take this job?" she asked.

"Good question. I've been asking myself the same thing." He was silent for a few moments, staring at his computer. "I guess the challenge," he said. "And the mission. And I was tired of figuring out better ways to blow people up."

"Is that what you did at DoD?"

"Pretty much. Or at least building smarter ways to do it. Trying to only kill the bad guys. Not always possible."

Jenna smiled and said, "At least we minimize collateral damage here."

Josh chuckled. "I guess it would have helped had Andre told me about you when he hired me."

"What, you expected you'd work directly for Andre?"

Josh didn't answer.

"Well, if you haven't figured it out by now," she said, "Andre's a bit mercurial. And clear communication is not his strong suit either. He just expects everyone will figure it out. And if not, he gets rid of you."

"Is that what's going to happen to me?" Josh asked.

"I don't know," she said. "But it might help if you stopped giving me the stiff-arm and worked with me. Like a partner."

"Like a partner," Josh repeated.

"Yes, like a partner. We can help each other. And instead of building up all this animosity, if I'm doing something wrong, tell me. How else will I learn?"

Wow, saying she wanted to learn instead of trying to come off like she knew everything. Maybe they could work together after all.

"That's fair, Jenna. Feedback should be two ways."

"Thank you, Dr. Brodsky."

"Josh," he said, and smiled. "It's probably time you called me Josh."

Jenna smiled back.

Josh's computer screen flashed a message:

```
NAVEEN:
Where can I find you?
                                    JOSH:
                                    Conf B
```

"Everything okay?" Jenna asked.

"It's Naveen. I think he's coming down."

Jenna opened the door. "I'll leave you to it."

"No, wait," Josh said. "Stick around. Let's hear what he's got."

Jenna smiled. "I just need to use the ladies' room. I'll be right back."

Josh took a long exhale. This had been a confrontation he'd tried to avoid since the day Jenna was assigned. Avoiding confrontation was a survival skill he had honed throughout his life, like a zebra fleeing a lion. But she had cornered him in his conference room, delivered a blow that was all too common in his fifty-five years.

You're like a wall.

Those same words he'd heard throughout his life—words that set off triggers in his head.

"He's like a wall!" his mother had snapped one night to Josh's father in the supposed privacy of their bedroom. Josh was in eighth grade at the time, sharing a bedroom with his two younger brothers, who were fast asleep. His parents didn't think Josh could hear them yelling at each other. Or maybe they did. After all, it was a small apartment. If everyone could hear their neighbors arguing through the thin apartment walls, there was a good chance his parents knew the boys could pick up things loud and clear in the next bedroom. Either that, or they didn't care.

"I tell you, Joe, I can't get through to that kid," he heard his mother say. "He never wants to leave the house. Just sits around reading books all day long."

"What do you want from me?" his dad shouted.

"You're his father. And all you do is disappear."

"Disappear?" he shot back. "Going to work is disappearing?"

"Spend some time with your older son. Take him out of here, like you do with Donny. I can't stand looking at him sitting around all day. It's not normal."

"What am I supposed to do with him?" his father said. "If he wants to sit around reading, let him. He's in his own world."

That much was true. In those days, Josh inhabited the worlds of E. B. White, J. R. R. Tolkien, Jonathan Swift, and Jules Verne. Always taking his mind into far-off places. If he wasn't reading, he was taking advanced math textbooks out of the school library. Solving linear algebraic equations by fifth grade and studying quantum physics before his sophomore year in high school. That was his world. A world separate and apart from his combative parents and much younger brothers.

He was one of those rare birds who didn't need much sleep, and he used this to his greatest advantage. Still, graduating from high school in three years was more of a relief than a point of celebration. And when he was accepted to MIT with a free ride, he bought a one-way bus ticket to Boston and never looked back. Even after his father's accident, other than for the funeral, he rarely went home again. Instead, he poured what he had into his science. Into his work. The type of work where being a loner wouldn't hold him back.

Throughout his years at Defense, invariably, someone would try to change him. To "adjust" his personality to fit the social norms of the department. To make him more "open," "friendly," "interactive." He'd see the feedback on the occasional 360-degree review, almost exclusively from peers and superiors. Most of the comments were in polite corporate or military speak.

"Take time to get to know people. Learn to be more interactive. Be more revealing."

But occasionally, someone would express their feedback in harsher terms.

"Standoffish."

"Antisocial."

"Recluse."

All code words, but the meaning was clear. And when those themes were brought forth, things usually ended badly for him. Hopefully, he and Jenna had reached a détente of sorts, enough for him to focus on the mission without distractions.

Naveen entered, trying to catch his breath. What he said changed everything.

"We have an issue. It's really unbelievable. It was so well hidden. We're—"

When Jenna joined them, Naveen stopped.

"It's okay, Naveen," Josh said. "Tell us what's going on."

"Okay, mon. I'm not sure how it got there. It's very sophisticated."

"What are you talking about?" Jenna asked.

"At first we thought it was a bug. But it's not a bug. Well, it is, but not something we did ourselves. Whoever planted it is a pro."

"What?" Josh asked.

"Okay, sorry, mon, I just can't believe it. Someone infected CHERL with sophisticated pieces of malware."

"Malware?" Jenna asked. "Oh my god!"

"It blended in so perfectly with our code," Naveen said. "We couldn't detect it. We just stumbled on to one, and now we're finding them everywhere."

Josh stood. "What are they doing?"

"That's just it—nothing yet. The cybersecurity team is investigating. They're worried that these are sleeper cells that can be activated to copy or encrypt CHERL's code."

"Shit!" Josh said. "How did we get malware? I thought Sway had all these state-of-the-art security systems."

"I don't know," Naveen said.

Josh couldn't believe what he was hearing. "Naveen, make sure we save all the backup versions of CHERL's code."

"I'll go down and get an update from security," Jenna said. "I'll need to brief Andre in the morning."

She looked at Josh and added, "Let's go do this together."

CHAPTER
EIGHTEEN

IT WAS HIGH NOON, and the signature pages were lined up in the Peabody & Munson boardroom, stretching down both sides of the long oak table. Twenty piles, five pages deep, lined up like white tiles. Copies for the lawyers, investment bankers, regulators, lenders—each to be signed by the CEOs and general counsels of Virtual Bank and Peachtree. Six junior associates placed Montblanc pens atop each stack. The executives from Peachtree were gathered in a separate conference room down the hall. The VB team was on the opposite end of the building, in the Silverado Room.

Louie poked his head in to check on the VB team. Sitting there were the bank's general counsel, Joel Esposito; finance chief, Chris Jones; and the CEO, Peter Galloway.

"All set for the big day?" Louie asked.

Galloway, decked in full suit and tie, with a matching pocket square, was typing with one finger on his phone. Without looking up, he said, "We'll be with you in a minute."

"Okay," Louie said, looking at Jones, who shrugged and put his hand up.

"I'll be next door when you're ready," Louie said, mouthing the word *prick* as he walked down to check in on Peachtree. Galloway couldn't even acknowledge him, say, "Hello," or "thanks for getting us this far."

He was probably too busy scouting out vacation property on Sotheby's. Louie hated working with assholes like Galloway but considered it the cost of doing business. Every step of the way, the only thing Galloway cared about was his role in the new company and how much equity he'd get. The asshole never once inquired about what was going to happen to his own executive team, or any of the units that would get cut as part of the merger, which were many. Of the 20,000 employees of Virtual Bank, the Peachtree team had already identified over 7,000 eliminations, with more to come post-close. Of Galloway's top twenty executives, eight would lose their jobs on day one, seven would take on roles with lesser responsibility and lower compensation, and five would be in roles similar to what they had premerger. Esposito and Jones, who were about to sign the paperwork closing the deal, were in category two. But Galloway had made sure to negotiate very well on his own behalf. He wouldn't run the new company, but his role would be president of the combined entity, with a sizable compensation increase. He'd have to work in the new unit for three years while his equity vested, and then he'd go off into the sunset with enough money to retire ten times over. Not to mention lifetime use of the corporate jet, office space, and a digitized personal assistant. Galloway had been unsuccessful in retaining his human personal assistant, rumored to be providing him with some very personal services in the back of the corporate jet. Still, Virtual

Bank's CEO was highly motivated to get this deal completed.

Louie stood outside the Peachtree conference room, overhearing a heated exchange coming from within. He knocked and walked in. There were over twenty people around the table. Their conversation stopped when they saw him. At the head was Evans, looking serious.

"Hello, Louis," said the Peachtree CEO. "Come on in."

"Wow, quite a crowd for a closing," Louie said.

"Well, that's just it, Louis," Evans said. "We figured we'd have one last go-around on this breach issue. I don't like what I'm hearing."

Louie looked around the room. He recognized Peachtree's CFO and general counsel, both in suits and ties, but had never met any of the other twenty or so people, clad in jeans, sneakers, and a colorful assortment of tees and polo shirts. Papers and charts were scattered across the conference table.

"Exactly what is it that you're hearing?"

"It appears there's been an intrusion at Virtual, son," Evans said.

"What are you talking about, Darrell?" Louie said. "We've been all over this territory."

Evans motioned toward the people around the table.

"I'm afraid it's real, Louis. And I think Virtual knows it too. But that's another story. This is my tech team. Best in the business, I think. Show Louis here what we've been looking at."

A heavyset woman stood and walked her tablet to Louie.

"We ran our intrusion-detection software during the due diligence last month," she said. "We found no evidence of a breach of any kind. We thought we took down all the detection software when we cleared out after due diligence, but someone forgot to pull this one out that was monitoring the customer information systems at Virtual. The dashboards were being sent daily to our security team, who noticed something peculiar when they reviewed yesterday's end-of-day scan."

The tablet displayed a chart listing each of VB's systems, with a color-coded scheme across the horizontal axis showing days of the week over the past two weeks. Most of the days on the chart were green, with the occasional box filled in as yellow. That all changed the previous day. The boxes on the chart were all bright red.

"What am I supposed to make of this?" Louie asked.

"It says what it says," Evans said. "The customer systems have been breached. Virtual has a big problem on their hands."

Louie stared at the charts in front of him. His heart rate picked up.

"Darrell, can I talk to you outside for a minute?"

The six-foot-five Evans slowly lumbered out of his chair and followed Louie into the hallway.

"Darrell, this is crazy," Louie said. He felt a bead of sweat drip down his back. "This deal needs to close."

Evans folded his arms in front of his chest, grimacing.

"You need to get a grip, Louis. I'd look like a fool with my board if I signed those papers now, not to mention my team in that conference room. Let me ask you something: did you know about this? Is that why you're pressing to get this done?"

"What!" Louie said, louder than he'd intended. "I know nothing about a breach. You think I would jam you up like that?"

"I don't know. You seem pretty jacked up to get me to sign those papers."

"Because it's a good deal!" Louie said. "Come on, even if there is a breach, how bad can it be if it just happened? And nobody's heard about any customer impact? Don't you think something would be public somehow?"

"I don't know," Evans said. "But I feel like someone's trying to snow me, and I don't take kindly to being snowed."

"If you think you're being snowed, let's go talk to them," Louie said. "They're right down the hall."

"I'm not sure I want to talk to them right now," Evans said. "My team is pretty sure those sombitches knew about this."

"Forget it," Louie said. "You stay here. I'll go."

Louie scurried to the Silverado Room. Galloway was still pecking away at his phone.

"Peter, we need to talk," Louie said.

"Just a few more minutes," Galloway said. "I'll be right with you."

"Peter, this deal may be off!"

Esposito and Jones turned. Galloway looked up, placing his phone on the table. "What?"

"Peachtree's intrusion-detection software shows a breach of your systems. They say customer databases may have been compromised and that you have to know about it."

"What software?" Jones asked nervously. "We reviewed all their reports after the due diligence. It was clean."

"They left their software running after due diligence," Louie said. "They meant to take it down, so they claim. The breach showed up in the past few days."

Galloway looked over at his lawyer. No words were exchanged, but Louie could see the CEO was looking for guidance.

"No data has been stolen from our systems," Galloway said slowly, deliberately. Louie did not like how carefully he chose his words.

"You're not convincing me," Louie said.

"I'm telling you, no customer data has left our environment," Galloway said.

"You need to tell them that. Evans is listening to his tech team, and they say they've detected a break-in. Are you telling me there wasn't a break-in?"

"I didn't say there hadn't been a break-in," Galloway said. "I just said no data has left our systems."

"So you *have* had a break-in?" Louie asked, his voice rising. "You didn't think you needed to disclose a breach to the public? And to the guys down the hall, who are about to merge with your bank?"

"We're in the process of trying to resolve the issue," Esposito said. "We don't think it's elevated to a disclosable event."

"Guys, what the fuck is going on?" Louie shouted. "Stop with all the bullshit!"

"I can assure you that no customer information has left our systems," Esposito repeated. "We are very confident of that."

"Okay, cut the finely parsed words," Louie said. "These guys are about to walk. The whole deal is cratering. I asked you, what the fuck is going on?"

Esposito and his boss exchanged glances. Esposito nodded to Galloway.

"Our customer data is securely in our systems," Galloway said. "We have complete access to our data."

"Then what's going on?"

"There has been an intrusion. Nothing's happened yet. We detected that a bunch of malware has been dropped into our systems. But we're clearing it out. There's no problem."

"Are you sure?" Louie asked. "Then let's get your CTO on the phone so he can tell Evans that."

Esposito nodded to Galloway again and said, "I think we can do that." Before Galloway could make the call, Esposito's phone rang.

"Slow down, Steve," Esposito said. "We were just talking about that. Hold on. Peter is here with me." He put the phone on the table and introduced Louie to their chief technology officer, Steve Cannon. "You're on speaker, Steve."

"Yes, Steve," Galloway said. "I'm right here."

"There's been an unfortunate update," Cannon said. "The malware has been activated."

"Activated!" Galloway's face turned red. "To do what?"

"It's an encryption attack. We've been locked out of our own customer databases. We just received a message demanding five million dollars. It says we have one week. If we can't remove this malware before then, we may never be able to unlock our files."

———

THAT NIGHT, Louie opened the door to his apartment, placed his keys on the table, and kicked off his shoes. His head throbbed from the long day in the stuffy conference room. He wanted to go into the master bathroom medicine chest to get three Tylenol but was afraid he'd wake Vicki. Instead, he padded over to his home office, flicked on the desk lamp, opened the bottom drawer, and pulled out his Prozac and a small bottle of scotch. He slid into his leather chair, washed down the Prozac with four quick sips of scotch, and reflected on his predicament.

What a shit show. The whole deal was about to go up in flames.

"There's no guarantee the hacker will remove the malware, even if we pay," Esposito, Virtual Bank's general counsel, had said when Louie finally got the two banks together in one room. Evans was livid but agreed to give VB a week to resolve the issue, or Peachtree would walk away.

"I've got plenty of other fish to fry," Evans told Louie privately. "Plenty of other investment banks are bringing me good deals. With trustworthy partners. Without any baggage."

The threat was clear. The malware had to be disabled and Virtual's security walls needed to be firmed up in order to get the deal across the finish line.

The hallway light flicked on, startling Louie. Vicki appeared at his office door. She stood in her pajamas, holding a piece of paper in her hands.

"Hey, babe," Louie said, sliding the bottle of scotch behind his desktop monitor.

"Don't give me 'Hey, babe,'" she snapped. "Where were you?"

"I was at the office," he said. "I texted you."

"That was at two o'clock this afternoon. You said the deal was closing. You didn't say anything about going out partying."

"No party," Louie said, slouching in his chair. "No closing."

"Why do I smell scotch? Where were you?"

Louie slid the bottle farther back. "I told you—at the

office. The closing blew up. I mean, it's derailed. We're trying to get it back on track. Why are you up so late?"

Vicki padded over to Louie and flipped the paper onto his desk.

"I was waiting for you to talk about this," she said.

Louie picked up the paper. It was from the bank that held the mortgage on their apartment.

Dear Mr. Brodsky:

You are hereby notified that your payment of $55,382.96, representing two months past due, has not been received. If said payment is not received by April 1, the undersigned shall invoke all remedies under the mortgage agreement, including, but not limited to, foreclosure proceedings.

"It's a mistake," he said, sounding unconvincing, even to himself.

"Is it?" Vicki moved around the desk and stood over him. "I called the bank. I tried to transfer money from our savings account to pay for this, not knowing what was going on." Her eyes were locked on him. "They said our savings accounts have a zero balance," she said, her anger visible. "All of them."

"Vic, take a deep breath."

"Where's all our fucking money, Louie?"

"I moved a bunch of stuff around," he stuttered. "I forgot to tell you about it. I didn't realize I left our bank accounts empty. I'll fix it in the morning. It's no big deal."

"Moved money around?" she asked, her face turning red. "Why are you moving money around? Where?"

"Vic, calm down," he said, hands raised as if trying to push back her onslaught. "You'll wake Jess."

"I'll calm down when you tell me what the fuck is going on."

"I told you. I moved money out of our bank to our other accounts. We're getting more interest at some of the online banks, that's all."

"Bullshit! What online banks?" she said, her arms flailing. "You never told me about any online banks. This letter says we haven't paid them in two months. Sign on to those fuckin' online banks right now and show me where our money is."

"What's going on, guys?" Their twelve-year-old daughter, Jessica, stood in the doorway.

Louie came from around his desk and put his arms around her.

"Hi, sweetie, I feel like I haven't seen you in days," Louie said, holding on to his daughter as if she were a shield.

"Hi, Daddy. Is everything okay?"

"Everything is fine, baby." Louie pushed Jessica's hair to the side and kissed her over and over on her cheek, the sucking sound making her giggle. "Daddy, staaaap."

"Sorry, I can't help it if I miss you," Louie said.

"I miss you too. What are you guys fighting about?"

"It's nothing," Louie tried. "Everything is fine. Mom and Dad are just having a small disagreement."

Jessica pulled away and walked over to her mother, who was wiping her eyes on the sleeve of her pajamas.

"Mom?"

"It's okay, Jess," Vicki said, regaining her composure. "I'm fine. I'm sorry we woke you. Go back to bed."

Jessica looked at both of her parents. "You sure?"

"We're fine, honey," Louie said. He guided her toward the door. "How's school?"

"Let her go, Louie. She needs to be up early."

"Will I see you in the morning?" Jessica asked her father.

"No, sweetie," he said. "I've got to get back to the office early again tomorrow. I'm sorry. But I'll call you after school. I promise."

"Okay," Jessica said hesitantly. She looked back at her mother. "Are you sure you're okay, Mom?"

"Night, honey. It's okay. I love you."

Louie closed the door and motioned his wife toward his desk chair.

"Sit down, Vic," he said, his voice barely above a whisper.

Louie saw her staring at the bottle of scotch tucked behind the monitor.

"Rough day," he said sheepishly.

Vicki rolled her eyes.

"I'm gonna fix it, okay?" he said. "I am fixing it."

"Where's the money?" she said sharply.

"It's just temporary, Vic," he said. "I promise."

"What does that mean?"

Louie rubbed his hands together. "We have a temporary cash squeeze, okay? It means that more money is going out the door than is coming in. For now, at least."

"I don't understand," she said, speaking in a monotone. "When did this start? I thought we had so much money."

"My salary is nothing," he said. "You knew that. It covers the basics. But the mortgage, car leases, vacations —all that comes out of my bonus money. I get paid for the deals I bring in and close."

"Eat what you kill," she said, parroting the line she'd heard forever.

"Exactly. But I haven't closed a deal in a long time. We've been living off my bonuses from three years ago."

"Why haven't you told me any of this? Why have you been lying?"

"How have I been lying? You know what's been happening at work. When was the last time you heard me close a deal?"

"I never knew that our money was running out. You're the one who handles the finances. Anytime I ask if we're okay, anytime I ask anything about money, you blow me off. You tell me not to worry, you've got everything under control. You should have told me."

"I never thought this drought would last so long," he said softly. "I thought I had it under control."

"Louie," she hissed through clenched teeth. "The bank is going to throw us out of our fuckin' apartment!"

"They're not throwing us out," he said. "Calm down. I can tap into our line of credit. Just to get us over the hump."

"Credit line?" she said. "I don't understand. How did we run out of money so fast?"

Louie knew he couldn't answer his wife's question. As he fingered his phone, he remembered he hadn't checked today's race results.

Vicki leaned her head back and looked up at the ceiling. Blinking her watery eyes, she said, "You never should have taken this job."

Louie glared at his wife, his demeanor no longer subdued and apologetic. "Great. That's helpful."

"It's true," she said sharply. "Look at everyone who stayed at Goldman. The Benjamins just bought a big house in Marco Island. He was your year, right? So was Jeremy Michaels. They're always taking vacations on his personal jet."

"Now you care about having a personal jet?"

"No, Louie. I just care about not being evicted from our fucking apartment. That'd be enough for right now."

"We've been through this, Vic. I was going nowhere

at Goldman. The politics were cutthroat. That wasn't me. I'm a deal guy."

"Well, maybe you need to be a little more cutthroat. And where are the deals, Mr. Deal Guy?"

"So supportive." He sneered.

"Don't get so defensive," she said. "This is fucked-up. You work your ass off. I never see you, and now you tell me we don't have any money."

"Don't overreact for a change. I've made plenty of money. Just not in the last three years. I'm not the only one. The whole firm has hit a dry spell."

"Oh, just not in the last three years. That's a pretty long time, wouldn't you say? Maybe it's time you found a new job?"

Louie stood up and slowly moved around the desk to store the scotch back in his desk drawer. "Look, I got this," he said. "The deal I'm working on now, it's a big one. It puts the firm back on the map. It puts *me* back on the map. And it's a big payday. Enough to pay off this mortgage. And we'll have enough cushion for another three years."

"Didn't you just tell me that the deal was derailed?"

"Vic, I'm telling you. This deal is going to go through. And it will get me back in the winning column. There'll be more to come."

"What if there's not? I can't live with a sword over our heads."

"I will get this deal done," he said.

Whatever it takes.

CHAPTER
NINETEEN

DONNY CHECKED into the Floral Park Motel after picking up Chinese takeout and a six-pack of Miller. He threw his shoes off, plopped on the bed, washed down a few mouthfuls of General Tso's chicken, and checked his messages. Still nothing from Ana. He had emailed her and sent her numerous text messages over the past two days. But for whatever reason, she remained silent. He clicked on the contact list from Horizon's coding class and texted the two students who were with them at Gibson's that night.

"Haven't seen her since Monday," one responded.

"Nada," from the other.

Where did she disappear to? Or was she already blowing him off, fishing elsewhere for an alternative partner? There wasn't much he could do about it from this shitty motel. He would track her down when he got back. But he wasn't going home without those diaries.

He spilled a forkful of rice all over the blanket, promptly brushing the grains onto the discolored carpet, where they stood out like white mouse droppings. He kicked whatever he could underneath the bed.

He opened the diary he had pilfered from Maggie's closet, and on the very first page, dated January 1, 1959, he was struck by the penmanship. The way she looped her *l*'s: clean, distinctive, and very legible. There was no mistake. This was his mother's.

It was a surreal experience reading the thoughts of his then eighteen-year-old mother. But as the pages turned, he realized that while the handwriting was the same, this was the work of a person far different from the mother he knew. She seemed happy, carefree. Mature for her years but not much different from what he would have expected from any high school girl. Comments about her friends. Which teachers were nice, which ones were mean. Crushes she had, but nothing that ever merited a third mention. Donny knew that his parents had married in June of 1960, when she was just twenty. Other than the fact that they had been fixed up by his grandparents, he never knew much about that time of their lives.

Halfway through the diary there was still no mention of any boy named Joe Brodsky. However, the year before she got married, his mom started writing about a different boy she had her eye on. His name was Tommy.

Tuesday, July 7, 1959

Met this very cute boy on Nostrand Avenue today. I was strolling with Maggie and Natalie, and we went into Jahn's for an egg cream. We sat at a booth and Maggie said our waiter kept looking at me, but I don't think that's true. He did

have a beautiful smile. And these blue, soulful eyes.
I must say, my heart skipped a beat.

Wednesday, July 8, 1959

Maggie and I went back to Jahn's for an egg
cream. That boy was working the fountain, so we
sat at the counter this time. And he came over
and served us. I was so nervous, I could barely
breathe. His name tag said Tommy. Maggie said
he looks so mature. He was looking over at us the
whole time we were there, but I was afraid to look
up. I kept my head down into my egg cream. I
didn't dare look up. I ran out of there as soon as
I was finished.

Donny chuckled. Jahn's became a frequent destina-
tion for Mom and her friends over the next few weeks,
giggling about her infatuation with this Tommy guy. But
then things got more interesting toward the end of the
month.

Saturday, July 18, 1959

Maggie came with me to Jahn's again and we
took our usual seats at the counter. After order-
ing, Maggie left to go to the bathroom. Tommy
came over and started talking to me. Said he
hadn't seen me in a few days and wondered if I
lost my taste for egg creams. He asked me my
name, and I could barely speak. He said his name
is Tommy Vitola. Asked me if I liked the movies,

and I said of course I did. He asked if I liked Paul Newman. He said he was a big fan and he wanted to be just like him someday. Then he asked me if I would go with him to see Newman's film that was replaying at the Albemarle Theatre. He said it's called Cat on a Hot Tin Roof. I told him I had never heard of it. As soon as I said it, I was so angry with myself. What a fool I was. I just didn't know what to say. He asked if that meant I wasn't interested in the movies and I said of course not. I would love to see it. So we're going next weekend. I hope I can catch my breath.

Sunday, July 26, 1959

What a wonderful day. What a wonderful movie. Elizabeth Taylor was so beautiful. It was so intense, I couldn't catch my breath. I kept looking over at Tommy. He was mesmerized. I wasn't even sure if he knew that I was there, sitting next to him. But when it was over, he looked at me and asked if I liked it. Of course, I said. We sat there talking about the movie while everyone else left the theatre. He knows so much about the movies. I felt like an idiot. When the theatre was completely empty, we sat talking for a long while. When we were about to get up, he took my hand, stared at me with those hypnotic blue eyes, and gently kissed me on the cheek. My legs were so weak, it took all of my strength to rise from my seat. He

walked me home, talking the whole time. But I
said goodbye to him when we were a block away. I
couldn't risk my family seeing us. He said he wants
to see me again. I'm so afraid.

"Holy shit!" Donny said, loudly enough for his neighbors at the motel to hear him. Tommy Vitola? *Vitola*! His mother had had the hots for an Italian guy? The mother who grew up in a strictly Orthodox Jewish household? He never knew. She always said she'd never dated any guys before Dad. Donny skipped ahead to find their next encounter.

Monday, August 3, 1959

Met Tommy again yesterday. We took a long
walk on Ocean Parkway. I was so nervous that
someone from the Temple would see us and tell my
parents, so we walked away from the neighbor-
hood. Tommy has a very bad limp, which he said
came from a bad car accident when he was
twelve. He told me he's twenty and tried to enlist
after high school like everyone else, but was 4-F.
He's been working at Jahn's and other jobs, living
with his parents, trying to save enough money to
move to California. He wants to get away from
having to work in his father's business. I asked
him what his father did for a living but he
wouldn't tell me. It doesn't really matter. He only
wants to be in the movies.

Donny read her entries for the rest of the summer and into the fall. His mother saw Tommy Vitola often, and her feelings were growing stronger with each passing week. She started recording steamy petting encounters parked at Brighton Beach. Donny found one particularly shocking entry in the middle of October.

Sunday, October 11, 1959

We went all the way last night. I can't believe it. Tommy said I'm so mature for a high school girl. He said it wasn't his first time and I was as good as anyone he's been with. I was so relieved. I didn't want him to think of me as a high school girl. But it all felt so right. So perfect.

Unbelievable. His mother had lost her virginity at nineteen. Not married. Not with Dad. In the back seat of a car. Ugh! His mother had fallen head over heels for this guy. And best he could tell, she did it without her parents finding out anything about it.

From October through early December, they talked of running away together. Heading to California so he could be in the movies. How could this be true? His parents would marry in another six months, but in December 1959, his mom was about to run away with an Italian lover? But then things became clearer over the last few pages of the diary.

Friday, December 11, 1959

I snuck out to see Tommy again last night. It was after 1 in the morning, but I was very quiet.

We drove down to Coney Island and parked next to the beach. The moon was full and it lit the ocean for as far as our eyes could see. We just sat there, listening to the ocean. I leaned into his shoulder and stared out at the water. I feel so happy. I just want to be with him all the time. We're trying to be so careful. My parents will kill me. But I don't really care what they think anymore. I can decide for myself who I want to be with. And he's just so handsome. With that pompadour he looks like a real life movie star. And he is so kind to me. He loves me. He hasn't told me yet, but I know he does. We talked about running away again. Just loading our belongings into his car and driving away. I wonder what it will be like being married to a movie star? He's been checking the bus schedules—he doesn't think his car can make it all the way to the West Coast. But he wants to save more money before he's ready. I'm going to go with him.

Sunday, December 13, 1959

Last night was very bad. Tommy snuck into my room. He climbed up the fire escape and I let him in the back window. We didn't think we were making any noise but I guess the bed creaked. Dad opened the door and found us. He lost his mind. Tommy wrestled free and climbed out the window and down the fire escape. Mom tried to pull Dad off me but he slapped me pretty hard.

Wanting me to swear I'd never see him again. But I didn't. I wouldn't say that. I'll be staying home from school tomorrow. I don't want my friends to see me with a bruise on my face. But I have to get back to school. And I have to see Tommy.

So Grandpa slapped her around, Donny thought as he finished his fourth beer. He wondered how often that happened.

Monday, December 14, 1959

Home all day today. I dared not leave my room. Mother brought me some soup because I couldn't really chew. I lay in bed daydreaming. Picturing our life together in California. Palm trees, beaches. I want to live by the beach. I love the water. Maybe I can get a job near the water. Wouldn't that be wonderful?

Tuesday, December 15, 1959

Mom helped me with some makeup and I went to school. I went over to Jahn's after school. I just had to see Tommy. He was so angry. He could see the bruises on my mouth, even with the makeup. I lied to him and said that I fell, but he knew. I pleaded with Tommy. We have to get out of here. Let's just go to California. He said he's trying to save more money and that we could leave soon. I have some money. It's not a lot but who cares? I know I can get a job out there. But I must get away from this crazy family before I go insane.

Wednesday, December 16, 1959

My face looked a lot better today. I didn't need any extra makeup. Tommy hates when I wear too much lipstick or mascara. But he didn't even get a chance to see me today. I went to see him at Jahn's but his friend Billy said he didn't show up for work today. That's odd. I hope he's not home ill. I'm afraid to go to his apartment after school, in case his mother stayed home from work to take care of him. Hopefully he'll feel better tomorrow and I can see him.

Thursday, December 17, 1959

Billy said that Tommy didn't come to work again today. I was worried all day. No one has seen him for two days. I walked by his apartment building, but there was a police car out front. I saw a young girl that looked like Tommy. Must be his younger sister. She was standing with an older couple. Tommy's parents? I was afraid to go too close. I was so frightened. Did something bad happen to Tommy?

Friday, December 18, 1959

Tommy's gone. He took his father's car and left. He left two days ago. The police found the car

in Pittsburgh, parked across from a bus depot.
Nobody knows where he is. But I know. He's on
that bus to California. He left without me. Did he
ever intend to take me? Was it all a joke to him?
Did I mean anything to him? I'm heartsick. Just
like Elizabeth Taylor.

Donny put the diary down and scraped the bottom of the Chinese food container. Mom, a jilted lover. In love with an Italian boy. The same mother who drilled into him and his brothers how important it was to marry a Jewish girl. Who said she would never accept anything but a Jewish girl. Could this really be the same mother who almost ran away with a Catholic boy? There were only five pages left in the diary. Her writing became shorter, less frequent, like she was losing interest in writing down her thoughts. But her last two entries had a common thread. And that thread was what he was looking for.

Saturday, December 26, 1959

The Brodsky family came over last night. I
didn't know why. Shabbat dinner is usually just
family—cousins, aunts, and uncles. It was
Christmas Day. I thought maybe they came over
to play cards. But we didn't play cards. I didn't
know why they would come over with their entire
family. All five of their children came. I recognized
their oldest, Joe, from school. He's in my grade.
Very quiet. He didn't say much. I think he plays
basketball, but I'm not too sure. I couldn't wait

for dinner to be over with. But they stayed very late. My father and Mr. Brodsky disappeared for a long time. They went off into the den. I could smell the cigarette smoke coming from beneath the door. They both reeked of scotch when they finally emerged. And then my mother came to tell me this morning. Now I know why they were here. They were here to see me. The Brodskys came to Shabbat dinner to meet me. For Joe to meet me. I didn't even say two words to him last night. Mom told me Joe is coming back tomorrow, alone. I'm to host him with cookies and tea. And I'm not to be rude to him. I have no strength.

And then, on the last page:

Thursday, January 14, 1960

It's been almost three weeks. I promise not to neglect you. I just couldn't put my thoughts down. I have no thoughts. I'm a blank. The days have been a blur. I don't feel anything. I go to school.

I come home. I close my bedroom door. I do homework, but not most of it. Mostly I just stare. Stare at the walls. Stare out the window. Stare at myself in the mirror. I feel nothing. Mom's been worried about me. Doesn't like me sitting in my room so much. Last night she made me come downstairs and sit and watch her play mah-jongg with her friends. I didn't care. I stared at them playing, but I wasn't there. She keeps telling me to snap out of it. Snap out of what? What am I in? Joe's been trying to talk to me at school. He seems nice. My mother told me not to be rude to him again. I have no strength to fight this.

CHAPTER
TWENTY

THURSDAY

"ANDRE'S READY FOR YOU," said the voice of
Andre's personal assistant, the audio seeming to come
from behind the waiting room sofa.

Josh stood and took a deep breath, followed by a long
gulp from the company-issued water bottle made from
recycled bamboo.

"Lynn, what kind of mood is he in?" Jenna asked out
loud. She had told Josh she'd learned not to give their
mercurial CEO upsetting news on one of his legendary
bad days.

"He's fine now," replied the voice. "He's currently
testing some new capabilities."

"New capabilities?" Josh asked.

"It's okay," said the voice. "You may go in. Let him
know you're there."

Jenna opened the door to the cavernous office. Andre
was stumbling from his bookshelf to the window and
back, with a set of oversize darkened goggles wrapped

around his head. His hands were in the air in front of him as if he was trying to blindly feel his way. Jenna cleared her throat.

"Jenna? Is that you?" Andre asked cheerfully.

"Hi, Andre," she said. "Yes, Josh is here with me. Where are you today?"

"Barcelona!" he said. "Have you ever been? It's beautiful. I'm making my way through the Sagrada Família. Spectacular piece of engineering. Want to see?"

"No, Andre," Jenna said. "I've seen it in person. It's brilliant, I agree."

Andre ripped the headset off and handed it to Josh, smiling like a kid who has just met his favorite Disney character.

"Dr. Brodsky, you must see this," he said. "It's our latest release. I think it's absolutely the best virtual reality device we've ever created. I'm telling you. I was right there in that basilica! And I was speaking with visitors from all over the world. Outstanding!"

"Maybe next time," Josh said. He sat next to Jenna on the sofa.

"Suit yourself," Andre said, tossing the headset on his conference table. "What's going on?"

"Let me get right to the point," Jenna said. "It looks like CHERL is under attack."

"What?" Andre snapped. "Attacked? By what?"

"We're trying to find out. But someone or something has placed malware into various parts of the system."

"Malware? That can't be true. Our cybersecurity is state-of-the-art. How the hell did that happen?"

"We're not sure yet," Jenna said.

"Where's Torres's team?" he asked. The chief operating officer oversaw cybersecurity.

"His team is all over it, as are my guys," Josh said. He glanced at Jenna. "I mean, our guys."

"What's the malware trying to do?" Andre asked.

Jenna explained the sleeper cell theory, that the malware was lying in wait to be activated for whatever the intended purpose, most likely encrypting or copying the code.

"Copying? It must be the Chinese," Andre said, banging the table with his fist. "Or the North Koreans. Damn it, we kept this project top secret. We knew the Chinese would steal anything to do with AI."

"We don't know if it's the Chinese," Jenna said. "If it's a foreign operation, Torres thinks it's most likely the Russians—they're skilled at making it look like someone else. He's trying to trace the IP address. To see where it came in."

"Is Torres looking at all our vendor systems?"

"We're looking at everything," Josh said.

Jenna added, "Vendors, partners—"

"What about employees?" Andre asked. "It could be an insider."

"We have to consider the possibility," she said.

Andre looked at Josh. "You suspect anyone on your team, Dr. Brodsky?"

"Not a one," Josh said, without hesitation. Truth was, he hadn't considered anyone from the project. But Andre and Jenna were both staring at him.

"Let's pull all their emails," Andre said. "Search history, phone logs."

"In progress," Jenna said.

Josh knew he shouldn't be surprised. Still, he wondered why she hadn't told him Torres was checking on his team?

"Good," said Andre. "We've got to stop this dead in its tracks."

"I also think we should put a temporary freeze on code development," Jenna said. "At least until we rule out employee tampering."

"Nonsense," Andre said. "I want you to keep everyone working. The Secretary of State is coming next week. And I want that crap removed."

Andre rubbed his forehead, which still had a red mark from the virtual reality goggles. Josh could almost see Andre's brain at work, calculating the odds and repercussions of the various outcomes.

Andre's personal assistant spoke. "Andre, I have Hector Torres on the line. He asked me to interrupt."

"Put him on speaker."

A moment later, the brusque voice of the COO was on the phone.

"Andre?"

"Hector," Andre barked. "I just heard about CHERL. What's the status?"

"It looks like our hacker knew we were on to him, Andre. The malware was activated a few minutes ago. CHERL's neural networks have all been encrypted."

Josh felt a chill run down his back.

"Goddammit!" Andre rose and walked behind his desk. "You think you can break the key?"

"We're trying. But Andre, whoever did this also sent a message."

Andre placed his hands on the desk and leaned over. "We're listening."

"They want five million dollars. All in Bitcoin. When the Bitcoin is in their account, they'll provide the key to release the encryption."

Andre was now looking directly at Josh. "Let me be clear. I will not pay a dime!"

"But Andre," Jenna started, "that doesn't seem—"

Andre held his hand up and said, "Hector, I'm paying your cybersecurity team to keep our systems secure. I want a full report on how this happened. But for now, get down there and break that encryption key!" Then, looking at Jenna and Josh, he added, "That means the two of you too. I want everyone on this."

Torres said, "Will do, Andre. But I need you to pick up the private line for a minute."

Andre pushed in his earbuds. "What?"

Josh watched and listened to Andre's side of the conversation. Andre let out a long exhale and said, "It's not the money, Hector…Yes. That's exactly right, where does it end?…Uh-huh…You think you can trace it back?…You did?…Really?"

Andre stared at Josh, then turned his back. Andre whispered, "No, I didn't know…You sure that's where he lives?…Okay, yes, check it out…Yes, I agree. We've tested Pearl enough. Let's see what she can find out."

Andre slowly removed the earbuds.

"What did he say?" Jenna asked.

"Ah…" Andre said. "He just wanted me to know he was all over this thing."

Josh stood to leave. Andre wasn't telling them something.

"Oh, and Brodsky. We need you to go down to see the People Experience team. We'll need a full debrief. Torres alerted them to expect you."

"Now?" Josh asked. There would be plenty of time for finger-pointing later, but from the glare on the CEO's face, he knew better than to argue the point. A glare that made his stomach churn.

CHAPTER
TWENTY-ONE

AFTER A MIND-NUMBING morning with the technologists from Virtual Bank and Peachtree, Louie needed a break. He had been sequestered with over thirty cybersecurity and IT experts, trying to steer discussions toward brainstorming ideas and solutions. What he heard was mostly finger-pointing and recriminations. Clearly there was no quick fix to remove or disable the malware. Six hours in the poorly ventilated conference room was enough. When he suggested everyone break for lunch, the two teams simply left the room, debating where to eat as they made their way toward the elevator. He had no intention of joining in. He had other things to do.

He gripped his phone and texted his psychiatrist, Dr. Jacobs: "Can you talk?"

Thirty seconds later, Louie's cell phone rang.

"What's going on?" Jacobs asked. "I have an appointment about to start. Are you all right?"

"I don't know," Louie said. He had trouble catching his breath. "I'm just feeling a little jumpy, you know. Like my nerves are on edge."

"Is something creating more stress than normal?"

"I guess you can say that," Louie said. "I hate to bother you. The Prozac usually keeps things in check, but I have a lot weighing on me. Do you think you could up the dosage a bit? Just for a few days, to get me over the hump."

"Louie, you haven't been here for a couple of months. I can't assess what's going on over the phone. Why don't you come in tomorrow for a full evaluation and we can figure it out?"

"I can't tomorrow." Louie covered the phone and cleared his cracking voice. "Can I come over now?"

There was a pause on the line before Jacobs said, "I have an opening in an hour if you can get here."

Figuring that he wouldn't be missed by the tech teams, Louie bought a sandwich in the cafeteria and called a ride service, arriving thirty minutes later at Jacobs's office. The last place Louie wanted to be right now was in his shrink's waiting room, but he took a seat and ate his lunch. He stared at a wall full of photographs, each showing Jacobs, trim and fit, on his exotic vacations, surrounded by the smiling and happy faces of his wife and three kids. Louie quickly ate his sandwich. He needed to keep this session short too.

Jacobs finally came and escorted him to his meeting room.

"What's going on?" Jacobs asked.

Louie closed the door and sat in the brown leather chair. "A lot's going on, doc."

"That's not unusual for you."

"It's coming at me from all directions," Louie said. "Maybe you can adjust my meds? Just to take the edge off?"

"Work or family?" Jacobs asked. For years, Louie

would visit Jacobs every other week, delving into all aspects of his life, especially during the period when he had managed to stay away from the racetrack. But other than an every-other-month check-in, they hadn't sat down for a really deep discussion in over a year.

"Vicki found out about my financial problems."

"I see. How'd she find out?"

"Foreclosure notice."

"Foreclosure notice," Jacobs repeated. "How'd that happen? You said you were managing things."

"I was. I mean, I am. I've got a very big deal coming through."

"That sounds promising."

"It's just taking longer than I thought," Louie said, pulling a stray hair off his slacks.

Jacobs was silent.

Louie finally said, "The mortgage company doesn't usually get on my case about being late. They just take the money out of our savings accounts. But the accounts were empty."

"How did that happen?" Jacobs asked.

"I lost track."

"And your wife found out?"

"Yep."

"We talked about being straight with her," Jacobs said.

"I know—avoidance."

"Avoidance," Jacobs repeated.

"What can I say? That's how I survived growing up. At least I can't blame my mother anymore."

"Why is that?"

"She died. Funeral was last weekend."

"I'm very sorry to hear that."

There was a pause in the conversation. Louie's phone

rang and he quickly silenced it, saying, "Sorry. There's a conference room full of people probably looking for me. I should try to get back soon. Can you—"

"Before you go, I want to get back to Vicki. These are pretty significant problems to keep from a spouse. That's probably why you're feeling edgy. How did she react?"

"Calm, as always."

"What happened?"

"Opened up a whole bunch of stuff," Louie said. He mimicked his wife's voice: "'You should have stayed at Goldman. Everybody that stayed is making tons of money. Why don't we have a plane?' How's that sound?"

"I can see how that would make you anxious."

"She didn't make me anxious," Louie said, staring out of the window.

"Depressed?"

Louie shook his head. "Mostly pissed. She said maybe I should think about doing something else. Maybe I'm not cut out for this."

"What do you think about that?" Jacobs asked.

"It's bullshit."

"We used to talk about that. You've said that maybe this career choice is not for you."

"But that's just talk," Louie said, leaning forward. "We were just talking. You and me. I was just talking out loud with you. We were going through what was in my head."

"Just tossing things around," Jacobs agreed.

"That's right, just tossing things around. I can have those doubts. I can talk to you about that. Those are my doubts. I don't need to be hit with them when I'm out *there*."

"Have you ever thought about sharing those doubts

with Vicki? Part of what's agitating you is you're keeping so much from her."

"That's just how it is," Louie said, sliding back. "I never learned how to share my feelings."

"We've been through that too."

"Yeah," Louie mumbled.

"Vicki must be frustrated," Jacobs said. "Maybe she's trying to be helpful. Maybe she'd be supportive of a change in your career choice."

"Sure, as long as I can afford a personal jet, I can do anything I want. I'm sure it's easy to change careers at forty-seven."

"Do you really think she wants a jet?" Jacobs asked.

"No," Louie said softly, staring out the window again. "She just doesn't want to get evicted."

"That seems reasonable."

"I hate feeling like I've let her down," Louie said. "I hate feeling like I can't do this."

"That's also been a running topic for us," Jacobs said.

"I know. Fear of failure. Feeling inadequate. Looking to prove myself, over and over."

"We need to spend time figuring out where that's coming from," Jacobs said.

"Right," Louie said, looking at his watch and standing. "But not right now. I've got to get back. Do you have enough information now?"

Jacobs paused.

"You'll have to put me in a straitjacket if I can't get this deal done," Louie said.

"You're not gambling, right?"

"No, not a thing," Louie said. This was not the time to open up about that.

A few moments passed.

"I'll call in a minor adjustment to your medication. I

don't think you need anything major. But I want you to come in again next week."

"Promise. I'll be in a much better place after this deal closes."

Louie returned to his office and made a detour to hit the vending machines. He carried cold coffee and Fig Newtons to his desk and pulled out his personal computer. In the time it took him to wolf down the stale snacks and coffee, he was able to open ClubTrack, and place four different bets of $10,000 each. A couple of long shots had a chance to bring him current on his mortgage and pay down the home equity balance. As soon as he hit the enter key on the bets, he felt some of the stress leave his body. Hopefully, whatever Dr. Jacobs was calling in would take care of the rest.

He tossed the coffee, put away his laptop, and made his way to the conference room. As he approached, he heard a loud argument taking place behind the closed door. The conversation came to a halt when he entered. All eyes were fixed on Louie.

Esposito, VB's General Counsel, finally spoke. "We've been trying to reach you."

Louie reached for his phone and saw he had three missed calls. He had forgotten to turn it back on.

"Sorry, guys," he said. "What's up? Did you figure out how to delete the malware?"

"No, Louie," Esposito said. "But we do need to access your computer."

CHAPTER
TWENTY-TWO

DONNY WAS in a foul mood after another sleepless night. He tried to order room service, but the lady at the front desk told him to walk across the street and pick from McDonald's or Wendy's. He brought the Egg McMuffin and coffee back to his room and watched CNN in bed. During commercials, he posted nastygrams on a reporter's blog. Well, she had it coming, standing there smirking in front of the Texas governor's mansion with a red "Breaking News" banner crawling across the bottom, as she breathlessly spit out the latest on the sex scandal.

"Wolf, reports are surfacing that a second woman is planning to come forward, sometime later today, and that she has specific, credible evidence of her three-year affair with the governor."

Naomi Rodriguez. So smug. So sure she had the scoop to bring down the governor. Dragon slayer. He grabbed his laptop, logged onto Naomi's blog, posting every nasty adjective he could think to combine with the word *bitch*. Anonymously, of course.

Pressing the enter key left him feeling refreshed, like

he'd taken a warm shower. His head clear, he checked his email and voice messages one last time. An empty in-box made it official: Ana was gone. Fuck her. Even if she returned to class on Monday, he swore to himself he wasn't getting involved with this broad—he would put the entire Ana episode out of his mind. OneNiteFrenz was more than adequate for his short-term needs. Besides, he needed to focus on a more immediate mission.

He took a shower and shaved, wanting to show a clean-cut, harmless-looking face to Maggie. Calm and ready to do some good old-fashioned sweet-talking, sure he could convince her to turn over his mom's diaries. The level of detail he found in just the one diary was incredible. He hoped his mother had written in as much detail about his father's accident.

He instructed his rental car to park in front of Maggie's house at three-thirty p.m., assuming Richie would be long gone.

Donny rang the doorbell. There was no answer. He rang again and waited, picking at a decaying gray shingle on the side of the door.

"Can I help you?"

A male voice. Again, formal but friendly. Maggie playing with her robot assistant again.

"I'm here to see Maggie."

"This is Mrs. Berman's residence," the voice came back. "What is your business?"

"It's Donny. I was here yesterday."

"Mrs. Berman is about to take her afternoon nap. Can you come back in about two hours?"

"But Maggie is expecting me," Donny said, worrying that Fred might be set to overprotective mode.

A pause, then, "Please face the door."

A moment later, the door opened.

"Mrs. Berman will be right with you. I'm allowed to delay her nap another thirty minutes—that's all."

"I won't stay long," Donny said.

"Please wait in the living room. It is to your left."

Donny walked past the grandfather clock and into the living room and immediately noticed that the tables that were cluttered the day before were completely barren. He entered the living room, now sparse except for the furniture. All the pictures on the mantel were gone. He heard a slow double *clump*, signaling Maggie was making her way toward him. As she approached, he could see her eyes were already glassy. Instead of the cane from yesterday, she was now leaning on a walker.

"Hi, Maggie."

She appeared not to recognize him.

"It's Donny," he said, pointing at his chest. "Remember? Ruth's son. I was here yesterday."

"Oh, Donny, honey. I wasn't expecting you. I was just getting ready to lie down."

"I was worried you might be napping already," he said. "I'm sorry. I would come back later, but—"

"Later would be better," she said, her voice creaky. "I already took my pills."

"I know. I just don't have a lot of time. My flight back to Chicago is in a few hours."

She looked back into the room, then down at her feet.

"Well…come sit down," she said, sighing and nodding toward the kitchen. "I'll make some tea."

"Maybe just one cup. I really can't stay long."

"Oh?" she said, shuffling into the kitchen, leaning on the walker. "Do you have to get back to Manhattan?"

"Maggie, sit down. I'll make the tea."

"Oh no," she said. Donny could hear her muttering

to herself. "It's my kitchen. Where did I put those tea bags?"

Sleepy and disoriented. Just as Donny hoped, thankful he wouldn't need to use the sleeping pills he'd brought.

A few minutes later, they were sitting at the kitchen table.

"Any of those delicious cookies lying around?" he asked.

"I think I have some in the pantry," she said. "I'll get them for you."

"No, no," he said, holding her arm and guiding her back to her seat. "Just point me to the pantry."

Maggie blew on her hot cup while Donny fetched a bag of Chips Ahoy! cookies.

"It's good to see you again," she said. "When did you say you were here?"

"Just yesterday. Don't you remember? I was going to come back this morning, but you had lunch with Richie, right?"

"Oh, how did you know about that?" she asked, her sleepy eyes suddenly brightening. "We had such a wonderful day. He took me to a clothing store at the mall. Not that I needed anything. Then we went to the Peking Palace for lunch. I used to go there all the time with Selma and Faygie. Selma loved their lo mein. It was a little greasy if you ask me. She'd eat half the plate and take the rest home for dinner. Faygie and I would share chicken and steamed vegetables. Faygie loved those steamed vegetables."

"Used to?" he asked. "Did they move?"

"No, they're both gone," she said, staring into the steam coming from the tea. "Faygie died last year. I think Selma died three years ago. I can't remember."

She broke off a small piece of a cookie. "They're all gone," she said, looking up at Donny.

"I'm sorry. It must be hard losing old friends."

Maggie blew on the tea, staring blankly. "I was so tired after lunch with Richie. He had his friends clean out my house. He says it will make it easier to sell."

Donny shifted in his seat. "Oh, are you moving?"

"Richie wants me to move in with him. I don't know about that. I don't want to be a burden."

"I'm sure you wouldn't be."

"It's a brand-new house. He says he has the latest technology. He says the house would have eyes on me all the time. I'm not sure what that means." She leaned over and whispered, "It's a little much, if you ask me."

"What is?" Donny asked. "And why are you whispering, Maggie?"

"Shhh." She put her finger up to her lips, then whispered, "All this." She waved both hands around the room, adding, "I don't like to talk about it in front of them. I think they get insulted."

"Who?" Donny asked, leaning back and surveying the room.

"Fred. And Wilma," she whispered. "They think they're perfectly capable of taking care of me. I don't think they were happy when Richie told me why I had to move."

Donny leaned back, surveying the quiet room.

"Won't it be nice to have family around?" he asked.

Maggie sipped her tea. "It does get lonely," she said, no longer whispering. "But I've lived here for forty-five years. This is my home. All my memories live here."

Donny stared out the window. He chewed nervously on a cookie. "Good memories are…good."

Maggie looked up, her eyes suddenly clear and

focused. "Your family went through a tough time," she said.

"Really?" he said, his tone turning sharp. "What did my mother tell you?"

"Enough."

Donny forced a smile. Maggie knew things, but she wasn't saying. If he wanted answers, he had to get those diaries. He thought about asking for them again, but he didn't expect her answer to be different from the day before. As if reading his mind, she looked at him and placed her hand on his arm. She became clear-eyed and alert.

"Just leave the past alone," she said. "You won't find what you're looking for. Those are not memories you want to dig up."

Donny pulled his arm away. Who was Maggie to decide what he should know and shouldn't know? "You know a lot, don't you, Maggie? My mother shared it all with you."

Maggie pulled a small tissue from her flowered house-dress and dabbed at her eye. She crumpled and dropped it on the kitchen table. The hazy and unfocused glaze returned to her eyes.

"Maggie," the male voice was back. "You do need to take your nap now."

Maggie looked up through half-shut eyelids. She glanced at the digital clock on the oven. "Oh my," she said. "It's so late for my nap. No wonder I'm feeling so tired."

"I'm so sorry," Donny said, gathering himself. Time to get what he came for. "I've overstayed my welcome. Of course. You look exhausted."

Maggie pushed herself up from the table and tried to lift her tea, but her hand shook.

"You can leave it." Donny grabbed the cup and put it back down. "Go take your nap. I'll clean up here and let myself out."

"Okay, honey," she said. She was eyeing him curiously. "But you don't need to clean up."

"It's not a problem. You mind if I sit and finish my tea first?"

"Oh," she said. "I guess so."

She turned and reached gingerly for her walker. "Are you coming back tomorrow?" she asked.

"No, Maggie. I have a flight back to Chicago tonight."

She nodded and shuffled down the hallway to the master bedroom without saying another word. Donny sat and nervously finished his tea. After a few minutes, he quietly rinsed the cups in the sink, returned the cookies to the pantry, and listened. Silence. He reached for the panel by the kitchen light switch and pressed the button marked "Assistant Pause."

"Fred?" he called out. No answer. "Wilma?"

He took off his shoes and tiptoed down the hallway to look in on Maggie. She was out cold. He quietly closed her bedroom door and made his way to the hallway closet. He listened again. No sound from the direction of Maggie's bedroom. He slowly opened the closet's louver doors, stopping each time the hinges let out a slight creak. When the door was completely open, he looked from side to side and dropped to his knees, holding his head, and began hyperventilating. The closet—that just the day before had contained old dresses and shoes, a pile of tattered blankets and pillows, and the four boxes containing Ruth Brodsky's sixty-plus years of recorded memories—was completely empty.

Donny searched Maggie's house, moving from room

to room, closet to closet, less and less aware of the noise he was making. He examined every room and closet except for the master bedroom, where she was in a deep sleep. No sign of the diaries. In fact, most of the closets were empty.

"He had his friends clean out my house," Maggie had said.

———

DONNY OPENED the door leading to the attached garage and found two trash bins. A few feet in front were three large bags with a handwritten note taped to the top: "For Goodwill pickup."

Donny tore open the top of each bag and felt around. Nothing but folded clothing. Tossing the bags to the side, he threw the lids off the bins, which were packed with bulging black bags. He ripped opened each bag and rummaged through the insides. More old clothing mixed in with rusted electronics, broken picture frames, and piles of old shoes. When he tore open the final bag, his body froze as he stared into a mass of shredded paper. He emptied the contents onto the cracked cement floor, frantically pulling tiny slivers up to his eyes. He tried to make out piece after piece. In just a few minutes, the garage floor was covered in confetti. But all of the shreds were either typed or printed materials. Nothing that resembled handwritten words, only bank statements and other financial records.

Two sealed boxes were pushed against the rear cinder block wall. Donny ripped open the first, which contained the shredder. The second contained a pile of unused tools and a half-empty carton of black garbage bags.

Donny left the mess in the garage and went back

inside the house. Maggie was still asleep, but it was close to five o'clock. How much longer until she woke? He could wait around to ask her about the diaries, but something told him that Richie didn't involve her in any part of this cleanup. Besides, if it was up to her, Donny wasn't leaving with those diaries. He had to speak to Richie before flying back to Chicago. If the diaries weren't in the house, where had Richie taken them?

He pulled open kitchen drawers and cabinets, looking for some type of address book. Nothing. But he knew where she probably kept all her phone numbers. He went to the kitchen wall and pressed the "Assistant Activate" button on the wall pad.

"Fred," he whispered, "what's Richie's phone number?"

Fred didn't respond.

"It's okay, Fred," Donny said. "I just want to tell him I was here and how well Maggie seems to be doing under your care."

Still no response.

Donny continued, as if he was talking to himself, "There's no real reason to move her from here. She seems to be getting the best of care. But what do I know?"

After a pause, "Sir, I must ask you to leave."

Donny hurried out the front door and scrambled into the passenger seat.

"Just drive," he instructed, and the car shifted into gear and pulled away just as a police cruiser was fast approaching from the opposite direction. Donny ducked behind the seat backs, wondering if Fred called 911 when he was rummaging in the garage or when he reentered the house. Once Donny was safely away from the neighborhood and merging with traffic on Union Turnpike, he typed into his phone's search engine "podiatrist Richard Berman New York." Two office numbers showed on his screen. He clicked on the first.

"Dr. Berman's office," the receptionist answered. "Can I help you?"

"Yes, er, hi. Is he there, please?"

"Dr. Berman's with a patient right now. Can I help you?"

"It's very important that I speak with him. Do you know how long he'll be?"

"Dr. Berman will be with patients until six-thirty. He usually returns calls after hours. Are you a patient?"

"No, actually, I'm an old friend, kinda," Donny said. "But…it's about his mother."

"His mother," she said, her tone concerned. "Is Maggie all right?"

"Yes, yes. I just came from seeing her. She's fine. But I have something very important to discuss with Dr. Berman."

"About his mother," she said.

"Yes, that's what I said," he snapped. "About his mother."

"What did you say your name was?"

"Don. Don Brodsky."

"Don Brodsky," she repeated. "Hold on, please. Let me see if he can take the call."

After a few minutes of listening to Muzak, the line picked up.

"This is Richard Berman. Who is this?"

"Hi, Richard. This is Donny Brodsky. Remember me? Ruth Brodsky's son?"

"Donny? My assistant said it was something urgent to do with my mother. Is everything all right?"

"Yes, she's fine. I didn't mean to worry you. We just had a nice cup of tea together."

"Tea. You had tea with my mother," Richie said.

"That's what I said. We had a very nice visit."

"She didn't mention she was seeing you," Richie said. "I was with her all morning. But listen, if my mom's okay, I have a waiting room full of patients."

"I'm sorry. I won't keep you. It's just that I'm here in New York, and she was telling me about my mother's diaries. I'm sure my mother would want me to have them. Do you know where they are?"

"That's why you pulled me away from my patients? To ask me what I did with your mother's diaries?"

"I know it sounds crazy. But I'm here today and I have to get on a flight. Do you know where they are?"

"Wow. Josh told me about you. You're unbelievable," Richie said. "Look, she told me they were your mother's, and she wanted me to keep them in my house. But she said that about pretty much everything. She won't miss all the stuff I threw out. Anyway, if I knew you were in town, I would have given them to you, I guess. But I didn't. Listen, I gotta go."

"You threw them out?" Donny asked, his voice cracking. "But I didn't find them in her garbage cans."

"You went through her garbage cans?"

"Please, just tell me where they are," Donny pleaded.

"You'll have to ask Josh," Richie said. "He's the only one of you I've kept in touch with. I shipped them to him this morning."

CHAPTER
TWENTY-THREE

JOSH PASSED the empty receptionist desk and entered conference room A-1 in the Corporate Annex, the same building where he'd been processed as a new employee the previous year. One calendar year since he'd joined Sway Inc., but it felt like ten. While the location resembled the room where he spent his first morning filling out paperwork for payroll and benefits, the decor was starkly different. Replacing the inviting space to welcome new employees was a room more suited to cooling a row of overheated computer stations, consisting of white tiled walls and a sterile, raised floor. The windows that he remembered overlooking the campus pond and running track were gone. Nothing in the way of furnishings other than a single wooden desk and a straight-backed chair in the center. He poked his head out the conference room door. A stern-looking receptionist named Veronica had returned.

"When was this room redone?" Josh asked.

"Oh, I didn't see you go in, Dr. Brodsky," Veronica said. "I'm not sure about the room. I've only been with the department since last week. Please go back in and have a seat. Pearl is waiting for you."

"Oh. I didn't see her," he said.

"Pearl conducts all of our security debriefs."

Josh scratched his head. The automated invite for "People Experience debrief" had shown up on his calendar just as he left Andre's office. Jenna insisted that this was purely protocol, but Josh wasn't so sure. This was more likely some type of damage control, having him speak with Pearl, obviously a neutral third party from the People Experience group. He walked to the side of Veronica's desk, grabbed one of the chairs, and started carrying it back to A-1.

"I'm sorry," Veronica said. "Where are you taking that?"

"We'll need an extra chair," he said.

"That won't be necessary," she said. "Please put that back."

"But there's only one chair."

"Dr. Brodsky?" a female voice came from the conference room. "Please, come in. We're ready to start."

Josh looked at the receptionist, who motioned for him to enter. He walked over and peered in. The room remained empty, except for the table and chair.

"Come in and close the door, please, Dr. Brodsky," came the voice from the room. "I'm ready to begin whenever you are."

Josh slowly entered and looked around. Great, he thought. They dragged him all the way down here just to do a conference call.

"Pearl?" he asked.

"Yes, Dr. Brodsky, please sit down so we can get started."

He closed the door and eased himself into the chair, folding his hands on the table.

"Thank you, Dr. Brodsky. How are you today?"

"I'm fine," Josh said. "I didn't realize we were doing this as a phone call. Are you located in a different city?"

"I'm right here, Dr. Brodsky. I'm right here with you."

Josh shook his head. He started to rise when Pearl said, "Oh, I see you're confused, Dr. Brodsky. Let me introduce myself. I'm PEARL, the Performance-Evaluating Artificial Intelligence Review Leader."

"Review leader," Josh repeated to himself as the reality slowly set in. The voice: young and friendly yet extremely crisp, almost scripted.

"You're AI?" he asked.

"Yes, Dr. Brodsky. Sway launched me just this week as part of a new suite of people systems."

People systems? Josh felt like the walls were shifting. CHERL wasn't the only secret project Andre was funding, though Josh had heard a rumor that People Experience was developing their own artificial intelligence applications. He studied the room more closely. In the far corner, he spotted a miniature lens buried in the wall. He squinted and made out similar devices in the side and rear corners of the room.

PEARL continued, "This allows management to get right to the core of issues without all the emotion. Much more effective. I hope you'll agree."

"Listen," Josh said, rising from the chair, "I'm sure you'll do a fine job. But I have a lot to do, and maybe we can try this later this year, after you've been through the shakeout period."

"I can assure you, I am well out of beta testing. I am version 8.0, to be exact. Andre asked specifically for you to be one of our first subjects, given your comfort with artificial intelligence."

Strange that Andre hadn't mentioned anything about "Pearl" being AI yesterday, he thought.

"I'm one of the first?" he asked.

"Yes, indeed. Andre's planning on a full-scale rollout starting next week. Would you like to see an employee video announcing our program?"

The wall on the side of the room began retracting, revealing a large monitor. Josh put both hands up, indicating surrender.

"No need," he said, lowering himself into the chair. If Andre wants to roll out his new toy, who was he to argue? The timing sucked, but Josh was certainly curious to see how this AI application worked.

"Let's give it a go," he said.

"Excellent. I'm ready too. First, may I call you Josh? Or do you prefer Dr. Brodsky?"

"Josh would be fine."

"Thank you, Josh. How do you think you've been doing here during the past year?"

"I thought I was here to be debriefed on the intrusion," he said.

"Yes, that's true. But it's important to baseline first with an employee."

Interesting, he thought. Baselining, just like he and Naveen did with CHERL. But why conduct an evaluation first? Whatever—Josh just wanted to get through this quickly.

"I think I'm doing fine," he said, leaning back.

"But how would you evaluate your performance?" PEARL asked.

"I don't know," he said, shifting in his seat. "Scale of one to ten, I'd say…"

"No, please. I would prefer if you just tell me in your own words. I'm fully capable of scoring your responses."

"So you want me to just start talking?"

"Yes, please," PEARL responded. "Just comment about your performance."

Josh stared into the lens in the far corner. He had worked on hundreds of artificial intelligence applications over the past twenty years. Precision-guided missiles, war-gaming, hunting terrorists, and now the CHERL project to bring back important figures from the past. He was comfortable with it all. So why did he feel like these lenses were burning a hole in his head?

"Okay, well, I think it's been a challenging year," he began, measuring his words carefully. "It was a big change for me, getting used to working in the private sector. I assume you know I used to work for the government."

"I have your full history," PEARL said. "You said you were ready to leave the Department of Defense."

"When did I say that?"

"During your interview with Andre, before you joined Sway. It was in your second session together."

Of course she would have a full transcript of all his interviews, along with his full history in DC, most of which was in the public record. So were the names and background of every colleague and superior he ever worked for at Defense. PEARL could be using that infor-mation to cross-reference profiles and assess their impact on Josh's work habits and behaviors. Probably dissected his every paper, public presentation, and dissertation going back to his MIT days. Yet PEARL was still looking for more input from him. He told himself to proceed cautiously. Stick with generalities.

"That's correct," he said. "I was truly done with DC."

"How is your work environment here different from that of the Department of Defense?" PEARL asked.

"Well, for starters, the pace is faster here," he said. "It took a while to get used to."

"How did the change of pace impact your performance?" PEARL asked.

"I didn't say it did. I don't think my performance changed because of the pace."

"Yet you said it was a challenging year," PEARL responded, "getting used to working in the private sector. I assume you mentioned it because it was something you think we should know."

"I was just trying to answer your question," Josh said, leaning forward and clasping his hands on the desk. "You asked me to put things in my own words. It's different here, faster paced, but I don't think it mattered. I've performed well. That's what you wanted to know, right? How do I think I've performed?"

"Yes, Josh," PEARL said. "I understand. What about the people you've worked with here? I have here that you stated that it was critical that you, and I'm quoting here, 'work on intense challenges with extraordinarily brilliant people in order to operate at peak performance.' Did I get that right?"

He wouldn't have said that in a job interview, but it sounded like him. Then he remembered: the profile that the corporate psychologist performed before he joined. The one Andre said all senior executives must agree to before being hired. Five hours of probing his entire history, his likes and dislikes, his work habits. So much for confidentiality. With all this data, PEARL was probably compiling an analysis of his strengths and weaknesses that was more on point than anyone he'd ever worked for or encountered. But if PEARL was a performance-evaluation system, why was he being asked to speak to it about a ransomware attack?

"Sounds like something I would have said. I assume you have the transcript. But the people here are great. Very talented."

"Would you say they are extraordinarily brilliant?" PEARL asked.

"They're good people," Josh said, wringing his hands.

"So you don't think you've been operating at peak performance?"

"I didn't say that," Josh said.

"But you said you needed to work on intense—"

"You're taking everything literally," he interrupted, standing and pushing back the chair. Someone should assign a coder to work on PEARL's nuance engine.

"Are you all right?" PEARL asked. "You look irritated."

"I'm fine," he said, pacing the room, now understanding the purpose of the lenses. He had assumed Sway personnel were observing, but it was PEARL who had eyes on him. "I'm telling you the people here are just fine. I'm operating here just fine."

"Please calm down. I'm only trying to base—"

"I know," he said. "Baseline. You're trying to baseline. I get it. Can we just move on?"

"Please sit back at the table," PEARL said. "I want you to be comfortable."

"I am comfortable. All the same, I'd rather stand and finish this up." Josh paced the room with his head down.

"Very well, but please don't walk around as much. It's more difficult to discern changes. Our systems are very carefully calibrated."

Josh stopped and stared at the lens in the far corner. PEARL was almost certainly evaluating his visual cues, assessing not just verbal feedback but his body language, possibly his facial expressions, with a visualization engine. He went over and examined the table. The top appeared to be normal wood, but he felt around and could feel a difference in various spots, as if sensors were embedded.

"I'll try to slow down," he said, moving away from the table.

"Thank you," PEARL said. "One more question about the people, and then we can move on. Do you like the management team here at Sway? Andre? His executive team?"

"I like everyone," he said. "As I said, they're all good people."

"No one you're angry with or upset with?"

Josh shifted his weight. He thought PEARL might be probing the turmoil he'd had with Jenna, but he saw little benefit in rehashing it.

"I think I've had my share of professional disagreements," he said, crossing his arms. "Nothing out of the ordinary. But I think we're in a good place now."

PEARL didn't respond right away. After a few seconds, Josh said, "PEARL? Are you still there?"

"Yes, Josh. Just give me a moment."

A moment? This AI system needed a moment? They were high-speed supercomputers processing every word instantaneously, running thousands of potential pathways and responses in milliseconds. These systems didn't need "a moment." Perhaps his evasiveness about Jenna was unexpected—or being checked against other, potentially conflicting data. Before he could offer any clarification, PEARL came back.

"Josh, what about the change in mission from what

you were used to working on at the Department of Defense? I'd like to understand if what you're working on has an impact on your performance. The mission or mandate?"

"You have to believe in what you're doing," he said.

"Did you believe in your mission at the Department of Defense? Working on all those missile systems?" PEARL asked. "All that destruction. That had to be difficult."

Josh walked up to the camera in the far corner and put his face up to the lens. "Destruction? You mean my mandate to defend the citizens of the United States?" he asked, his voice rising.

"Please move to the back of the room, Josh."

"*That* mandate?" he continued, his nose almost touching the lens.

PEARL said, "Building all those precision systems that would be used to kill."

"We killed only when necessary." He turned and headed toward the door. "That was the point of our precision systems and using artificial intelligence—to avoid collateral damage."

"Collateral damage," PEARL repeated. "You mean destroying innocent life? How did that make you feel?"

He stopped and looked around the room. He wasn't schooled in organizational theory or behavioral science. But one thing he knew for sure: PEARL was trying to rattle him. To break him down.

"Where are you going with all of this?" Josh asked. "I thought I was here to debrief on the CHERL hack."

"I'm trying to add perspective to our assessment. Understanding whether your behavior varies if you have a disagreement on mission or with your superiors."

"I had no disagreement with our mission," Josh said. "We were defending the country."

"What about the CHERL project?" PEARL said. "Do you believe in our mission?"

"Of course I do."

"You believe in the benefits of being able to speak with leaders from the past?" PEARL asked. "People who are long gone?"

"That's our mission, isn't it?" Josh asked.

"You have no moral quandary about what you're doing?"

"I wouldn't be here if I did."

"No issues with the people," PEARL said. "No issues with management, and supportive of our mission. No moral dilemma. So you want to see CHERL be successful."

Josh found it hard to believe what he was hearing. The aggressive probing, trying to see if he was disgruntled. To see if he had a vendetta. Trying to rattle him about his time at Defense. They weren't doing a debrief. They were looking for a culprit.

"I am one thousand percent dedicated to CHERL's success," he answered slowly, flatly. "Since the day I arrived, I have been nothing but focused on the team and our mission."

"That's very clear, Josh. You seem calmer now. I didn't mean to upset you before."

Yes, you did, he thought.

"I'm not upset," he said, sitting back at the table, clutching the arms of the chair. "But let me ask you something."

"Yes, Josh, as soon as I'm finished with my baseline, you'll have a chance to ask me some questions."

"With all due respect, PEARL—and I do respect

what you're trying to do. I respect what our People Experience team is trying to do. You're a very innovative AI application. In fact, you've studied and analyzed everything about me, I'm sure. I don't think any more baselining is necessary. But tell me, what exactly are you trying to find out with these questions?"

PEARL didn't respond. Another one of her moments.

Josh stood and pushed the chair back. "PEARL, unless you tell me what this is all about, this session is over."

As Josh stood and turned for the door, PEARL said, "The session is not over yet, Dr. Brodsky."

Josh tried to turn the door handle, but the door was locked. He turned back to the room.

"Do you want me to bring kidnapping charges? I suggest you unlock this door."

PEARL did not respond. Another pause. Another moment. She hadn't anticipated this type of pushback, Josh surmised.

Finally, she asked, "Were you accessing CHERL from your home computer?"

Josh rested his fingers on the door handle.

"From home?" he asked. "If you've studied my work patterns, which I assume you have, you know I rarely work from home. In fact, you would know that I rarely *go* home. I practically sleep down in that dungeon."

"I do see that."

"And if I ever do work from home, on those rare occasions, it's always on the corporate-issued laptop, which has all the latest security features. I'm fully authorized to use it remotely. I'm sure you know that too."

"We have a record here of two separate access events from your home computer."

"Not possible," Josh snapped.

"Just a few days ago, your home IP address was used to access CHERL."

Josh leaned his back against the door, resting his chin in his hand. He exhaled a long breath and tried to recall the last time he was home. And then he remembered. The night of the demo for Andre. He went home without his office laptop. Naveen had called him, wanting him to sign in to CHERL so he could show off his Gandhi application. He had in fact signed in. But what difference did it make?

"Okay, I did forget my corporate laptop a few nights back," he said. "I signed in, but very briefly."

"What about the second access?" PEARL asked.

It was only that one time. Nothing bad could have happened in the five minutes he was signed into CHERL. Let's just move on, he thought. "There wasn't a second access," he said. "I'm certain of it."

Another pause. Finally, PEARL said, "Dr. Brodsky, we believe the malware hack of CHERL was initiated from your home computer. On the second access."

"That's crazy. You think I would sabotage my own project?"

"The malware came through your home system," PEARL said.

"It wasn't me."

"But you accessed CHERL on that very same day—"

"It wasn't me!" Josh shouted, pulling on the door handle. "I hope you got what you were looking for. Now, if you'll excuse me, I have work to do."

Another momentary gap in questioning ensued, an obvious quirk in PEARL's processor.

"How do you explain the malware coming from your home system?" PEARL asked.

Josh turned back to face the camera. "I have no idea," he said.

Then, looking up at the ceiling, he said, "And by the way, you should have just come and asked me. Instead of putting me through this bullshit interrogation."

After a few more moments of silence, PEARL said, "We'd like to finish our investigation, and we'd like to keep this internal to the company. For now."

"What investigation?" Josh asked. "This is nuts."

"Then you will help us clear this up?"

"I'm all for that," he said.

"We would like to conduct a full forensic search on your home computer."

"I barely use my home computer. There's nothing on it."

"Then there's nothing to hide."

"Fine. Let me out of here. I'll bring it in with me tomorrow. I've got to get back to work. Andre's expecting a completed product, and I'm sure he won't be happy if I can't finish because his android was holding me hostage."

"It would be better if we can come pick it up," PEARL said. "Our team knows how to best secure the system for transport. We'd like to do it right away."

"You mean, right now?" Josh asked.

"Security is waiting outside. If you just go to your car and drive home, they'll follow you and secure the device."

Josh's head was pounding. He took in deep breaths, trying to control his rapid heart rate. De-escalate. Think. But he was incredulous. He had left the Defense Department to escape the destructive application of artificial intelligence. In CHERL, Josh saw an opportunity to use AI for the good of mankind. But this application, this interrogating bot, represented something on the dark side. Unless...

"Let me ask you something," Josh said. "You have my background. My entire history. You know everything about me. And what you don't know, well, I'm sure you've supplemented your information. You do have an inference engine, right?"

PEARL did not answer.

"So fill in the blanks, PEARL. Think. What's your assessment?"

Silence.

"Are you still there, PEARL? I want to know if your assessment is that I had anything to do with the hack and ransomware."

After a few more moments, PEARL said, "I am not authorized to release that information."

"There must be something you can tell me," he said. "At the very least, do you think I'd have a reason to do this? Have you found anything in my profile that would tell you I'm motivated by money?"

Again, silence. Josh waited, hoping that these pauses meant PEARL was performing some type of rapid recalibration.

"PEARL, I'm asking you. Is it your assessment that I have any reason to sabotage, steal, or lock up CHERL code?"

"Dr. Brodsky…" Followed by another pause. "It does seem to be against your profile."

Josh let out a deep breath. "Thank you, PEARL. Whoever developed you knew what they were doing, and—"

The door behind him opened, and Jenna and Torres rushed in.

"I figured you were probably watching this charade," Josh said, moving past his boss.

"It's not a charade, Dr. Brodsky," Torres said, stepping in front to block his exit. "We have to follow where the data leads us."

"Well, you heard PEARL," Josh said, pointing back toward the room. "You heard where the data leads. It doesn't fit."

"That's not what PEARL found," Torres said. "Whatever she said, it was a very preliminary finding, at the very least."

Josh put his hands out. "She just said this didn't fit my profile," he said, his voice rising. "Her AI engine is obviously smarter than the two of you."

"We need to perform a forensic examination on your home computer," Torres said.

"In the meantime," Jenna added, "you need to stay away from the office."

Josh smirked. "I'm so glad we opened up to each other, Jenna. I'm glad we're partners," he said sarcastically. "Or was our conversation last night part of your investigation too?"

"I didn't know anything about this last night," she said.

"Well, I can't be away from the office. CHERL's locked up, and Andre's meeting with the Secretary of State next week. I have to figure this out."

"Andre is aware that you'll be out of the office," Jenna said. "Naveen is covering."

"Ah," Josh said, nodding. His biggest fear, and that of Naveen and his team, was apparently about to be realized.

"Have you told the team yet?" Josh asked. "That they'll be reporting to you?"

Jenna leaned against the wall, ignoring Josh's question.

"The security team is waiting for you outside," Torres said.

"This is crazy!" Josh said. "How could anyone think I would do this to my own project?"

Torres looked at his watch. Josh barely used his home computer. Let them see for themselves. He had nothing to hide.

"I'll bring it to you in the morning," Josh said. "You're not making a scene in front of my home. The whole neighborhood will be watching."

Torres shook his head. "It has to be now, Dr. Brodsky. Security will follow you. We'll use an unmarked car. No flashing lights."

Josh looked toward Jenna, hoping for some type of support, but her eyes stared at the floor. He shook his head and exited the room, his thoughts clearing as he made his way to the parking lot with two security guards in tow.

He wondered who was setting him up.

CHAPTER
TWENTY-FOUR

LOUIE PACED in front of his office window. The streets below were deserted, the workday long ended. Next door in the Peabody & Munson conference room, things were anything but quiet. The last time he was allowed to enter, the room was a frenzy of motion as IT and cyber engineers examined the firm's internal systems, with special attention to the computer belonging to Louie.

He was startled by a quick knock on the door. Peabody made himself comfortable on the sofa while Louie discreetly returned his flask of scotch to a desk drawer.

"Our client says the fingerprints are pretty clear," Peabody said, rubbing his hands together.

"Come on, Jon. You don't think I really hacked into my own clients' computer systems?"

Peabody grimaced, not answering.

"How the fuck would I even know how to *do* something like that?" Louie asked.

"I'm not sure," Peabody said. "But I agree. The only

reason they haven't called the feds is I told them there's no way you could do this on your own."

"Thanks. I guess."

Peabody peered at Louie over his bifocals. "But I know money's been tight, Louie."

"Come on, Jon. You think because I haven't signed any deals, I'm going to extort my own client?"

Peabody's severe expression slowly morphed into a forced smile. "They'll know soon enough. It shouldn't take them too much longer," he said. Then, adding a snicker, "In fact, they're checking *my* computer too. I guess you never know."

"Yeah," Louie said.

He had been struggling to remember anyone who might have accessed his computer over the past few days. Phil and Susan spent a lot of time in his office, but Louie had all the standard password protections. As far as he knew, his associates never came near his PC.

"If it came through my computer," Louie said, "someone probably hacked me first."

"Why would someone come through you to get to Virtual Bank? Who would know they're your client?"

Louie shrugged. While all deals were strictly confidential, there were always rumors about which bankers were working on transactions. But nothing was ever publicly disclosed until the ink was dry. A hacker could have thrown darts and randomly landed on a big target like VB. Another knock on the door and Virtual Bank's head of corporate security, Lance Strauber, appeared, followed by five others, including the CEO, Peter Galloway.

"Gentlemen?" Louie asked.

"Well," Strauber said, "it looks like whatever infiltrated VB's system, it definitely came from your computer."

"That's bullshit!" Louie said, banging his desk. "Come on, you guys know me. Why would I do this?"

Peabody wiped his bifocals with his tie.

"We can't say that you did," Strauber said.

"Then who did?" Peabody asked.

"We do have one question for you," Strauber said to Louie. "There's one email that came into your system that we can't trace. We can't even find it. We can see that you received it, but it's gone."

"Maybe he deleted it," Peabody said. Louie could practically feel his boss sliding his chair away from him.

"No. We can see all his deleted files," Strauber said. "When reconciled with his in-box, there's one we can't account for."

"I have no idea," Louie said. "I get a ton of emails."

"It probably carried an attachment that you opened. We've heard about this type of infiltration. They use something called a dropper. When opened, it plants malware on your computer, allowing the hacker to take over. He does what he came to do—remotely using your keyboard so it looks like you. In this case, accessing VB and planting the second malware that piggybacked along. What may be unique about our hacker is when he's done, everything disappears. The malware, the email, the attachment, they all delete themselves. Barely leaves a trace."

"How would I know a dropper?" Louie asked.

"It could be anything. A spreadsheet or a letter. Any document, like a presentation of some sort. It would have come to you a couple of days ago. Probably from someone you trusted, since you had to have opened it to release the virus."

Louie tried to maintain a calm exterior, but an icy chill ran down his spine.

"Any memory of opening up an unusual attachment?" Strauber asked.

"Let me think," Louie said, remembering the business plan. "Creating an AI Boot Camp," or something of the sort. That ungrateful son of a bitch! Donny wasn't seeking investors—he was tricking him into loading his fucking malware. The guy who could never make a go of it, no matter how many times he tried. Blaming the world for all his troubles. Borrowing money and never paying it back was one thing. How could he stoop so low? Extortion! Louie couldn't wait to turn around and give Donny's name to these security guys. To tell them about the business plan attachment, and where to find Donny. He was busting to say Donny's name out loud. All he had to do was turn away from this window and say, "My brother Donny sent me a business plan two days ago. I opened the attachment. He's your hacker. I'm sure of it. Throw his ass in jail!" They would issue an arrest warrant, take Donny away, force him to delete the malware, put him behind bars, probably for years. The Virtual Bank deal would proceed. Louie would collect his big fat fee, pay off his mortgage, and resume his place as a star investment banker at Peabody & Munson. He and Vicki would be back on easy street. All Louie had to do was give them the name.

Louie turned to Strauber and stopped. What if it was just a coincidence that the hack happened around the same time Donny sent his file? Maybe Strauber was wrong. Anyone could spread something unknowingly. Maybe the hacker just got lucky. How could Louie lead them to Donny until he knew for sure?

"Businesspeople are always sending me emails,"

Louie said, flatly. "I get stuff all the time. I can give you a list of my contacts. Could be any of them."

Strauber shuffled his feet. "Yeah, we have your address book," he said. "I guess we'll start going through it." Looking at Peabody, Strauber added. "Anyway, that's all we know. Just wanted to keep you up to date."

As Strauber and the others turned to leave, he said to Louie, "Listen, if you think of anyone who might have sent you something, let us know right away. And whatever you do, don't try to handle this yourself. Hackers tend to be a volatile bunch, especially when they have your system by the throat."

Louie gave a quick salute and sat behind his desk, as far away from Peabody as he could find.

"You should go home, Louie," Peabody said. "At least until we sort this out."

"Just the same, Jon, I'd like to stick around. Those guys might have questions for me. I've got nothing to hide."

Peabody rose from his chair, approached Louie's desk, and said, "I don't think it's a good idea for you to be here right now."

Louie looked at his boss in disbelief although he told himself he shouldn't be surprised. Peabody had never been loyal to anyone other than Peabody.

"Fine, I'll work from home," Louie said. "Give me a few minutes to put some things together."

After Peabody left, Louie retrieved the flask of scotch, then took his phone from his pocket to call Josh. But after downing two swigs, he decided that he had to know if Donny was really behind this—and if he was, to talk sense into him before it was too late. Convince his brother to delete the malware and disappear, just like his fucking drop in email, or whatever Strauber called it. No one would ever be the wiser. Donny could disappear from his life, too, for all Louie cared.

He would just call Donny. Confront him and find out the truth. But Strauber's warning played in his head. The last thing Louie could afford was to spook his crazy brother into doing more damage. Fuck it. He could be careful, he'd be sure not to accuse him directly. Provide Donny with enough information that he would know they were on to him, maybe even admit it.

He took another swig of scotch and dialed, startled to hear his brother's voice after the first ring. "Hey, Louie."

Louie tried to sound cheerful. "Hey, man. How ya been?"

"Whaddya want, Louie? I'm in a hurry." Donny's voice was almost drowned out by the blare of a siren.

"Nothing. Just checking in," Louie said loudly. "Sounds like you're on the road."

"You're just checking in?" Donny asked. "When was the last time you just called to check in?"

Louie forced a chuckle. He felt the scotch doing somersaults in his stomach. "Donny, man. You make it sound like we never talk. We talk. We're both busy, that's all."

"Aha."

"How's that business plan coming?" Louie asked, wincing from the cracking in his voice.

A few moments of static, after which Donny spoke. "You're too late."

"Wait. Why am I too late? What did you do?"

"I'm not getting into it with you now," Donny said.

"What did you do?" Louie asked through clenched teeth.

"Why didn't you tell me about Mom's diaries?" Donny asked.

"Diaries?" Louie asked, shaking his head. "What kind of diaries?"

Donny sounded agitated. "You know exactly what I'm talking about—handwritten diaries. Don't tell me you didn't know about them."

Keep him calm, Louie told himself. Donny was obviously trying to throw him off.

"Donny, I swear, I don't know what you're talking about. I've never heard of Mom keeping any diaries."

"And they're pretty detailed," Donny continued. "Going back to her childhood."

"We cleaned the whole apartment out, remember? There were no diaries."

"They weren't there," Donny said.

"I know, that's what I just said."

"Mom never wanted to marry Dad," Donny said.

"What?"

"Did you know Mom had an Italian boyfriend in high school? Lost her virginity to him? But he moved away without telling her?"

Bring him back to earth, Louie told himself. "Donny, why'd you want me to review that business plan?"

"She was gonna run away with him, but he left without her. Her parents practically made her marry Dad."

"Interesting story, Donny. But listen—"

"*Interesting story*? That's all you have to say about Mom trying to run away with an Italian boy? I just told you she never wanted to marry Dad in the first place."

Donny had either lost his mind or had concocted this elaborate story to evade Louie's questions. "What did you put in that attachment?" Louie shouted.

"And I bet there's stuff in there about what happened

with Dad," Donny continued. "About what really happened."

This was going nowhere.

"Listen, Donny. Forget the fuckin' diaries."

"I'm not forgetting the fuckin' diaries, Louie!" Donny shouted. "I want them back!"

"Fine," Louie said, taking another swig from the flask. "Good idea. I'll come to Chicago. We can read them together."

"I told you, I don't have them. But they're mine. I found them first, and I'm gonna get them back."

"Okay, great. We'll get them back. Sure. But I have to talk to you about—"

"I gotta go," Donny said. "I'm at the airport."

"Airport? Wait, Donny. The business plan!"

"Don't sweat it, bro. I knew you wouldn't invest. I just wanted you to see what I was working on."

The line went dead.

"Fuck!" Louie shouted. That son of a bitch!

His next call went to Josh's voice mail. "Josh. Where the fuck are you? Call me back. It's really important!"

Louie sat at his chair, elbows on his desk, rubbing his temples, his mind swirling. He picked up his phone, clicked on ClubTrack, and glared at the screen, but his fingers couldn't move. He wondered if the pharmacy had his new prescription ready. He grabbed his briefcase and headed for the door.

If he didn't hear back from Josh before midday tomorrow, he would tell VB's security team all about Donny.

CHAPTER
TWENTY-FIVE

FRIDAY

AFTER CIRCLING for the past hour, the Airbus A300 made its final approach to San Francisco, flashes of lightning reflecting on the low clouds. The captain was too busy steadying the aircraft to make status announcements; the flight attendants were nowhere to be found. The whine of the engines drowned out all noise, other than that made by a five-year-old who was crying and kicking Donny's seat back. The plane finally touched down, to a round of applause from the relieved, bleary-eyed passengers. It was four a.m., and Donny, exhausted and sweaty from the ordeal of the past twenty-four hours, limped off the plane.

When he left Maggie's house yesterday, he immediately called Josh, leaving a message. "Josh, it's Donny. I know Richie Berman sent you a package. He meant to send it to me. I found it first—it's mine. I'm on my way out to you to get it. I'll call you when I land, and we can arrange for a pickup. Don't screw with me, big brother. Those diaries are mine."

And just before he arrived at JFK the previous evening, his younger brother had called, apparently having had a change of heart about investing in the boot camp idea. But the last thing on Donny's mind was the business plan. Ana hadn't responded to any of his messages all week. He had texted and called her daily, but still no reply. Either she used her unique gifts to line up another "partner," or her AI boot camp was bullshit from the beginning. Either way, she was playing him, lying to him—just like everyone else. What a sucker he was. She was doing him a favor by disappearing.

Donny checked into the La Quinta Inn. Richie's package probably wouldn't arrive at Josh's before midmorning, so he had time to get a few hours of sleep. In fact, if Josh was at work—where else would he be—the boxes might still be sitting in front of his brother's home, where Donny could lift them and drive away. He had trouble closing his eyes even after his head hit the pillow.

"Just leave the past alone," Maggie had said. That's because she knew his mother had written the truth. She had always lied about what happened to the father who nurtured him. The father who was there by Donny's side through his athletic triumphs and defeats, as well as that dark day after Donny's knee surgery. The day that ended any hope of a college scholarship, let alone a professional football career.

He felt a sharp pain in his bad leg, thinking back to the agony he felt the day he realized that the life he had envisioned was in shambles. While that day was almost thirty-five years ago and the painkillers he'd been on made him groggy, he still had vivid memories.

"Mr. Brodsky, can we speak to you in private?" the doctor had asked Donny's dad.

His father returned a few minutes later, visibly upset. "I need to step out," he told Donny. "I'll be right back."

Donny remembered his growing anxiety when minutes passed, and then hours. Where was his father? Donny called the apartment, but there was no answer. By the time his mother arrived at his hospital room three hours later, Donny was in a complete panic.

"I have terrible news," she said, shaking. "Your father's gone."

Gone? Donny remembered hearing that word and initially thinking his father had left home. Had left his family. While his mother was speaking, Donny couldn't comprehend her.

"Head-on collision with a lamppost," she said. "I was driving...swerved to avoid oncoming car..."

Another vivid memory. His mother had no visible injury. Not even a scratch.

The questions lingered for years. The doctors would never disclose what they told his father that day, causing him to leave the hospital. "Privacy," they said. They could only assure him that their discussion had nothing to do with Donny's injury. His mother had said she had no idea. The police report corroborated her story, even though the one witness said there was no swerving car. Louie and Josh never questioned any of it, but they were lying to themselves. Those diaries were Donny's last chance to find out the truth. Whatever his mother had to say, he would find out soon.

Donny woke up hours later and surveyed his hotel room, momentarily forgetting where he was. His alarm had never sounded. It was already one o'clock.

CHAPTER
TWENTY-SIX

JOSH WOKE up wondering if he had made a mistake by letting Sway's security team confiscate his computer the previous day. He kept telling himself he had nothing to hide. They would find no vices hidden in his search history, which was limited to obscure technical topics, local takeout listings and world news reports. They'd find no malware or suspicious emails. He made a point of always following the cyber protection protocols drummed into him during his years at Defense.

Still, he was unsettled by the recollection of the security goons who had followed him home. They pushed past him like he was some kind of criminal.

"We can take it from here, Dr. Brodsky," said the first guard as soon as Josh opened the door. And with gruff precision, the man unplugged his computer and packed it into a padded black bag.

They were out his door within three minutes, after the taller guard handed Josh a receipt. As they drove off, Josh stood outside and saw trailer park residents lined up along the road, all watching the van marked with a large

"Security" emblem and flashing yellow strobe lights. So much for Torres's promise of not drawing attention.

He rolled out of bed and padded into the kitchen. He opened the refrigerator and winced when he saw a lone brown bag of Mexican takeout, probably fermenting for weeks. Not much of a breakfast. He grabbed his car keys, planning to head to the local drive-through for a bacon and egg sandwich with hash browns.

Coming down the steps, he noticed two large FedEx boxes beside his trailer's clamp-on steps. He assumed they were mistakenly delivered and probably belonged to one of the neighbors. Josh was one of the few residents of the community without the normal parade of Amazon and other retailer-branded packages showing up at their doorsteps. He ignored the boxes, certain the facility manager would help him find the rightful owner of the George Foreman Grill or whatever else they contained.

When he returned with his breakfast, he examined the packages again, turning one on its side to search for the correct recipient. He scratched his head when he read his own name and address printed on the label. In the sender section, it read "Richard Berman." What could Richie have sent him? He struggled to carry the boxes into the trailer.

He grabbed a knife and sliced open the tops. Inside were piles of neatly stacked notebooks, with a single envelope containing a note: "Hi Josh, hope you are doing well out in sunny California. Sorry to hear about your mom. Not sure why she left these at my mother's house, but I found them stuffed in her closet. Been packing Mom to move in with me. It's time. Anyway, thought you'd like to have. All the best, Rich."

There were dozens of notebooks, each labeled on the front cover with "from" and "until" dates. The first one, with a bold "Number 1" printed on top, started in March 1955 and ended in October 1955. The second notebook, started in February 1956 and ending in December 1956, was labeled "Number 2." When Josh opened the first notebook, his mother's distinctive handwriting hit him in the gut.

Sunday, March 3, 1955

> *Dear Diary—It's so good to meet you. My friend Natalie bought you as a birthday present. I don't know what type of things I want to say, but I'm looking forward to telling you all about myself. I am fifteen years old, and I live with my parents and my two older brothers, Ben and Harry. Harry's getting married next year.*

Diaries. These were his mother's diaries. He had lived at home for almost eighteen years, and never in all that time had he ever witnessed his mother writing in anything resembling a diary. She never wrote anything more than a shopping list. But here they were, two boxes of notebooks, almost one for every calendar year.

For the next few hours, Josh sampled various portions. The level of detail was incredible. She had written an entry for nearly every day of the year. He wondered when she did her writing. In the morning, before anyone was awake? At night, when they were all asleep? The diaries contained pages of specifics about her good days, her bad days, and everything in between. About her dreams and aspirations, which seemed to shift over time. In some parts, he clearly recognized his mother's voice, but some sounded like it had been written by a total stranger. He had to laugh. Here he was, the AI expert, making it possible for politicians to speak to great leaders from the past, now sitting here with material that would take him two years to read.

But there was one diary he wanted to read in detail. Throughout Josh's life, he hadn't spent a lot of energy thinking about his father or about the accident that had taken his life. Their mother's account had always seemed straightforward. The police investigation never went beyond the crash scene. A driver had swerved into her lane, causing her to steer her car into a lamppost. Case closed, but not to Donny. Josh always believed that all of Donny's doubts about their mother's story came down to one thing—that he could never accept that their father was dead. If there was more to her story, the details would have to be in these diaries.

Josh made a fresh cup of coffee, sat in his kitchenette, and started reading the notebook dated 1988. He skimmed through the early parts of the year to see if anything unusual led up to August 16, the day his father died. Several entries brought a heaviness to Josh's chest.

Sunday, March 27, 1988

Haven't heard from Josh in three weeks. The last time we spoke I asked him his plans for the summer, but he said he planned to spend the summer at MIT working with some professor. He wasn't sure if he was coming home for Passover. I'm not calling him again. Whenever I call, he gives me one-word answers. He never asks to speak to his father. I wonder if he'll ever come to visit again.

Friday, July 1, 1988

Excited to see Josh this weekend. Nobody wants to go except me but how else will I see my son if we don't go to him? Josh didn't seem to care if we come or not, but that's Josh. I want to see him. If the only way we can is for us all to pile into the car and drive to Boston, then we're going. It took a lot of convincing but Joe finally agreed. I don't care if Donny misses a summer practice with the football team, we're all going.

Tuesday, July 5, 1988

What a miserable weekend. I never thought I would be so happy to be in my stuffy apartment. Josh barely said two words the entire time we were with him, which wasn't much. Out of nowhere he had an important exam to study for. What professor schedules a test for the week after a holiday weekend? In the summer session? Joe took Donny to see the New England Patriots practice, leaving me and Louie without a car. We took the T into Boston and walked around, visiting some of the historic sites, but Louie wasn't very interested. Josh met us for lunch on Sunday. He was a little more talkative without his father around.

Josh had a vague memory of that weekend. Of his

mother's insistence that the entire family would be coming. He had no recollection of a lunch with just Mom and Louie. But that was a long time ago. It was also the last time he saw his father alive. Josh skimmed through the remaining July and early August entries, finding nothing unusual. He stopped to read what she'd written the day before the accident.

Monday, August 15, 1988

I just came from Coney Island Hospital. Donny will have surgery in the morning. The doctors said they won't know how badly his knee is damaged until they go in and look around. I'm glad I wasn't at the game when it happened. I could never take seeing my kids in pain. Seeing Donny at the hospital was bad enough. My neighbor Judy was at the game. She said Donny slid awkwardly into second base. She said he was out by a mile so she wasn't even sure why he bothered to slide. But he got all twisted up with the bag and the shortstop. They carried him off the field. Joe drove him to the hospital. By the time he called me, Judy had already told me what happened. I couldn't even look at Joe when I got there. He insisted that Donny play baseball this summer, saying that all the best athletes play multiple sports. But Donny wasn't being offered a college scholarship to play baseball. They want him for football. Why risk the injury? But nobody listens to me. I hope the doctors can fix him.

Josh turned the page. His mother didn't write again for an entire week.

Wednesday, August 24, 1988

Shiva ended yesterday. I'm glad everybody is finally gone, but the apartment feels so quiet now. Donny and Louie have been in their room all day. They come out to eat. I don't need to worry about food for a while—there's plenty left. So much left over that I had to give it to Judy to keep in her refrigerator. Louie can walk down whenever he and Donny want something. Josh went back a few days ago. It was fine that he didn't stay the whole time. He was here most of the week. At least he helped Donny, who's still not getting around the apartment very well with that big cast on his leg. He won't tell me if his knee is feeling any better. He hasn't spoken to me since the funeral, since I came to his hospital room to tell him. I tried to comfort him but he was inconsolable, crying, distraught. Thankfully, he didn't ask a lot of questions about the accident. He just wanted to know why his father left the hospital so suddenly. And why I picked him up. Where were we going? I told him his father had called and asked me to pick him up and take him home. But I know Donny didn't believe me. He barely speaks to me. His father was his entire world. It's been one week since the accident. That day is a blur. I remember, but I don't want to remember. It all

*happened so fast. I always knew that Joe had an
explosive temper. He kept it under control most of
the time. He lost it with Josh that one time, but
other than the occasional spanking, he never
hurt us.*

Josh rubbed the scar on his ear, trying to remember, but he had a very foggy memory of that time of his life. He just always understood that he needed to stay clear of his father. Josh continued reading.

*But he came at me so fast. As soon as I
picked him up from the hospital, he confronted
me. I wasn't prepared. I mean, I was always
prepared. I always knew this day could come. And
now he knew. I don't know how. I have an idea
but what does it matter? I didn't try to lie. I
don't know what I thought would happen, but I
didn't anticipate this. It all happened so fast. He
put his hands around my neck. I never thought he
would try to kill me.*

What? Dad tried to kill Mom? How? Josh turned the pages, searching for answers. There had to be more. What did their father confront her with? The answers must be in here. Josh read the following pages in detail for another hour. She wrote about getting Donny and Louie ready for the school year, about Donny removing the cast and walking with crutches, about Donny refusing to speak to her. She wrote about her new job at an eyeglass factory on Emmons Avenue.

He read as much as he could, but her 1988 diary

contained no further mention of the car accident, or what sparked his father's rage.

Josh's phone rang. It was Louie.

"Louie! You're not going to believe this!"

CHAPTER
TWENTY-SEVEN

LOUIE LEANED over the bar at his favorite watering hole. "Lemme have another one, Sal," he said. It was Friday at noon, early in the day even by his own standards. Not so for the dozen tourists and shift workers scattered around the tavern, all in high spirits. Needing a quiet place to regroup, he walked his scotch to the back corner and found a dimly lit booth.

The cell phone message he'd received a few minutes earlier from Peachtree's CEO was quick and to the point. "No progress—out of time."

Darrell Evans and the Peachtree team were leaving the conference room, and the city, where they had been sequestered for three days. "Deal off the table," Evans said, along with any chance for Louie's payday.

Louie rubbed his eyes, absorbing the news. Did he really have any choice other than to tell Virtual Bank's cyber team what he believed? What he knew about Donny?

Louie checked his cell phone in case he had missed a

return call from Josh. He drained the scotch and dialed his older brother one last time.

This time, Josh answered.

"Louie! You're not going to believe this!"

"Josh, what the fuck?" Louie said in a loud whisper. He turned his back and cupped his hand beside his mouth. "I've been trying to reach you since yesterday!"

"Yeah, er, well, I've been tied up. Lots of crazy stuff," Josh said. "And seems to be getting crazier by the minute. You're not gonna believe—"

"Crazy? You don't know the half of it. Our brother's gone off the deep end. Bonkers."

"What are you talking about?"

"He hacked into my client's database. He's extorting them for a ransom payment!"

"Slow down. Donny? There's no way."

"Asshole came in through my work computer. I opened his document for that fuckin' training business he's starting, and he planted encryption code. He wants them to pay him five million dollars, or the bank's customer files will be completely locked."

"Wait," Josh said. "What makes you think it was Donny's business plan?"

"Security says there was an attachment that dropped the malware into their system, and it came from my computer—and it happened on the same day I opened Donny's document. Come on, that's not a coincidence!"

The line was silent.

"Josh? You still there?"

No response.

"Josh!" Louie said.

Louie heard Josh clear his throat. "Do they think you had anything to do with it?"

"Well, it came through my office computer, so in their

minds, that makes me a suspect. But they haven't arrested me. Not yet. I don't know what to do!"

"When's the last time you spoke to him?" Josh asked.

"Yesterday," Louie said. "He admitted he sent me that file. I couldn't believe it. Said he wanted to show me what he's capable of."

"He admitted it?"

"Not straight out. I was warned to be careful. I was afraid I'd scare him into doing something more deranged."

"What else did he say?"

"All he really wanted to talk about was some fantasy about Mom having diaries."

"Hold on. How did he find out about the diaries?" Josh asked.

"What? You knew about them?"

"I'm staring at boxes filled with her notebooks," Josh said. "I was just reading them."

"They're real?" Louie asked. "How'd you get them?"

Josh was silent for a moment, then said, "I need to check something. Call you right back."

"No, don't fuckin' hang up!"

The line went dead.

"Shit!" Louie shouted. An off-duty Con Ed lineman at the bar glanced over his shoulder. Louie snapped his fingers toward the bartender and pointed to his empty glass. Before his scotch was refilled, Josh called back.

"We've got big trouble," Josh said.

"I told you that."

"He's on his way here," Josh said.

"What? To California? Why's he coming to *you*?"

"Donny found out Richie Berman sent me Mom's diaries. I'm not sure why, but Maggie had them. Donny says they're his, and he's coming to get them. But listen,

Donny got into my system too. He's made the same ransom demand at my company. But I didn't connect the hack to his attachment until now."

"Holy shit!" Louie said. He gulped his scotch. "Our brother's a psychopath."

"Hold on," Josh said. "Let me think."

"I tried to get him to talk about that business plan. Feel him out. But like I said, he just wanted to talk about the diaries."

"So you haven't told anyone at your office? About your suspicions?"

Louie stood and signaled for his check. "Not yet."

"Okay. That's good."

"But I'm heading back there now," Louie said as he threw a twenty on the table. "I'm outta time."

"We can use the diaries to our advantage," Josh said. "Huh?"

"I said, we can leverage the diaries."

"What do the diaries have to do with anything?"

"I don't think they have anything to do with what he did," Josh said. "But he's always been obsessed about what happened with Dad. He must think these have the answers he's looking for. Why else would he be flying out here?"

Louie slid back into the booth, whispering, "Did you find anything?"

"There's a lot in here, Louie. Mom didn't describe the accident, at least not in the portions I've been able to read so far. But Donny was right to be suspicious."

"Why? What'd she say?"

"She said Dad tried to kill her."

"What the fuck?" Louie shouted, loudly enough that several patrons stopped their conversations. Louie turned away.

"That's all she said, Louie. I didn't find anything more. At least not yet."

"That's crazy, Josh! Why would Dad try to kill her? Where did that happen?"

"I assume in the car, but who knows? The answer may be somewhere in her diaries, but maybe not. I read her 1988 diary, and it's not in there. It's possible we'll never know. Unless…"

"Unless what?" Louie asked.

"Louie, I have to go. My security guys just grabbed my computer. I'm assuming they'll find the same thing on mine that they found on yours. If they tie this to Donny before we get to him, he'll be screwed."

"Good. He'll have to take that crap off, and I can close my deal."

"Listen, Louie, it's possible Donny's been right all these years. Mom definitely lied about what happened, or maybe why it happened. At least what led up to the accident. Donny knew her explanation didn't make sense."

Louie rubbed his eyes. "This doesn't change anything, Josh. Donny's still fucking us over, and I'm out of time."

"I have an idea," Josh said.

"Me too. I'm calling the feds."

"Not yet," Josh said. "Can you get out here?"

"You're kidding me, right? I've got a fuckin' five-alarm blaze going."

"We'll get him to unlock our systems," Josh said. "We just can't let anyone get to Donny before we do. We can convince him to remove his malware and provide the encryption keys. If I'm right, I think we can make a trade of sorts."

"You think he's gonna give up his millions for the diaries?"

"I think we can do better than just the diaries.

Besides, you just said it—we don't have a lot of time. It will take us weeks to study those diaries. I know how to get him answers in a few hours, even if Mom didn't write about the accident. But I need you here."

"I can't come to San Francisco. If I disappear now, everyone here will think I'm guilty for sure."

"Then make something up," Josh said. "I can't do this alone. I'll text Donny and hold him off until Sunday. I'll tell him I'm out of town for a few days. I need some time to get this set up."

"Set up what?"

"Just get here tomorrow. Text me your flight info, and I'll pick you up. Right now, I've got to get these diaries out of here before Donny shows."

―――――

"YOU'RE GOING WHERE? This is the strangest story I've ever heard," Phil Calpers said. "An investment banker negotiating ransom terms with a hacker?"

Louie rose from the sofa in his office and started packing his briefcase with papers. Secretly meeting with the hacker was the only story he could invent that would possibly explain his absence for the weekend.

"It makes no sense," Calpers said. "You're telling me this guy broke into your computer to plant malware on our client. Now he wants to break bread with you? How did he know you were involved with VB in the first place?"

Louie zipped his briefcase. "He didn't say. We've got shitty security here, that's pretty obvious. The guy just said he knew he could get to Virtual through Peabody & Munson. Now he's willing to negotiate a lower ransom payment, but only with me."

"What did the boss say when you told him?" Calpers asked.

"I *haven't* told him," Louie said. "You can tell him for me. But only after I'm gone, so he can't stop me. Wait until tomorrow."

"Louie, you're not James Bond. This sounds crazy. Crazy dangerous."

"He's a hacker, not a serial killer. You've got to buy me a few days. That's all I'm asking for."

Phil shook his head. Louie had to raise the stakes.

"The hacker told me that if he so much as smells anyone but me, he'll publish all the personal information of Virtual's customers. Account numbers, Social Security numbers, security questions. Our merger deal is done for good if that happens."

"Jeez."

"I promise when I'm back and VB's system has been cleared, we'll go after him. I'll get as much information as I can. We'll still throw his ass in jail. But after I'm back."

Louie opened his file cabinet and removed his overnight travel bag, kept at the ready, with a change of clothes and toiletries to carry him through out-of-town emergencies.

"If this backfires…" Calpers began.

Briefcase and travel bag in hand, Louie stopped at his office door and said, "Backfires? How much worse can things get?"

Calpers slowly nodded. "You think VB will pay if the ransom is lower?"

"I don't know if they will. That's why you have to stay on those technology teams. If anything happens, text me right away."

Louie steeled himself for one last task. As he exited the office building, he dialed his home number.

"How are you going to California?" Vicki asked moments later, her tone sharp. "I thought you were barricaded in your conference room."

Louie rambled about last-minute complications with an investor in San Francisco, a venture capital fund that wanted to deal only with him. He threw in a few other excuses, pretty much anything that popped into his head.

"I'll just be a day or two."

"What about the mortgage company?"

"I'll call them again on Monday morning," he said, his nails digging into the seat cushion.

"You said you'd call them yesterday."

"Things are in motion," he said. Truth was, there was no use calling the bank again until there was money in the account. He just needed a couple more days.

After several moments of silence, Vicki said calmly, "I've been thinking about all of this."

"You and me both."

"No, I mean it," she said, her tone soft. "This is just lunacy. You're working your ass off. Jess and I never see you, and—"

"Vicki, not now, please."

"Hear me out. You're stressed like a madman, and you still have to juggle our bank accounts to pay our bills. Something's not right. I know it."

"I'm fixing it."

"Until the next time," she said.

"Vic, I—"

"I think we should sell this place," she said. Even with the highway noise, Louie could hear her voice cracking. "I don't care where we live. We can get a small house in Jersey. I don't want you staying at that firm. They're sucking the life out of you. Next thing I know, you'll tell me you've been gambling again."

Louie grimaced, feeling as if a vise was tightening on his skull.

"Louie?"

"I'm here." Louie squinted into the glare of the oncoming headlights as the taxi crossed the RFK Bridge. "Listen, I'm at the airport. Please. I've got this. I'll call you tomorrow."

"What's happening?" she sobbed. "What's happening to us?"

"Come on. Please don't cry. It's gonna be okay. You've got to trust me," he said. She didn't answer. Louie listened for a few moments as his wife quieted her tears. "Vicki?"

"I meant what I said," she said. "I love you."

"Me too."

He hung up, stretched out, and exhaled. What else was he supposed to tell her? That this trip was a long shot, a Hail Mary pass to keep them afloat, with longer odds than any bet Louie had placed over the years? Which reminded him. He opened ClubTrack on his phone, checking on his other long shot—the bets he had placed on the afternoon's races. He slumped when he read another disappointing result.

He was now betting on whatever plan Josh was dreaming up. They had to finish in the money.

He wasn't moving to some shithole house in New Jersey.

CHAPTER
TWENTY-EIGHT

DONNY INSTRUCTED the driverless rental car to stop on the side of the road. He had been driving around Palo Alto for the past hour, searching for his brother's home, but the only match to the address in his cell phone was a trailer park called Sequoia Mobile Homes. Donny was about to call Josh when a text message flashed across his screen.

> JOSH:
> Out of town until Sunday. Text
> me where you're staying. Will
> pick you up Sunday morning.

Sunday morning? Donny didn't plan to spend the weekend playing California tourist. He had the car proceed to the trailer park and pull into the gravel access road, passing several mobile homes, most appointed with neat gardens, American flags, and barbecue grills. He found his way to Unit 12, which had none of these exterior accoutrements. In fact, from the outside, it looked to be unoccupied.

Donny exited the car and knocked on the door.

"Ain't here," said a woman's voice from behind him.

Donny turned and faced the trailer in the next lot. In the doorway was a short elderly woman in a faded blue housedress. Large curlers held up her white hair, and a cigarette dangled from her lips.

"Excuse me?" he said.

"I said, he ain't here. Mostly ain't here."

Donny approached the woman. "Do you know who lives here?"

"You another cop?" she asked.

"A cop?" Donny said, surprised. "No lady, not a cop. I'm looking for Josh Brodsky. Does he live here?"

"Who's askin'?"

"Er…an old friend."

The woman came down the three metal steps, the screen door slamming behind her. She took a drag on her cigarette and squinted through the smoke billowing in front of her face.

"Does he live here?" Donny asked. "Josh Brodsky?"

"Seems so." She took another drag. "Postman mixes up our mail all the time. Yer friend's not very neighborly. Comes and goes. Mostly goes. But there was a whole bunch of cops here yesterday. Thought you was one too."

"What happened?" Donny asked.

"How should I know?" the woman said. "Just seen these guys follow 'im into the house. Come right back out carrying somethin'. Ain't here more'n a minute or two. What you call, plainclothes—no uniforms or nothin'."

"How'd you know they were cops?"

"I watch TV." She appeared to be insulted by the question. "Big black van, flashing lights. Looked just like the cops on the show. At least the big'un did. I'm sure they was cops."

"Did my broth—did Josh leave with them?"

"Nah. He stuck around for a few hours. Strange," she said, throwing the butt on the ground and stamping it out with her slipper.

"What was strange?" Donny asked.

"Don't see him much at all, then he's inside for a few hours today. Most of the morning. Gone by time I got back from makin' my rounds. I'm the manager here."

"Did he have anything with him when he left? Packages or boxes?"

"Didn't see," she said as she removed Marlboros from her housedress and tapped on the package. "Like I said, he was gone by the time I got back." Removing a lighter from her housedress, she added, "You think I spend all my time nosin' out my window? I got plenty things to do."

Donny looked back at Unit 12, thinking of Josh's text. If his brother was really out of town until Sunday, there was no reason Donny couldn't return after dark to get what he came for. He and his package could be on their way back to Chicago tomorrow morning.

"Thank you, ma'am," Donny said. "Listen, if Josh should come home, don't mention my being here. I'd kind of like it to be a surprise."

The woman let out a long plume of smoke.

"You know what those TV cops do? You know, when they want someone to stay quiet, or tell 'em somethin'? You ever watch TV?"

The woman looked up at the sky and rubbed the back of her neck.

Donny pulled his wallet from his back pocket and examined his billfold. He lifted a twenty and folded it over.

"Appreciate keeping our secret," he said, holding out his hand.

The woman's hand touched Donny's, and she discreetly put the crumpled bill into her dress pocket. She turned and walked back to her trailer.

"Haven't talked to him since he moved in," she said, waving over her shoulder. "Don't expect today will be any different."

FIVE HOURS LATER, Donny parked his car at the Palo Alto Diner, a quarter mile from the entrance to Sequoia Mobile Homes. He lifted an empty, oversize duffel bag from the car's trunk. The same duffel he'd purchased back in New York to carry his mother's diaries out of Maggie's house. He limped the remaining distance to the trailer park, a chilly evening wind whipping down the street. He slipped a black ski hat on his head as he walked down the dark gravel road toward Unit 12. There were no lights on. No car in front. Josh was definitely not home.

Donny came around the rear of Josh's trailer, staying out of the line of sight of the nosy woman in Unit 13. He helped himself to a lawn chair stacked in front of Unit 11 to help him reach the trailer's windows. The second window he checked was unlocked. Josh was so accommodating. It took a bit of effort for Donny to lift his overweight frame over the windowsill, but he was able to tumble into the unit after the third attempt, kicking the chair on its side.

Staying low, Donny turned on the pocket flashlight he'd bought at a convenience store.

He moved throughout the unit, searching behind two

coats hung in the minuscule front closet, underneath slacks and shirts in the bedroom drawers, socks and underwear in a plastic bin shoved under the bed. The bathroom contained piles of dust, soap scum in the shower, toiletries in the medicine chest. Moving through the kitchen, he searched the refrigerator and the limited cabinetry.

After an hour of searching, the diaries were nowhere to be found.

Donny crawled out of the window and dropped to the ground, landing awkwardly on his bad leg. As he limped back to his car, he called Josh.

CHAPTER
TWENTY-NINE

JOSH PROCEEDED UP THE LONG, moonlit driveway to a private home in Menlo Park, just north of San Jose. He had booked the house for a full week, using the keywords "secluded" and "spacious" on the rental app. "Peaceful, tranquil creek side setting on five secluded redwood acres. Spacious cottage with three bedrooms. Wi-Fi enabled. No other homes on the property." Hell of a place for a family reunion, he thought.

Josh found the key tacked underneath the second window, the owner's designated hiding place, and unlocked the front door. He flicked on the light, revealing a large wood-paneled living room with an oversize fireplace in the center. The space was surrounded by tall windows that looked out onto the large, wooded property. No curtains or shades to darken the room, the way he'd need it.

Proceeding down the hallway, he passed two small bedrooms, each with a twin bed and dresser. Neither room was large enough to set up his equipment. Making his way to the end of the hallway, Josh opened the door and entered the primary bedroom. He moved around, testing the weight of the king-size poster bed, which slid easily away from the wall. The small windows faced north and had a full set of dark brown curtains. This room would do just fine.

He returned to the car to retrieve the supplies he had procured at an electronics store: video cameras, speakers, microphones—all of the miniature variety—plus USB cables and a laptop with excess storage and a high-speed processor. He had also detoured to the hardware store and purchased duct tape and a package of zip ties.

After laying all the equipment out on the floor, Josh slid the poster bed to the far side of the room and dragged a dark pedestal desk to the center. He strung a fifty-foot extension cord across the floor, taping the female socket on the back of the desk. He set the laptop on the desk, plugged in, and texted Naveen. "How's the visualization engine coming?"

"No problem, mon," Naveen texted back. "My boy is making fine progress."

Naveen's college classmate, Ashwini, was an AI engineer on the People Experience team. He was happy to trade a copy of the engine behind PEARL's ability to read, interpret, and react to body language and expressions for some high-class weed. Even a rudimentary version would dramatically enhance their interactions with CHERL.

"The interface will be seamless," Naveen wrote, assuring him that all projects at Sway conformed to strict architectural guidelines, simplifying code transfer.

Josh had called Naveen only a few hours earlier, soliciting his trusted lieutenant's help. Jenna had unwittingly provided her encouragement by trying to explain Josh's absence. "Josh needs to take some personal time," she had told Naveen when Josh didn't show up for work.

"I got it, mon," Naveen had said when Josh explained his plan. The hacker might have encrypted the production code, but a backup version of CHERL dating back to December was still accessible. "She won't have all the changes and additions we've made since the beginning of the year," Naveen said, "but for what you're doing, it will still be like taking a Ferrari to the grocery store."

Josh was amazed at how quickly Naveen pulled everything together, even connecting CHERL to publicly available medical and accident reports from the prior fifty years—information that might enhance the system's knowledge of critical events. But Louie would be arriving soon, and Josh wanted everything set. They would need time to review the plan.

JOSH:
ETA?

NAVEEN:
Give me another hour.

Thx!

Josh returned to the task of setting up the room. He mounted the cameras in the four corners and connected them to his laptop using the house's Wi-Fi. Not satisfied with the speed, he unpacked and connected USB cables, which transmitted the images to perfection.

As he secured the cables to the table, his phone rang. It was Donny. Josh took a deep breath, telling himself to sound cheery, not to raise any suspicions.

"Hey, Donny. What's up?"

"Don't 'What's up?' me," Donny said sharply. "Where are Mom's diaries?"

"Don't worry," Josh said, startled by Donny's

menacing tone. "They're safe. You'll have them on Sunday."

"They weren't in your trailer."

"You broke into my trailer?" Louie was right. Donny had lost his mind.

"Nice home, by the way," Donny snickered. "Very classy."

"Ah, I don't live there. At least not anymore. It was temporary until I found a place. But that was pretty stu —" Josh stopped himself, not wanting to further antagonize his brother. Not this way.

"Yeah, I guess that probably was stupid," Donny said, "seeing that cops like hanging around. Why were those cops outside your place yesterday?"

The Sway security van. How long had Donny been watching him? Josh peeked out the window and saw nothing but darkness. If Donny had followed him here, Josh assumed, he would already be on the doorstep.

Donny laughed and asked, "What kind of trouble you in, bro?"

"Everything is fine with me. But I don't want to see you make trouble for *yourself*."

"You mean breaking in? Nah, I was careful. No one saw me. I really didn't want to wait around all weekend. With you saying you were out of town and all. But you can't be too far. Your neighbor saw you this morning. What's going on?"

"Just a misunderstanding. Nothing to worry about."

"That's good. I hate to think you were in trouble or anything. Do you have the diaries with you?"

"I told you," Josh said. "They're in a safe place. I'll give them to you on Sunday."

"And I told *you*. I can't wait around all weekend. Tell

me where you are, and I'll come get them." Donny paused, then asked, "Where are you, anyway?"

"Out of town. I can't tell you."

"Oooh, top secret, huh? Your company must take security very seriously."

Was Donny taunting him? Maybe Louie was right. It would be easy to just call the police. Have Donny arrested for breaking and entering, hold him until they could convince him to unwind his malware. But he could hear it in Donny's voice. Their brother was troubled. Instead of being angry, Josh actually felt sorry, remorseful. After all, Josh was the one who stayed away after their father died. He hadn't been there to console Donny after his knee injury ended his chance for a scholarship. No matter how bad his relationship with his father had been, Josh hadn't been around to comfort either of his brothers after Dad died. Josh was the one who remained in Cambridge to finish his degree at MIT, then moved on to DC and never came back.

"Tell me where you're staying," Josh said. "I'm flying in on Sunday morning. I can pick you up."

Donny didn't respond for a few moments.

"Go see the sights," Josh said. "We can go to my house together. You can get the diaries and be on the Monday morning flight back to Chicago—Sunday night, if you want."

A few more silent moments. Finally, Donny said, "What time do you land?"

"Around eight."

"Don't screw around with me, bro."

"I'm not screwing with you."

"I'm at the La Quinta. The one at the airport."

"I'll see you on Sunday morning," Josh said.

After he hung up, Josh slumped in a folding chair,

more convinced than ever that just trading for the diaries wouldn't change anything for Donny. Their mother had lied about the day their father died. But what Josh had read was just one small portion of her life, out of context compared with the vast details she had written over sixty-plus years, not to mention what was left unsaid. Unwritten. Why had she lied? Why did their father try to kill her, and was the car crash really an accident? If Donny didn't find answers in the diaries, there would be no telling what kind of mental state he'd be in as he moved on to his next victim. He would eventually end up behind bars, or worse.

Josh progressed rapidly through the room, completing and testing connections, his confidence increasing by the minute. CHERL was their best chance to fill in the missing pieces, and maybe change the course of Donny's life.

Naveen sent him another text.

> She's ready. I'm loading the
> diaries.

CHAPTER
THIRTY

SATURDAY

PIZZA BOXES and empty bottles lay scattered across the table in the kitchen of the rental house. Louie grabbed his third beer from the fridge, searching for relief from his throbbing headache. Every word of Josh's scheme hit him like a jackhammer.

"Just imagine, Louie," Josh said, gesticulating as he moved around the kitchen. "Imagine if historical figures could speak to us! Teach us what they know. Extrapolate from history to develop a better understanding of the future. Without concern for their legacy. Without any spin, or any agendas from biographers or historians. Just their knowledge and experiences."

The quiet, reserved, oldest Brodsky brother was as animated as Louie had ever seen him, speaking as if he were trying to convert him to a new religion.

"But we can supercharge them," Josh continued. "Supercharge them with information they didn't have at the time. Just think of the benefits. They can solve some of the most intractable challenges of our time!"

Louie rested his elbows on the table, rubbing at the pressure in his temples. "This is all very interesting. But what the fuck does this have to do with Donny?"

Josh sat across from his brother and smiled. "I told you, Louie—we have Mom's diaries. Detailed diaries, from the time she was fifteen!"

Louie shook his head. "And…"

"I'm telling you; Mom's diaries are rich but vague in many places. But we can add supplemental information. Not perfect, but CHERL knows how to fill in the gaps. I think it will work."

"Who the hell is Cheryl?"

"Our code name. Computerized Human Experienced as Real Life. CHERL. We built her to advise global leaders, help them think through the implications of huge, global issues. National security. Diplomacy. I know she's not designed for this. What did Naveen say? Oh yeah. It's like taking a Ferrari to the grocery store."

Louie glanced over his shoulder. "Naveen?"

"He works for me at Sway. He and my team fed every word of Mom's diaries into CHERL and merged them with massive amounts of data from contemporary secondary sources."

Josh explained more about the secondary sources his team was able to integrate into CHERL's data files. Historical records on US births and deaths, immigration by country and religion, along with tax returns to understand the context of their parents' financial life. Volumes written on the Jewish experience throughout the twentieth century. Plus, fifty years of New York medical and accident records.

"We even found profiles of similar women. We call them look-alikes. Very predictive of future behavior."

Slowly, the picture came into focus. Louie turned away, frightened of the person sitting across from him.

"Who's better than Mom to help us save our brother?" Josh asked, his hands extended.

Louie cleared his throat. "Are you out of your fuckin' mind? This is why you flew me out here? You're crazier than *he* is!"

"Listen to me," Josh said. "I'm telling you—"

"No, Josh. You listen to *me*," Louie said, unable to suppress a slow burn of anger. Donny was coming to this hideaway for the diaries, and Josh's big plan was to introduce them to a computerized version of their mother? "I really don't give a shit. You understand what I'm saying to you? I really, really don't. I thought we were just going to trade the diaries for the encryption key. He unlocks our files, and we're done. We're not playing games with your new toy."

"CHERL is not a toy."

"Oh, no? It's *real*? You're really gonna bring Mom back to talk sense into our brother?"

"Oh, it won't be her exactly," Josh said. "To some extent, she'll be more self-aware. And she'll understand more about what happened than our real mother did. A lot more."

"How's it gonna know more than the diaries?"

Josh was smiling. "I told you. We start with her diaries, but we know biographies and journals are always incomplete. That's where our inference engine comes in. It allows CHERL to extrapolate from the diaries and that supplemental information I told you about. Find connections that weren't laid out for us."

"Great. It makes shit up. That should help."

"No, no. Not at all," Josh said. "It's still Mom's facts. The diaries are the world as she saw it. The world that she experienced, or at least how she chose to record those experiences. It isn't necessarily the whole truth. CHERL fills in the blanks. She'll infer things that Mom doesn't describe, but with a high degree of certainty that they actually happened."

Louie shook his head, laughing to himself, but this was anything but funny. The dull throbbing in his head had morphed into a sharp pain, as if all the pressure he had been suppressing was trying to break loose. He felt his deal slipping further away, and with it, Vicki and Jessica, and everything they had built together. He came to California thinking he had to deal with one crazy brother. Now he had to bring a second one back to reality. He pressed his hands together, as if in prayer, saying, "This is not some fuckin' science experiment. This is my life you're screwing around with."

"I'm not screwing around."

"Go bring somebody else's mother back to life!" Louie shouted. "Or Mother Teresa, for all I care! I'm not waiting around so Donny can have a nice chat with our robot mom. When he gets here, we're gonna make him take that malware off VB's system. We'll give him the diaries. If he does that, he gets a get-out-of-jail-free card. That's all."

"Are you really prepared to throw him in jail?"

"If he doesn't unlock our systems? Damn straight I am. After what he did to me? To us? Why wouldn't I?"

"I don't believe you. You could have turned his name over to the FBI in New York, but you didn't. Why not?"

Louie rubbed his eyes and quietly said, "You told me you had a plan, so I held off. You asked me to come out here, so I came. But Donny can read the diaries about

Dad, and that can accomplish the same thing. He removes the malware; he gets the diaries. Simple as that."

"Don't you understand?" Josh said. "He might make the trade for the diaries. That solves our short-term problem, but it won't change anything for Donny, especially if Mom didn't spell out the details of what happened with Dad. What if the answers aren't in there?"

"I guess he'll be the same fuckup he is today," Louie said.

"He's troubled, Louie. I can hear it in his voice. I think he'll wind up in a gutter someplace, or worse. CHERL gives us the best chance of helping him. We'll all have a much better chance of finding out the truth and moving forward."

"I know how to move forward. As soon as Donny deletes the malware, I'll move forward onto my flight back to New York to close my deal. That's the only forward I care about right now."

Josh placed a hand on Louie's shoulder. "Don't you think this family needs to clear the air? It could do us all good to hear what Mom would have told us. Should have told us."

"This is about Donny." Louie shoved his brother's arm away. "He's the one with the demons."

Josh put his hands up, saying, "We all have our demons, Louie."

"Excuse me?" Louie shouted. "You've picked a hell of a time for a family intervention. Why do you care so much all of a sudden? I mean, where have *you* been all these years? I'm the one who's been propping up Donny. Taking care of Mom while you've been hiding in your bunker. Now you want to save us all?"

"You're right, Louie. I haven't been there for my

family. But I can't change my past. I can't change Donny's past either."

"I don't give a shit about his past," Louie said. "Or yours."

"This is not about me," Josh said. "Our brother is in trouble. He's lost it, for whatever reason. Whatever he's done to us, he's distracted enough to come all the way across the country to answer this one question that's been burning a hole inside him for almost forty years. And from what I was able to see in the diary, he wasn't crazy to question Mom's story. What else might we learn from the diaries? From CHERL? It may not be all good, for any of us. Shouldn't we be there for our brother when he finds out? Shouldn't we be together when we all find out?"

Louie folded his arms on the tabletop and rested his head on them. Josh was like a dog with a bone, on some kind of mixed-up quixotic mission to test his AI creation, to save their brother, and maybe even to strip himself of his guilt for having been in his own world all these years.

"And if it doesn't work?" Louie asked.

"Then what choice do we have? We'll do it your way. Tell him we're burning the diaries, deleting her memory from CHERL. And if he doesn't delete the malware, we'll call the feds."

Louie went to the window and stared into the dark woods. He wiped the perspiration that was now dripping down his forehead. Even if he wanted to make his own trade with Donny, who knew where this guy Naveen had stashed the diaries? Josh had left him with no choice but to follow along with his crazy scheme. But, Louie told himself, he wouldn't sit still for some type of elaborate family intervention. Donny would take his crap off

Virtual Bank's system quickly or Louie would shut down Josh's charade and call the cops.

"What do we have to do?"

————

THREE HOURS LATER, Louie was sprawled on the living room sofa with yet another beer, watching the business news channel. Josh called him to the master bedroom, where he was working to "put CHERL through the paces."

"I think you should stop with the beer," Josh said. "We'll need to be sharp tomorrow."

"Don't worry about me," Louie said. "Just make sure Mom is primed to go."

"We're close," Josh said. "I need to synchronize our voices with the facial recognition software."

"Oh, you mean supercomputer Mom won't just *infer* which one of us is the asshole?"

"Funny. Come over here and read this." Josh handed Louie a sheet of paper with various sentences, words, and phrases.

"Who am I speaking to?"

"Nobody. It's CHERL's natural language processor. Keep your head up so the camera picks you up, but speak into the microphone. Just use your normal speaking voice."

"Maybe I should sing."

"Read."

Louie read the first sentence. "I am speaking to my mother."

"Keep going."

Louie looked toward the camera and said, "Donny is a fucking asshole."

"That won't hurt, Louie. But could you stick with the script?"

After Louie finished reading the fifteen sentences, he asked, "How will she know when it's Donny speaking? He might not be recognizable after I bash his head in."

"Process of elimination," Josh said. "He'll be the default setting. The only voice and face she won't recognize. She'll know you and me."

"What will good ol' Mom sound like?" Louie asked.

"We pulled a female voice from our library. It's not her, but it'll have to do. I don't have any recordings of Mom."

"I do," Louie said. "I have her voice."

"Wait, what?"

Louie held up his phone. "Yeah, for some weird reason, I kept her voice messages. That's all that's left of her." He pressed a few keys. "She's right here."

"Louie, it's me. Call me back. I'm going out for a little while but call me back later. I have a question." Their mother's raspy voice with the Brooklyn accent was unmistakable.

"Fantastic!" Josh said. "Let me have your phone. I'll give it back to you in the morning. Why don't you get some sleep? Tomorrow will be a long day. You just be ready when Donny gets here."

"I'll be here," Louie said.

"And no mention of the ransomware until we get deep into our conversation. You have to keep your head. It could get intense. But the more real we can make it, the more revealing we can make her be with us, and the more it will drive Donny crazy—he'll want access to her so badly. Until we say so, he'll just have to sit here and listen."

"He'll never just sit still and listen," Louie said. "How are we gonna stop him from opening his big mouth?"

Josh pointed to the duct tape and twist ties on the desk.

"We're tying him up?" Louie asked.

"I don't see any other way. Just remember, Louie, like I said before, CHERL will know everything Mom wrote, and more. But this will be an earlier version of the system. This version doesn't have the code we wrote to fix a few things. CHERL may seem a bit more aggressive than how we remember our mother. She'll have no concept of empathy. Just be prepared—she probably won't pull any punches."

Louie chuckled. "Maybe we really will learn something."

CHAPTER
THIRTY-ONE

SUNDAY

AS DONNY STOOD outside the La Quinta Inn, he gripped his roll-on bag and leaned on the railing to support his throbbing leg. The consistent ache told him more rain was on the way. Donny had been cooped up and bored for two days, just waiting for Josh to take him to the diaries. At least his rendezvous, courtesy of OneNiteFrenz, had provided a bit of a distraction, even if the atmosphere at the La Quinta wasn't the best, and the bed a little creaky. Who cared if his neighbors got a cheap thrill? Better than the back seat of her Honda.

Now, at long last, the wait was over, a wait that extended well beyond the past two days. Donny had been looking for answers for three and a half decades. Thirty-five long years, trying to find out what had really happened to his father.

He checked his watch again, glanced up, and noticed a blue Taurus approaching. Between the mist and the wipers flapping back and forth, it was hard for him to make out the driver. As the car came to a stop, the passenger window lowered.

"Throw your gear in the back," Josh said.

Donny pocketed his phone, collapsed the handle on his travel bag, and tossed it, along with the empty duffel bag and his briefcase into the trunk. He lowered himself slowly into the passenger seat.

"Hi, Donny—good to see you." Josh extended his hand and smiled.

Donny gave his brother's hand a quick squeeze, saying, "You're awfully chipper."

"Not chipper. Just haven't seen you in a while."

"Yeah, well, you would've seen me if you'd made it to Mom's funeral."

"Let's not go through that again," Josh said. "How was the hotel?"

Donny repositioned his leg to get more comfortable. "Oh, beautiful. One of La Quinta's finest. Loved sitting around for two days in that dump."

Josh was quiet, his eyes fixed on the road ahead. Donny had been preparing for a lecture about "bad judgment" or "not respecting property." But his older brother never could say what was on his mind. Josh just drove along with an awkward, clearly forced smile plastered on his face. Donny told himself to take his punishment now, before they arrived at the house. He needed to avoid a bad scene that could slow his departure.

"Don't be pissed about me breaking into the trailer," Donny blurted. "I didn't hurt anything. Besides, you said it wasn't your home. Just storage."

"Doesn't mean it's okay," Josh said in a singsong voice, as if he was speaking to a child.

Donny could feel the car's sudden acceleration as they approached Highway 101.

"You told me you were out of town," Donny said. "I didn't want to wait around. I wasn't gonna take anything else. You really should remember to lock all your windows if you're so worried about break-ins."

Donny leaned over to see the speedometer. They were going ninety-two miles per hour. "And slow the fuck down!" he shouted as he pressed his own foot onto the floorboard.

Josh seemed to snap out of a trance as he slowed the vehicle. "Don't worry about it."

"Just yell at me already. I know you're mad."

"I told you," Josh said. "Forget it."

For the next fifteen minutes, they drove along in silence. Donny glanced at his brother every few minutes. While Josh no longer wore the weird smile, a slight row of perspiration had begun to form on his brow.

"You never told me why the cops were at your trailer," Donny said.

"Yes, I did," Josh said, exiting onto Route 84. "It was just a misunderstanding."

"What were they looking for?"

Josh bit his lower lip.

"You have nosy neighbors, Joshie." Donny locked his eyes on his brother. It was fifty degrees outside, only slightly warmer in the car, but Josh was now noticeably sweating.

"Why are you examining me?" Josh asked, looking back and forth from Donny to the road.

"Why do you look so nervous?" Donny asked.

"Nervous? I don't know. Do I look nervous? I guess I'm kinda nervous about reading Mom's diaries too."

"Did you read any of them?" Maybe his brother had already discovered some truths.

"A few. Some of the early ones. Too many to read. I didn't have time."

"Did you find anything about Dad? Did she write about what happened?"

"There are forty notebooks, Donny. I've just been too busy trying to deal with a crisis at work."

"Oh? What kind of crisis?"

Josh made a right onto Oak Grove Avenue in Menlo Park and stopped at a red light. He turned and faced Donny and said, "You're really a piece of work."

Now Donny knew there had to be something else on Josh's mind. The smile his brother had greeted him with twenty minutes earlier was long gone.

Donny watched the neighborhood change from strip malls to small homes, then to larger, more secluded residences. They turned down a long gravel driveway that seemed to go on forever. Josh drove slowly, stopping in front of a beautiful, rustic house, surrounded by a dense cluster of trees.

Donny rolled down the car window. "Very nice, bro," he said. "This is more of what I'd expect from a Silicon Valley big shot. Really freaked me out thinking you were living in a trailer park."

"Let's go in," Josh said as he got out of the car and bounded up the porch steps. "Mom's diaries are inside."

Donny walked to the back of the car, motioning for Josh to pop the trunk.

"We'll get your bag later," Josh said.

"I need my stuff." Donny knocked on the trunk twice. "I have some work things I might have to deal with too."

Josh reached into his pocket and pressed the key fob, then disappeared inside while Donny removed his briefcase and the empty duffel bag. He limped up the stairs and crossed the transom, saying, "I didn't see you as the rustic—"

His feet went out from under him as he was hit below his bad knee, sending a sharp pain up his side. A flurry of arms and legs pounced on top of him. Startled, Donny began swinging his fists wildly, believing they had stumbled into a home invasion.

"Hold him down!" he heard someone shout.

"Stop hitting me, you motherfucker!" cried a second voice, a voice he recognized instantly.

"Louie?" Donny shouted, his heart pounding. "What the hell are you doing?" He stopped punching, trying to see behind him, but was quickly pinned to the ground.

"Pull his arms back," came the first voice. It was Josh's. Stunned by the realization, Donny gave up the fight, and within seconds, his wrists were bound together. He was finally able to twist around to see Louie sitting atop his knees, while Josh wrapped several large zip ties around his ankles.

"You're out of your fucking minds!" Donny yelled. "Take these off me!"

"Let's get him in the back room," Josh said over Donny's protest. They lifted their brother from under his armpits.

"Hold on a second," Louie said. He reached for something on the kitchen table and tossed it to Josh.

Donny kept shouting but was suddenly muffled when Josh secured a piece of duct tape over his mouth, making it difficult to breathe. They dragged him to a dark back room, the only light coming from a single lamp in the corner. The dark brown curtains were tightly drawn. After dropping him into a folding chair, Louie, his face beet red, waved a fist in Donny's face, and said, "You fuckin' son of a bitch!"

Donny tried to speak, to ask what was going on, his attempts completely muffled by the tape pressing against his lips. He struggled to catch his breath, his heart pounding in his chest. Their potential rationales raced through his mind like a rapid-fire slideshow. All of this because of his trailer break-in? This couldn't be about his trolling. Why had his brothers lost their minds?

Once they had him seated, Josh bent down in front of him, face-to-face. "Listen to me, Donny. I need you to calm down. Everything's okay. We're just going to have a nice conversation here—"

Louie pushed his way in and shook his fist again, saying, "Unless you want to delete your fuckin' ransomware right *now*!" The stench of beer forced Donny to turn his head away.

"Louie, that wasn't the plan!" Josh shouted.

Louie slumped into another chair and looked at the floor, his face going from red to purple.

What ransomware? What the hell was Louie talking about? Donny looked around the darkened room full of miniature cameras, wires, and speakers. He tried to talk again but could only manage a series of groans. Josh sat down at the desk and flipped open a laptop and started typing. Suddenly, a humming sound came from the speakers, followed by a voice. A distinctive, elderly, female voice, with an unmistakable Brooklyn accent.

"Hello, boys. It's good to see you all together."

Donny's eyes widened as he looked back and forth from Josh to Louie. A recording of their mother? Something they'd made before she died? But with the next words from the speaker, he knew this was no recording, her voice jolting him as if he had been hit with ten thousand volts of electricity.

"But why is Donny tied to that chair?"

CHAPTER
THIRTY-TWO

JOSH ADJUSTED the shades and switched on the recessed lights. Donny was slumped back, quiet, maybe in shock from what he had just heard. Louie sat on the other side of the room, nervously tapping his foot.

Josh glanced up, speaking toward one of the miniature cameras in the corner. "It's Josh. Can you hear me?"

"I know who you are," came their mother's voice from the speakers. "And I hear you fine."

Donny straightened, his eyes suddenly alert but bewildered, a muffled moan coming through the tape covering his mouth.

"I asked why your brother is tied to that chair," she said. "What did he do this time?"

"See, asshole," Louie said to Donny, his words slurring. "She's figured it out already."

"Watch your mouth, young man," she said. "You're not too old to have your mouth washed out with soap."

Louie started laughing, but Josh shot him a stern look. Louie placed a hand over his mouth.

"Now remove that tape from Donny's face," she said.

"It's for his own protection," Josh said, fascinated by the effectiveness of CHERL's new vision. Naveen had outdone himself. "We'd like him to just listen to us talk for a while, if that's okay with you. He'll be fine like that, right, Donny?"

Donny was silent, unmoving, his eyes conveying both fear and confusion.

"*Thaz* better," said Louie, keeping his hand over his face to conceal his smirk. "See, Mom? Josh is right. He's fine. Don't worry 'bout him."

"Don't tell me not to worry about him, Louie," she said, her tone sharp. "And why are you slurring your words?"

Louie stopped smiling and leaned back. Josh rolled his eyes and said, "It's okay. Louie didn't mean anything. He's worried about Donny." Josh turned to Donny. "We're all worried about you. We want to help, but you have to help us too."

"'Cause we don't understand how you can try to extort money from your own brothers," Louie said, adding, "You fuckin' asshole."

"Louie!" Josh shouted. He lifted his youngest brother by the shirt and pulled him into the hallway, shutting the door. "What's wrong with you?" Josh whispered through clenched teeth. "We had a plan!"

Louie placed his hands on his head, whispering, "Fuck him."

Josh smelled the stench of beer. "How many did you have already this morning?"

"I'm fine," Louie said. "I'll be fine. *Lez* get back in there."

Josh grabbed his brother's shirt again. "Louie! Come on, man! Straighten up! She's watching you. Listening to everything we say. No more crap about the hacking until we're deep into the dialogue."

"I got it, I got it," Louie said. He pushed past Josh and reentered the room.

"What's wrong with all of you?" she said when Josh returned. "Why is Louie so upset?"

"Sorry," Josh said. "We're all right. We're just here to help Donny. Right, Louie?"

Louie dropped to the folding chair and gave a thumbs-up.

"But I'm sure this is all very shocking to Donny. He may not believe you're really here. Would you mind if we just start with a few questions?"

"Questions?" she said. "About what?"

Josh started as he did every AI session, with some basic baselining facts. "Let's start with your name and birth date."

"You never did remember my birthday, Josh," she said.

"Of course I do. I'm just trying to make sure we're all working from the same knowledge base."

"Okay. I'm your mother, Ruth Brodsky. I was born on March 3rd, 1940."

"And who and when did you marry?"

"I married Joseph Brodsky on June 12th, 1960."

"That's great," Josh said. "And Mom, when did you die?"

"I died last week, on March 17th."

Louie raised his palms in a questioning manner. Josh mouthed, "From public records"—one of hundreds of external files and databases Naveen had culled, based on Ruth Brodsky's profile. As Josh scribbled notes, he could see that Donny's breathing had become more rapid. His brother had better not suffocate before they were through.

"Just a little more baselining, Mom," Josh said. "Tell us about your childhood. About your parents."

"My parents," she began. "My parents were tough. You boys thought I was tough on you. You had it easy compared to what I went through."

Josh thought he detected a sneer in her tone. "Did you get along with your parents? Were you a happy child?"

"Happy? I never thought about my childhood as a happy time. It was a rough time for me. My parents never thought their job was to make me happy."

Josh motioned toward Louie, who was leaning back, appearing uninterested. "Louie, what do you want to ask?"

"Uh, yeah, Mom," Louie said, a sarcastic emphasis on *Mom*. "So what made your parents so tough?"

"What made them tough, Louie?" she asked. "I was the only girl in a house full of men. My father was the king. If you stepped out of line, he was quick with the back of his hand."

"Our grandfather hit you?" Josh asked.

"My father hit all of us," she said. "Whose father didn't in those days?"

"How about your mother?"

"My mother was totally subservient," she said. "Whatever my father said, that's the way it was. That's the way it was for that generation, back then. Women had no say. Women had no influence. I promised myself, I'd never be like her. That would never be my way of life."

Josh recalled bits and pieces of his mother's childhood story, anecdotes about growing up in an Orthodox Jewish household. She never expressed any real sentiments about what it was like, or how she felt about her life or her parents. To Josh, hers was just a series of bland stories. Whenever he questioned, pushed her to explain, her refrain was consistent: "That's just the way it was." But she obviously had no reluctance sharing these thoughts and emotions with her diary.

"I was a straight A student. A good girl. When I was young, I was the girl my parents expected me to be."

Donny was motionless, apparently mesmerized by her tale, while Louie was glassy-eyed, slumped in his seat. Over the next half hour, their mother pieced it all together, transporting them back in time. She told them how she'd spent her childhood, appearing to her parents as the good, obedient daughter. She helped with the household chores. She was polite. She was deferential to her father and submissive like her mother. She proceeded through her early teens, which was when she slowly started to show her rebel side. Silently, at first, with small acts, always out of sight of her parents.

"My friends and I. We smoked cigarettes in the alley-ways, ate non-kosher foods. My parents never knew. I lied to them about everything."

She lied about everything. This was quite an admission, Josh thought, unsure how much of this was from the diaries and how much was CHERL's inference engine at work. More important, what was Donny thinking? Josh thought he would let this all sink in when she continued, "There was only one place I could be myself. Only one place I could say whatever I wanted. What I really felt. Only one place where I could tell the whole truth."

"Where was that?" Josh asked, expecting her to reveal a special high school group or secret club.

"It wasn't actually a place," she said. "It was when I wrote in my diary."

Donny's eyes widened, and he squirmed, trying to sit up, struggling again with the twist ties.

"It was my liberation. My salvation. My diary was… my confidant!"

A sense of excitement coursed through Josh when he saw Donny's reaction. These weren't stories she created to entertain herself. She wrote her truth.

"I could tell it anything—anything I did that my parents couldn't know about. Going to the movies. Hanging out with non-Jewish boys."

"Hmmmm. Hmmmmm," Donny moaned, pulling on his ties so violently that his chair made a deep scratch on the oak floor.

"Calm down, asshole," Louie said. "Be a good boy and you'll get your chance."

"The movies?" Josh asked as he scribbled more notes.

"The movies," she continued, Donny now still. "We were not allowed to see movies. My father thought the movies were improper, that they would mold the way his children would think, away from religious teachings. At that point, I really didn't care if my parents found out, but they never did. I had a friend, and we'd sneak into the movies all the time."

Josh motioned with his hand to get Louie to engage.

"Uh…" Louie said. "How old were you when you started doing that?"

"Nineteen," she said. "I was frightened the first time, but it was so exciting. We saw *Cat on a Hot Tin Roof*. Paul Newman was wonderful. After that, we saw so many movies. Elizabeth Taylor, Joanne Woodward, Marilyn Monroe. All so beautiful. So glamorous. Strong women. The movies were my door to the world they lived in. The world I wanted to be a part of."

"Keep going," Josh said. "So your parents didn't approve of you seeing these movies?"

"They never found out," she said. "That was a good thing. I can't tell you what they would have done, but they never found out."

Louie pointed to the computer for Josh to mute the microphone and join him in the hallway. "This is unbelievable," Louie whispered once the door was shut, but Josh could tell this was feigned excitement. "I think Donny Boy is sold. Let's make the trade."

Josh understood that he still had two brothers to sell on CHERL's reality. "Not yet," Josh whispered. "It's still early. Let's keep going. There's plenty more to cover. At least we know Donny wants to hear about her dating habits."

"Come on, Josh. It's getting late. We've been going at this for almost an hour. We don't have to go through her whole fuckin' life story."

"Just a few more hooks," Josh said. "Did you see him go crazy when she talked about dating non-Jewish guys."

Louie scratched his head and said, "Yeah, I guess that was the one thing he told me he read about."

"We'll save that for later," Josh said. "Let's keep this going. See what else he's interested in."

From inside the room they heard her voice. "Donny, where did your brothers disappear to?"

"We should go back in," Josh said.

"How 'bout we fast-forward a bit?" Louie asked. "To where we're all part of the story?"

Josh whispered, "Okay. Let's just stay away from talking about Dad for now."

Louie gave a thumbs-up and led the way back in. Josh sat and punched a key to unmute the speakers and said, "Sorry, Mom, we're back. Let's—"

"Let's talk about us as kids," Louie interrupted. "Maybe some things we didn't know." He looked at his oldest brother. "What was Josh like as a kid?"

Josh glared at Louie, who shrugged and whispered, "Just trying to get this moving."

"You were quiet, Josh," she began. "Always brilliant. Always stayed very much to yourself. Funny thing, you started speaking at an early age. Babbling at first, then real words and sentences. You talked all the time."

"Josh was a talker?" Louie said, smirking. "Who would've thunk it?"

"But then, when you were around four, things changed."

"What changed?" Louie asked.

"He stopped speaking so much," she said. "At least to me. To us. It was like he put on a protective shell."

Josh shifted in his chair and stared at the floor as he rubbed the scar behind his ear. He didn't want to make these sessions about his own childhood. There was no point in dredging up his own past. He had sealed off that part of his life a long time ago, determining at a young age how to deal with the outside world, making sure no one could hurt him. He now needed to quickly regain control of the conversation—to change the topic, explore areas more important to Donny. But something stopped Josh from interrupting, held him back from saying the words that would send her off in a new direction. A curiosity he hadn't expected. Both of his brothers were staring at him.

"Protective shell?" Louie asked. "What was he protecting himself from?"

"Well, from your father, of course," she said. "But Josh, you didn't need to worry. I knew he would never hurt you again. Not as long—"

"Whoa!" Louie shouted. "Hold on. What? Dad? He never hurt us. At least not physically. You were the disciplinarian. That's the way I remember it." Louie turned to Josh. "What is she talking about?"

Josh felt behind his ear again, the eight-inch scar permanently elevated. Interesting how quickly she went to that day, he thought. He didn't remember much. About what got his father so mad that he threw him against the wall. So mad that his father busted his head wide open behind his right ear, the wound a lifelong reminder—a warning—for him to steer clear of his father, which he did until the day Dad died. Josh could talk about it now. Why not? She couldn't hurt him. No one could hurt him.

"How'd you know he would never do it again?" Josh finally asked.

"Because I told him that if he ever hit you again, if he ever laid a hand on any of you—on any of us—I would kill him."

"Holy shit," Louie whispered, glancing at Josh.

"I was so angry, I almost took you and Donny and left on the spot," she continued. "I had already lived through my own father's crazy temper. I wasn't going to watch it happen again."

"I never knew any of this," Louie said to Josh.

"It was before you were born," their mother said.

"What did Dad do to you?" Louie asked Josh.

Josh had never spoken about the incident, not even the faint memories of his baby brother crying next to the crib. Not about his father's fury.

"Why didn't you?" Josh asked his mother, ignoring Louie's question. "Just take us and leave?"

"He begged me," she said. "He begged me not to leave. He said it would never happen again. But I should have left him. Things were already no good with us. I could have gone too. I wanted to go."

"This is crazy," Louie said, rubbing his eyes.

"I was afraid," she said. "I don't know of what—just afraid. He stayed away from you, Josh, after that, so I thought everything would be okay. And you stayed away from him too. You kept company with your books. That's pretty much how you were until you left for college. It was like you both knew that being together would lead to no good."

She paused.

Josh felt unnerved by CHERL's version of events, but he pushed himself to focus, as he always did, to regain control of his emotions. A practice he had honed throughout his life. But as hard as he tried to concentrate, a question nagged at him.

"Why did Dad get so mad at me?" he asked. "What did I do?"

"Wait," Louie said. "You don't know?"

Their mother didn't respond.

"*Mom!*" Josh said, sharply.

She began, slowly, almost hesitantly. "I left you in the bedroom together. You and Donny. You would sit and play with your puzzles while Donny took a nap. I was in the kitchen making dinner. Donny was colicky so I needed that quiet space when he napped. You were easy, Josh. You always stayed in the bedroom with your baby brother while he napped. I never worried about leaving the two of you alone, until…"

She paused again.

"Your father came home from work early. We heard Donny crying in the bedroom. Your father said he would go to him while I warmed a bottle. That's when I heard all the screaming. When I came in, you and Donny were wailing, your father was yelling. There was so much blood on your face, Josh. But Donny was okay. Just a bruise on his head. I held you both, and we rushed to the hospital. Thank goodness you only needed stitches."

Josh felt the scar again and asked, "What did he say I did?"

"Donny was fine," she said. "He was just scared."

"What did I do to him?" Josh asked.

"Your father said that when he came in, you were in Donny's crib, and Donny was on the floor, crying. He had a large welt on his head, but he was fine. Your father flew into a rage. He was so protective of Donny from the day he was born, but I had never seen that side of your father before. He must have thrown you so hard that you cut your head on the corner of the wall."

Josh had no memory of doing anything to Donny. He wondered whether this was really how things had happened, or whether it was CHERL's inference engine at work. His only indelible memory was of his father, whose presence would forever elicit a fright in him so intense that he had to turn away every time he entered the room.

"I always thought it was an accident," she continued. "You wouldn't hurt your baby brother. You were always happy to play alone in your room. Reading by yourself, even at a young age. But your father always protected Donny." She paused, then said, "Josh, you just weren't the kind of son your father wanted. I think that had a lot to do with what happened."

Josh stood and parted the curtains, staring into the woods, trying to clear his mind. It had to have been an innocent accident, a child's idea of horseplay, and an overreaction by a volatile father. What reason would there have been for a four-year-old to hurt his infant brother?

Josh wondered what his therapist in DC would have said about all of this. But that was for another time. He had had enough for now. He hadn't planned for this to come up, but he hoped it demonstrated CHERL's authenticity —to both Donny and Louie. And her inability to hide the truth, even if it might have been inferred by a super-computer.

He was about to pull the tape from Donny's mouth when she continued. "We had so much trouble conceiving you, Donny," she continued. "I think that explains part of your father being so overprotective. We had tried and tried for years. I didn't know what was wrong. But after a while, I didn't care if I ever became pregnant again. Your father used to say I wasn't trying hard enough, as if I could do this on my own, or I could do more than he could."

She paused.

"Mom?" Louie said. "Are you still there?"

"So I tried harder. Then I got pregnant with Donny."

Donny tried to speak again, managing only an animal-like grunt.

"Quiet down, Donny," Louie said, holding his hands out, anxiously whispering to Josh, "Quick break?"

Josh looked at Donny, who appeared to be in a trance, exhausted. This needed to be over soon. It was time to get Donny to remove his malware, decrypt the files. "Okay," Josh said. "Five minutes."

When Louie stood and said, "Mom, when we come back, I want to talk about me," Josh knew that his youngest sibling was now a believer.

CHAPTER
THIRTY-THREE

LOUIE TWISTED the top off a beer and took a long swig, the cold brew calming his nerves, while Josh stared out the kitchen window. Three more gulps and he tossed the empty bottle into the sink, making a loud clatter.

"I think you've had enough," Josh said.

Louie removed another beer from the refrigerator. The past hour had left him shaken, second-guessing his own memory of his mother's death and funeral. He knew she was dead. This wasn't really her—CHERL was just a fabrication. A technological re-creation, he kept reminding himself. Their only purpose was to convince Donny to admit what he did and unlock the encryption of Virtual Bank's customer files. Louie would be on the first flight back to New York, to close his deal and replenish his finances. Donny and Josh could then finish any conversations by themselves. They could explore every nook and cranny of their parents' lives, for all he cared. Find out whatever they wanted to know. Once VB's files were decrypted, Louie planned to be long gone.

But Louie could not deny or fight the gravitational

pull coming from that room. In life his mother would never discuss the past. If this CHERL thing was revealing her truth, this could be his final chance to find his own answers.

"Was that all real?" Louie asked. "The stuff about you and Dad?"

Josh continued staring out the window. "I don't remember what happened. If she says it did, then it was real."

"Jeez." Louie had never seen their father's violent side, at least not physically. Any spankings were doled out by their mother, but nothing like what he had just heard. "A lot went down in our house."

"Look, I can take whatever she has to say," Josh said. "What's important is that Donny is reacting to our conversation, right? We can see the areas he wants to probe. I think he's ready."

"Hold on," Louie said. "I have a few things I want to dig into first."

"An hour ago, you were ready to make the trade."

"I know, I know…but…we might only get one shot at convincing Donny."

"We can't keep him tied up much longer, Louie. What are you thinking?"

Louie looked down and shuffled his feet. "I don't know…something. Something to prove your story wasn't just planted. That it wasn't a fluke."

Josh came over and placed a hand on Louie's shoulder. His big brother gave him a knowing look. "Is there something that you never got a chance to ask Mom?"

Louie didn't look up when he said, "Maybe."

"And you're okay if we're all in there with you?"

Louie walked away and placed the half-full beer bottle in the sink. What happened thirty years ago was between him and his mother—a secret they had agreed to keep, especially from Josh and Donny. He had kept his end of the bargain all these years, never divulging anything. But now, no matter how real she seemed in that room, their mother was dead. Why shouldn't his brothers hear what she had to say? It was now or never.

"Let's get back in there," Louie said.

When they reentered the bedroom, Donny's eyes were closed, his head tilted to the side.

"Donny!" Louie shouted. Donny's head snapped to attention, his eyes foggy.

Josh punched several keys on the computer. "We're back, Mom," he said.

"I don't like the way Donny looks," she said. "I want you to untie him."

"Soon," Josh said. "I promise. Not much longer. Let's just finish this first. Louie?"

Louie leaned on the back wall, gathering his thoughts.

"Mom," Louie began. "I want to take you back to those years after Dad died. But before we go there, I do have one question."

"Yes, Louie?"

"You said things were not good with you and Dad after what happened with Josh and Donny."

"No, they weren't," she said.

"You said that you wanted to leave him, but you didn't."

"That's right, I did want to leave him. He begged me to stay."

"Right, you said that already. I understand. But if the marriage was so bad, why bother having another child?" Louie looked up at the corner lens. "Why did you have *me*?"

She didn't respond at first. Then she began, her pace

slower than earlier, her inflection flatter, as if trying to carefully choose the right words. "You're right. After your brothers were hurt, things were not good between us. He was either working or on the ball field with Donny, and that was fine with me. I had my own life too. We lived under the same roof, slept in the same bed, but we weren't together much. Not in that way." She paused. "I certainly never wanted another child. Not with him."

Louie felt a sudden pain in his side, like he had been punched in the ribs.

"I had so much trouble getting pregnant with Donny, I never thought it could happen again. But I only gave in to your father that one time. It was a stupid mistake."

A mistake? Louie glanced at his brothers but quickly looked away and walked to the window. He pulled the curtain back and chewed on his lower lip, feeling like that small, insecure child all over again.

Then she continued, her tone softer, the words flowing more freely. "You were a very sweet child, Louie. I loved you. But I felt bad for you. Your father was so focused on Donny. Always with his ball games. Your father said he could tell you didn't have the same talent as your brother."

Louie kept staring out the window, saying, "I don't remember him ever trying to teach me much. The way he did with Donny."

"He did, maybe until you were about six. He said he knew very early. So I guess, using your language, he doubled down on Donny."

"Doubled down," Louie repeated to himself. She did remember. He again peered out the window, his reflected image shaking him back to the present.

"You wanted to be with them too. You wanted to be just like Donny, but he didn't really want you around much. That didn't stop you from trying. When you were younger, you were always trying to chase Donny around."

She paused again. Louie walked toward a corner camera and firmly looked into the lens, puffing out his chest, ready to get it all out. "I had some other talents, though, didn't I?"

"I didn't think so, at least not when you were really young. It wasn't like you could, or even wanted to be like Josh. You didn't particularly like elementary school—I think you were bored most of the time. Watched a lot of TV. Always had trouble concentrating on homework. But that changed after…"

She stopped.

"Are you still there?" Josh asked, punching keys.

"She's there," Louie said. He recognized his mother's avoidance tics.

Josh rapidly moved his fingers across the keyboard. "I don't know what happened."

"Mom," Louie said. "We're gonna talk about Dad's accident later." He nodded toward Donny, who was slumped over but alert. "We'll save that for Donny if he's a good boy. But let's talk about what happened after Dad died. About what happened to me."

Another moment and the speakers hummed. Josh removed his hands from the keyboard, and she started up again. "When your father died, I worried about you as much as I did about Donny. I just about gave up on your amounting to anything…"

Louie turned his palms up and said, "It's okay, Mom."

"I was just going to say how everything changed when we found out how good you were with numbers. I was so proud of you, winning all that money. You saved our lives."

CHAPTER
THIRTY-FOUR

DONNY'S HEART rate had finally slowed, but his hands were numb, his mind entangled with the cascade of events and revelations. Of one thing he was certain; Josh and Louie wanted him to believe in whatever this was, and that it, or someone, was watching them. Someone who had obviously not only read their mother's diaries, but who had also memorized them, internalized them. Become one with them. This could not be his mother, he kept reminding himself. He had seen her body at the funeral home, watched as her casket was lowered into the ground. He and Louie took turns shoveling dirt into the grave. Yet Donny shuddered every time his mother's high-pitched, nasal Brooklyn accent burst into the room. What had Josh done?

She was different in one stark way. His real mother had been a keeper of secrets, the biggest being the truth behind his father's death. But now the depth, and brutal honesty, that this version was willing to share was jarring, just like the one diary he had managed to read back in New York. Josh and Louie wanted him to believe in this portrayal, and they wanted him to stay and listen. Why else tie him down like a hostage? So listen he did, as whoever, or whatever, was on the other side divulged things that Donny had never known. And unless Louie and Josh were putting on the performance of their lives, they were ignorant as well. While he tried to tell himself every few moments that it was an elaborate deception, he found himself pulled in, continually glancing toward the bedroom door, expecting his mother to enter at any moment.

After she'd detailed her childhood and relationship with her parents, she'd come to the part in the diaries that he was very familiar with…

"Going to the movies," she'd said. "Hanging out with non-Jewish boys."

"Hmmmm. Hmmmmm." They *did* use the diaries! Donny tried to speak, only creating more moaning sounds, ignored by his brothers. "Ask about her friend Tommy!" It must be *him*! He started pushing his chair with his feet.

"Calm down, asshole," Louie said. "Be a good boy and you'll get your chance."

Donny stopped struggling, the zip ties cutting into his wrists and ankles with each movement. As his brothers delved into their own pasts, Donny found himself suspending his disbelief, transporting himself back to his childhood. He leaned back, steadied his breathing as best as he could, and waited.

"I was so proud of you, winning all that money," the voice had told Louie. "You saved our lives."

Donny looked at his younger brother, who slumped over, burying his head in his hands.

"When your father died, Josh, you were already at MIT, and a year later, Donny, you moved out and got the job at Kings Plaza. I was desperate for one of you to live at home with us and help out with the money. But Josh had another year of college, and Donny, well, by that point, you were just wrapped up in yourself. And you never believed me about your father, did you? You wanted to get as far away from me as possible."

Donny closed his eyes, recalling his anger all those years ago, feeling it return to him now.

"Forget about that," Josh said. "What was that about winning money?"

"I didn't know how we would manage. We had very little money. I worked, but I never could hold on to a steady job. I didn't like being told what to do. I guess the bosses reminded me of my father. Then an old friend had an idea. He said they were looking for a place to hold their card game."

Donny glanced at Louie, whose head was still in his hands.

"All the places they used to play had been busted too many times. He thought the police would never come looking in our apartment, and I would get paid just by being the host. It seemed pretty simple to me."

"Wait," Josh said. "These were just guys from the building playing some friendly poker, right?"

"They weren't from the neighborhood. They lived in Bensonhurst. And the games were not so friendly. They played for high stakes. Sometimes very high stakes. But I didn't mind. The higher the stakes, the more they would pay me at the end of the night."

A long silence followed. Donny leaned forward, studying Louie's face, but his brother was staring at the floor. Josh sat in stunned silence.

"Things got a lot better for us after those games," she

said, "especially when you started playing with them, Louie. And winning all that money."

Not a chance, Donny thought. Even their mother wouldn't let a teenager gamble with men. But all doubts disintegrated when Louie, rubbing his eyes, asked, "When did I start joining the game, Mom?"

"Just a few weeks after it started. I didn't see the harm in it. The men thought it was funny, at first. My friend staked you a little money, and I think by the end of the first night, you had fifty dollars. That was a lot of money back then."

"It came pretty easy to me," Louie said.

"I thought so too. I know they were letting you win, at least at the beginning, another way for them to put some money in our pockets. But after a few weeks, they taught you how to play on your own. They said you were calculating odds in your head or counting cards—I didn't know what that meant."

"You let them hook me in pretty good," Louie said.

"All I knew is that they paid me for using the apartment, and you were bringing in good money on your own."

Donny could not believe what he was hearing. Another one of his mother's secrets, except this time involving Louie.

His younger brother, his eyes still cast downward, asked, "Did you ever worry what the impact would be? Letting a young teenager gamble with grown men?"

"I wanted to stop you," she said. "But my friend said playing cards would build your confidence."

"Confidence?" Louie repeated, his face contorted into a sneer. "You let me gamble to build my confidence?"

There was a long silence, then she said, "Before that, you never excelled at anything."

Louie shook his head. "Excuse me?"

"Before your father died, you lived in the shadow of your brothers. Josh was the brilliant academic, Donny the star athlete. What did you have? But playing cards with those men—they did build you up. They showed you how to be great at something."

Louie rubbed his head in his hands.

"Don't look like that, Louie. It was not a coincidence that your grades started improving right around that time. Not just in math—in every subject."

Louie snickered.

"I never knew anything about any of this, Louie," Josh said. Looking at Donny, he asked, "Did you?"

Donny shook his head. He had always assumed his dad had left some money behind. He never imagined this was how his mother and Louie had got by.

"Mom made me swear that it'd be our secret," Louie said. "You think she wanted anyone to find out? Especially the two of *you*?"

"You didn't play poker with these guys all through high school, did you?" Josh asked.

"You heard her—we needed the money." Then, turning to face Donny, Louie added, "I don't remember either of *you* helping out."

Donny's eyes broke away from his brother.

"They didn't help out," she said. "My heart was broken for you, Louie. Everyone disappeared from your life. I was overwhelmed. Tommy and his friends were there for us when there was no one else."

Donny's heart jolted. Tommy? That couldn't be the same friend. The same Tommy that she'd pined over in the single diary he had pilfered from Maggie's closet? The Tommy who left her behind for a life in California? How was she still in touch with him all those years later?

Donny tried to move his mouth to free himself from the tape, desperate to ask his own questions.

Then she said, "But I did put a stop to those trips to the racetrack."

"Wait," Louie said, looking up at the camera. "How'd you know about the track?"

"You think I was blind? Of course I knew Tommy took you."

"Tommy said the track would be our secret," Louie said.

Josh mouthed, "Who's *Tommy*?" Donny wanted to tell him. Tell them both.

"I knew about it," she said. "Tommy said he wanted to show you how to make real money, but I told him to stop. He said you were more suited for poker anyway because you had a head for numbers. I was just glad you stopped with the horses."

Louie approached one of the cameras. He looked directly into the lens and asked, "Who said I ever stopped?"

"What?" she said, her previously steady volume now several decibels higher. "Tommy kept taking you to the track? Are you telling me he lied to me? *You* lied to me?"

"Don't sound so shocked," Louie snapped. "Best I can tell, you were both pretty good at lying. And he didn't lie to you. He never knew—I found my own way there. I found my own bookies too. There were plenty of characters hanging out at the track willing to take bets, even from a teenager, as long as they got a piece of the action. After a while I didn't even need to go to the track to place a bet. Bookies were everywhere." He pulled his phone from his pocket, waving it at Donny, saying, "Now I don't even need bookies. Online gaming gladly takes my money."

Donny felt dazed, light-headed, as if he was absorbing body blows with each new revelation.

"You shouldn't have done that, Louie," she said, her voice taking on an ominous tone.

"You're gonna lecture me?" Louie shouted. "You thought it *built confidence*, letting me gamble. Didn't you ever think I might not be able to turn it off?"

They heard a sudden click, followed by a humming sound, then silence. Josh typed furiously, calling out, "Mom? Mom, are you still there?" But there was no response.

"She's down," Josh said.

Louie sneered, "Guess she doesn't like the truth so much, after all." He placed his hand on Donny's knee and leaned in. "That's how it started for me, Donny. The hooks were set. Except the bets got bigger and bigger. I won enough at poker to pay my way through college. I didn't do too well at the track though, but I couldn't stop going. Oh, I thought I had it under control back then. I told myself I did. More lies, I guess. And once I started working as an investment banker, well, then I had *real* money to play with. I thought I had put away enough funds to carry me through any dry spell at work. Until gambling on the horses drained every penny I ever saved."

Josh walked over and placed a hand on Louie's shoulder. "I think we should take a break."

Louie pushed his arm aside, his eyes ablaze. "No, enough of this bullshit. I don't care about saving his ass. He needs to hear this."

Saving my ass from what, Donny thought?

"You see, Donny, things have really dried up for me at work. I haven't closed a deal in over three years."

He ripped the tape away, scorching Donny's face from ear to ear.

"Louie!" Josh shouted.

"But you know that system you hacked into?" Louie asked, as he dropped to a knee in front of Donny. "Where you planted your ransomware through that fuckin' boot camp business plan?"

Donny flexed his jaw, trying to let the burning subside. "What business pl—" Donny stopped midsentence as it all came together in rapid-fire succession. *Ana's* business plan? "Ransomware?"

That explained why she disappeared. The flirting, the partnership she dangled—none of it was real. That's why she pushed him to seek investors. To email her business plan to Louie and Josh. He had allowed himself to be used, sending a modern-day Trojan horse. Donny swallowed to suppress the taste of bile in his throat. His voice cracked when he said, "Louie, I…I didn't do it."

"Your target happens to be my payday," Louie said, moving in closer. "The payday I was counting on to get back on my feet." He pointed to Josh. "And Josh here, his company thinks he had something to do with another hack job too. They traced your malware back to his computer. Who knows, we might both get a chance to see the inside of a prison because of you. But you'll be in the cell next to us. I promise."

Donny felt the room spinning, everything out of focus.

"Our tech guys can't clear that shit off our system," Louie said. "Seems only you can. So thanks to you, our worlds are about to get busted wide open. Let me tell you what's about to happen."

"Louie, I—"

"Shh!" Louie stood and pulled his chair next to

Donny. "Just listen first. We're gonna burn Mom's diaries. We'll have a nice bonfire outside."

"You can't do that, Louie," Donny said. "I gotta—"

Louie placed his index finger over his lips. "Then Joshie here pushes the delete button on good ol' Mom. And you mister, are going to jail. You still wanna say you didn't do it? Or do you want to clear your encryption—forget your ransom, go get some help, and get a chance to talk to good ol' Mom here? Get your one chance to find out whatever you want to about how Dad died?"

Donny swallowed hard, his mouth dry as dust. "I'm...I'm sorry, Louie. I...I didn't know. I swear, I didn't. But I know where it came from. She's..."

Suddenly, the silence in the room was shattered by the sound of tires crunching on gravel. A flood of red and blue strobe lights streamed in from behind the drawn curtains. Heavy footsteps pounded on the porch, followed by loud knocks on the front door, and a husky, authoritative demand.

"Joshua Brodsky! It's the FBI! Stop what you're doing and open the door."

"Shit!" Josh said.

More urgent knocks.

"Shit!" Josh repeated.

"Well," Louie said calmly, standing over Donny. "Looks like we're all fucked now."

Then, a female voice from outside. "Josh. We know what you're doing. Please, open the door."

"Who the hell is that?" Louie asked.

"I'm not sure," Josh said. "But I think it's my boss."

CHAPTER
THIRTY-FIVE

"I'M NOT HURT," Donny said. An FBI agent was interviewing him in the kitchen, while Louie was being interviewed by a deputy in the back room. Josh could hear pieces of their conversations from the living room, where Agent Doug Farrell, tall and serious, was trying to comprehend what had been happening. If Jenna hadn't been alongside, explaining CHERL to Farrell, Josh was certain he and Louie would already be in handcuffs and under psychiatric evaluation, with theft of intellectual property and trade secrets leading the long list of allegations. He didn't want to think about the additional charges that could be leveled when they finished with Donny. For now, Agent Farrell was only interested in what they all knew of a mysterious hacker who had attacked several companies, including Sway and the CHERL system, with ransomware.

"Once we had your computer, it took us a while to determine what happened," Jenna said to Josh. She explained how Sway's cybersecurity team had retraced Josh's every computer step—every keystroke—to find the source, a shadow file that vanished on the day of CHERL's infiltration. "Hector Torres called the FBI when he found traces of that file."

"It was a very sophisticated hack," Farrell said. "She really made it look like the ransomware came from you."

"Donny's business plan," Josh said, rubbing his forehead.

"Whatever it was," Jenna said, "as soon as you opened that file, it planted itself on your computer. And once it was there, the hacker was ready. All it took was for you to create the pathway—the first time you signed into CHERL from home, they piggybacked along. After that, the original file vaporized. But not without leaving a small trace that Torres was able to use—a shadow was what he called it."

"We know the hacker's MO," Farrell said. "A Trojan horse is pretty effective, but it can take time and thousands of attempts to strike gold. This time, she found a quick and easy way in, leveraging a weakness in your defenses."

Josh glanced through the open kitchen door at the other FBI agent scribbling in his notepad, trying to keep up with Donny's debrief.

"We came looking for you once we realized what happened," Jenna continued. "The trailer park manager said she hadn't seen you all weekend. Naveen finally told me where to find you, once he knew you were no longer in trouble. At least, not for the hack."

"We thought it was Donny," Josh said, pointing his thumb toward the kitchen. Farrell raised an eyebrow when Josh added, "We thought speaking with our...I mean, we thought we could use CHERL, loaded with our mother's diaries, to...I guess we thought we could motivate him to remove whatever he put on our systems."

"Do you think Donny knew her?" Jenna asked. "The hacker?"

"My partner will find out," Farrell said.

Josh asked, "What makes you think the hacker is a woman?"

"We've seen her operation before, coming out of Chicago. Our bureau had her under surveillance. We know she and your brother were in the same computer class. Good-looking gal. We think she operates out of Portage Park in the suburbs. A lot of Eastern Europeans have settled out there."

"How did she know to go after CHERL?" Josh asked.

"We don't think she did," Farrell said. "She was probably just phishing, working through easy prey—you know, the naive and vulnerable."

Well, she had good targeting skills, Josh thought, peering at Donny in the other room.

"They got Louie too," Josh told them. "His client is Virtual Bank."

"Really?" Farrell said. "A bank? I guess our gal hit the jackpot."

Jenna explained that Torres's team was already working with the FBI to remove the ransomware from other companies hit by the scheme. Releasing locked files and software was relatively easy now that the encryption code had been cracked. "Any business that was hit, Andre wants Torres to help."

The agent who had been interviewing Donny came over and said to Farrell, "I think we're done here."

"What did you find out?" Farrell asked.

"It appears we have a young female hacker. Technically savvy. Very beautiful." Donny joined them as the agent continued. "Mr. Brodsky is voluntarily turning over his laptop so we'll be able to check out his story."

Farrell rose and put his notepad in his jacket. The third agent walked in with Louie and said, "Looks like we have another victim back east."

"I heard," Farrell said. "Look, I need the three of you to stay in town for the next few days."

"You holding us for this?" Louie asked, visibly agitated.

"Not unless your brother here presses charges," Farrell said. Donny shook his head.

"Then I gotta get out of here," Louie said. "I've got that same ransomware on my client system."

"Let me have the contact information for your client," Jenna said. "Our team knows what to do."

"That's tremendous," Louie said, smiling broadly now. As he wrote down the names and phone numbers of Virtual Bank's and Peachtree's IT leaders, Josh could practically see the tension leaving Louie's shoulders.

As the agents departed, Jenna motioned for Josh to follow her to the porch. A cold breeze rustled the surrounding trees.

"Andre told me to have those diaries deleted from CHERL," she said.

"I can't say I'm surprised," Josh said. He assumed their session with the diaries ended the moment he saw the flashing lights.

"I'll be calling Naveen to give him the go-ahead as soon as I leave here," Jenna continued. "Andre's pretty upset. He's not pressing charges, but he wants you fired. I think I calmed him down. I'm trying to get him to agree to some type of probation, or a reprimand, but you know Andre."

"Thanks." Josh hadn't thought much about his future over the past twenty-four hours, but he expected his short stint with Sway was about to come to an end. Still, it would be good to finish what he came to do.

"I can't make any promises," Jenna said. "But I'm trying." She walked to her car, turned around, and waved toward the house. "This was all pretty incredible, what you did here."

"Yeah, well, my brother has been through a lot. I guess all three of us have."

"How did she do? CHERL, I mean."

Josh put his hands in his pockets, bouncing on his toes to stay warm. "With the diaries? We only had a few hours, but best I can tell, she performed...well." Then, chuckling, he added, "I'm glad Naveen did more work on her empathy algorithm. She was a little rough."

Jenna smiled. "I'm not surprised. After all, that was old source code you were using."

"True."

"Did you and your brothers find out what you were looking for?" she asked.

"Not completely," he said.

"How good was the inference engine?"

"It was hard to tell what was in the diaries and what CHERL inferred. We would have to take our conversation further, spend more time studying the diaries, compare CHERL's output to what our mother wrote." Josh shuffled his feet, adding, "But I guess we ran out of time."

Jenna got into her car and started the ignition. Her window lowered.

"You know," she said, extending her phone out the window. "My battery is dead, and I'm pretty sure my charger is broken."

"Do you want to come in for a quick boost?"

"I really should get going," she said. "But I won't be

able to call Naveen right away. So I can't have him delete the diaries until I get back to the office."

Josh stopped shuffling his feet.

"I'm sure traffic is getting pretty bad," she said with a slight smile. "It will probably be an hour before I see him."

Josh nodded. She nodded back, shut the window, and drove away.

CHAPTER
THIRTY-SIX

DONNY AND LOUIE cleared the kitchen table of their half-eaten turkey sandwiches while Josh spoke on the phone with Naveen.

"Just text me when you're about to shut her down," Josh said. He pocketed his phone and gave Donny a thumbs-up.

"Are you ready for this?" Louie asked Donny.

"What more can happen?" Donny asked, wiping mustard from his shirt. "She can't make me feel like any more of a fuckup than I already do."

Louie wrapped his arm around his brother, and they walked to the back room. Hours earlier, Donny had been bound and gagged, unable to move or speak. But entering the room now, he felt even more vulnerable. He swept the zip tie clippings with his foot, forming a neat pile on the side of his chair, while Josh resumed his position by the keyboard.

"We're all set," Josh said. "Go ahead, Donny."

Donny rubbed his wrists, his skin still indented from the bindings. Listening to Josh and Louie interact with their mother had been bizarre, but he had been an observer, as if watching a play or a movie. But the idea of having his own conversation with her made him feel disoriented. He reached back to grab hold of the chair and eased himself down.

"Hi, uh…Mom?" He winced at the sound of the word.

"I'm glad to hear that you can still speak," she said. "And to see that you're not tied up anymore."

"I'm not sure about this," he whispered to Josh.

"Just ask her—" Josh started.

But Louie interrupted. "I'll get her going with a softball." He looked up. "Tell us, Mom, how did Donny spend his time as a kid?"

Josh grimaced and mumbled, "Too far back," but she immediately launched into her stored recollections.

"He always wanted to be playing on the streets with the other kids. The parks, playground—we always knew where to find you, Donny. On the weekends, after school, you would come home for meals, but as long as it was daylight, you were playing somewhere. Everyone wanted you on their team. It seemed like you grew stronger and faster every year. They said you were a natural athlete. I wished you'd spent as much time with your schoolwork, but your father never backed me up on that. He was so proud of you."

She described the teams Donny played on and his father's involvement with each. Donny waited for her to pause, uncertain how to interrupt. Josh seemed to be checking his watch every few seconds, as if warning that they could lose the connection at any moment. But as she continued, mixing in more comments about their father, Donny sensed her pace quicken, her tone more mechanical, as if she needed to recite her prepared remarks.

"Your father was always at your games. As soon as he got home, he'd find you. He wanted to coach you on everything. Sometimes before school, sometimes after dinner—it didn't matter to him." After a pause, she added, "He gave everything he had. At least to *you*."

Donny looked to Josh, whose eyes were focused on his laptop as he motioned with his hand to speed things along. Donny swallowed hard and said, "Mom, I need you to tell me what happened when Dad died."

When she spoke again, her tone shifted; there was an edge in her voice Donny hadn't noticed before. "I didn't think he cared what the rest of us did. He had his world, which revolved around work and you. He didn't realize I had my world too."

"I don't understand," Donny said, impatient with her evasiveness. Knowing he might never have another chance, he blurted out, "Why did Dad leave me so suddenly at the hospital that day? Why did you lose control of the car? What made you hit that telephone pole? Why—"

Josh put his hands up. "Whoa, slow down, Donny. One question at a time. She can't—"

"He thought football would be your life. Your high school coach started inviting college recruiters to see you play. And then your knee was mangled. The doctor came to see you and your father at the hospital. They didn't have the kinds of surgeries that could fix you back then. We couldn't afford it, even if they did."

"What did the doctor tell Dad?" Donny asked.

"Your father was distraught. You were beyond anything he had ever hoped for. He never thought either of our families had the genes for a star athlete. I could never explain it to him."

"Explain what?"

"You never believed me about your father," she said. "The police believed me. Louie and Josh accepted what happened."

Donny looked at Josh and said, "This thing is just as evasive as the real Mom!"

"Maybe it would help if you told us about the car accident, Mom," Louie said.

"That's right," Donny said, his voice rising. "Because nobody saw a car swerve into their lane. Nobody saw a blue Chevy. And none of you saw Dad's expression when he came back to my hospital room after speaking to that doctor."

She didn't respond.

Donny stood and threw his chair against the wall and screamed, "Answer me!"

Still, no response.

Josh said, "Donny, let's try a different approach. Why don't you take us through what you remember about the day of Dad's accident?"

Donny took a deep breath and sat on the floor, thinking back to that day. "Well, I was in my room, recovering from the surgery. I remember waking up and being in a lot of pain. Dad was sitting by my bed."

"Was Mom there?" Josh asked.

"No, I wasn't," she said. "I stayed home with Louie."

"That's right," Donny said, startled that she was engaging in his own recollections. "It was just Dad. The doctor walked in, told me they did what they could, but my football career was done. I broke down pretty hard. Dad was crying too. But instead of leaving me and Dad alone, the doctor asked Dad to step into the hallway. He said he wanted to speak with him in private. Dad walked out of my room. He came back looking ashen, like he found out I was gonna die or something. He wouldn't tell me what the doctor said, just that he needed to step out."

Donny paused. "He said he would be right back. As simple as that. That was the last time I saw our father." He looked up at the lens. "What else did the doctor tell Dad?"

She stayed silent. Donny lowered his head between his knees.

"Okay, Mom, you weren't there," Josh said. "But if Dad didn't tell you, what do you think the doctor told him?"

They waited for her response.

"She's still hiding it," Donny said, his voice shaking. "She's not—"

"He lunged for me, right there in the car. At a stoplight. He put his hands around my throat."

"What?" Donny shouted. Louie sprang from his seat, his eyes widened. But Josh sat motionless.

"I tried to push him off, but I couldn't breathe."

"Jesus," Louie mumbled.

"I felt myself blacking out, but then our car started moving. All I know is, I lost control and we crashed."

"This can't be right," Louie said, extending his hands toward Josh.

"When I came to, there were people all around the car trying to help us. They pulled me out, but your father was trapped. The passenger side smashed into the lamppost. He wasn't wearing a seat belt. The police officer didn't ask many questions. I made up a story about an oncoming car swerving into our lane."

"The blue Chevy..." Donny whispered. It never existed.

"The officer pointed to the red marks around my neck. He told me to use makeup to cover them up, so no one would see. He said he would write it up just the way I told him. I overheard him tell his partner that he knew what it was like growing up with an abusive father."

"Holy shit!" Louie said.

"Why?" Donny asked. "What made our father do that?"

She paused again.

"Mom," Josh said. "We're running out of time. You need to tell him."

Again, she was silent.

"Fuck this!" Donny rose and approached Josh. "Where are the diaries? I'll find it myself."

"I don't think you'll find it in there," Josh said.

"How do you know?" Donny asked.

"It had to be blood type," she said.

Donny turned toward the lens. "Huh?"

"Whose blood type?" Louie asked.

"Your father had given his blood the day before the surgery. I'm sure there was a discrepancy."

"I don't understand," Donny said.

"Coney Island Hospital had my blood type on record," she said. "I had delivered all three of you boys there."

"That's where I had my surgery," Donny said.

She continued. "Your doctors told your father you might need a transfusion during the surgery. I told him I would go to the hospital and give blood but he insisted that it had to be him."

"So he gave blood," Louie said. "What was the discrepancy?"

"My blood type was A," she said.

"Mine too," said Louie. Josh nodded slowly, indicating the same.

"Mine's type O," Donny said. "So?"

"Your father's blood type was AB," she said.

"Okay, what's the big deal?" Donny asked, not remembering much from his high school biology classes.

"He and I couldn't have given birth to a type O child."

Louie said, "There must be something wrong here. Donny, you sure you're type O?"

"He is," she said. "Donny is type O."

"*What*?" Donny paced around the room, his legs trembling, almost buckling beneath him. "What the hell is she talking about?"

"It all makes sense," Josh said.

Donny kept pacing, his head down, his eyes watery. "What are you saying?"

Josh and Louie sat silently.

"He's not my father?"

She didn't answer.

Donny felt as if the walls were closing in, his head about to explode, as he collapsed to the floor. He could hear Josh and Louie tending to him, trying to help him up. But he stayed on the floor, sobbing, attempting to process everything he'd heard.

"Donny," Josh said. "You need to finish this. We're almost out of time."

Donny wiped the tears from his face, and she started again.

"Your father found out. I was worried when he told me he was giving blood, but I couldn't stop him. He came at me in a rage."

Louie and Josh helped Donny sit up while she kept speaking.

"He called me and had me pick him up at the hospital. I knew something was wrong. His voice sounded odd. Like it wasn't even your father. He got in the car and told me to drive. He didn't say anything else, just to pull away from the hospital. When we stopped at a red light, about a mile from the hospital, he asked me."

"Asked you what?" Louie said.

"He asked me who Donny's father was. I knew right away that he'd found out. For once in my life, I didn't try to lie. I always knew this day would come. It had haunted me for years. I was exhausted from all the deception. Exhausted from denying it to myself. It all came out in a flood of words."

"How did you tell him?" Josh asked.

"I told him the truth. Keeping my secret all those years, it was like I was living a double life. One foot stuck in the world I was in, the other in the world that could have been. I never let go of either one. It was actually a relief telling him. Until he tried to kill me."

"So...who is my real father?" Donny asked.

"My high school boyfriend had been in and out of my life for almost thirty years."

"Holy shit," Louie said.

Donny's head sank to his knees. "Tommy?" he said. "Tommy's my father?"

"How do you know about Tommy?" she snapped. "Who told you?"

"Wait," Louie said. "*My* Tommy?"

"I read about him in your diary," Donny mumbled. "I thought he left you for California."

"He did, but he moved back five years later. I hadn't seen him or heard from him in all that time. He found me through Maggie. She had become good friends with Tommy's sister."

"You fuckin' whore," Donny muttered, shaking his head.

"I never stopped loving Tommy. I was shattered when

he left me, and I never got over it. When Tommy came back to me, I wanted to leave your father, but I never had the guts. We made each other miserable. Your father just wasn't the person I was supposed to be with."

"And you were taking all of this to your grave," Donny said.

"I couldn't bring myself to ever tell you, Donny. I just couldn't. I was weak. I never had the courage. I knew it would devastate you. You were never supposed to find out about that part of my life. Maggie swore she would keep the diaries from you."

"Why didn't you just destroy them?" Louie asked. "Why give them to Maggie?"

She paused, then said, "I wanted the diaries to be buried—in the casket with me, but then you boys would know about them. I just knew I couldn't destroy them. They were my memories. How can you destroy your memories?"

"Why didn't you go with Tommy after Dad died?" Louie asked.

"Tommy wanted me to, but I couldn't. I guess it was guilt, after the accident. Tommy tried to take care of me anyway. He thought he was helping me by helping you, Louie."

Louie shook his head.

Josh glanced at his phone. "Naveen just messaged me. This is it, guys. We're about to lose her."

They were all quiet. Donny was drained, but he wanted to say something—this would be his last chance to speak to her. He wanted to call her a liar, tell her that he hated her for taking his father from him for the second time in his life. His mouth opened, but he could not find the words. Instead, for the first time since he had entered the house, Donny noticed birds chirping outside.

A moment later, she spoke. "You were never supposed to find out any of this. It's all in the past. It's over. He was your father. Neither one of us was perfect. I wanted to leave him to be with Tommy, but I didn't abandon any of you, did I? I did what I had to do. I stayed. I made mistakes, but I did the best I could. And I didn't kill your father, even though he probably would have killed me. So stop being so obsessed with the past. Move on with your lives. You're not children—you're grown men! And all you have is each oth—"

The voice stopped.

CHAPTER
THIRTY-SEVEN

SIX MONTHS LATER

"YOUSE GUYS READY?" asked the harried waitress at the Manhattan Beach Diner, where impatient patrons called out from all directions. Josh couldn't take his eyes off her. She was in her late sixties, maybe seventy, certainly not attractive. But every restaurant back in Silicon Valley had tablets with menus integrated into their tabletops. He couldn't recall the last time he had given his food order to a flesh-and-blood waitress.

"How long have you been here?" he asked.

She cracked her gum. "Twenty-eight years."

"I thought so," Josh said, smiling. "You probably served me the last time I was here."

"Maybe," she said. "What'll ya have?"

Donny flipped through his menu. "Let's see…"

She closed her pad and hurried away to grab two plates of food that had emerged from the kitchen.

"You let her get away!" Louie cracked.

"It's okay, I'm not ready either," Josh said.

"Come on, guys," Louie said. "How much more time do you need? I'm starving."

"There's too much to choose from," Josh said. "What's good?"

"Forget the menu," Louie said. "We don't really have a lot of options."

"What do you mean?" Josh asked, as he turned the pages. "I see fish, and fresh turkey, and chicken parm, and—"

Donny chuckled. "Don't you remember? Mom and Dad never let us have any of that. Breakfast and burgers and tuna sandwiches. That's all we could afford."

Josh tossed the menu back on the table, nodding. "Well, this is a day for Mom, so I guess I'll have the burger."

"Me too," Donny said.

"If we can just get our waitress back here," Louie said, twisting around. "You can't ever send these waitresses away."

When she finally returned, Louie quickly ordered cheeseburgers and fries for each of them, iced teas all around.

"Make mine a chocolate milkshake," Donny said.

Josh glanced out the window. It had been unusually warm since he and Donny had arrived in New York the previous day, so the three brothers had lingered at the cemetery that morning, enjoying the bright sunshine.

It had been a beautiful day for a headstone unveiling.

Before driving away, they made sure the small hole they had dug next to their mother's grave site was filled in, the surface smooth. They sprinkled grass seeds Louie had picked up at a nearby nursery.

"It came out nice," Josh said. "The headstone inscription."

"Yep, short and sweet," Louie said.

"Did you come up with that last line yourself?" Josh asked.

"That was my idea," Donny said. "It was something Maggie said to me when I visited her last year. I don't remember much, I was so focused on the diaries. But that one phrase stayed with me. I thought it fit."

"It's perfect," Louie said. "But I made sure Vicki didn't think it was crass."

"Is she doing okay?" Josh asked as the waitress brought the iced teas and tossed three straws on the table.

"Vicki's a trouper," Louie said. "Once she wrapped her head around everything that happened, she was actually pretty supportive. Of a lot of stuff."

"She must be," Donny said. "I can't believe you got her out of Manhattan."

"It was her idea. We're closer to her folks now that we're in Jersey. She even hooked me up with a sponsor at the Bergen County Gamblers Anonymous group."

"That's great, Louie," Josh said.

"Yeah. He's pretty good at talking me down when I get the urge. Vicki's all over my ass too. I can't even play Go Fish with Jessica."

A busboy brought Donny's milkshake.

"How about the job?" Josh asked.

Louie sipped his drink, then said, "Working with Virtual Bank? It's different than I'm used to, that's for sure. I've been managing the integration with Peachtree —getting a chance to roll up my sleeves and do some real work. It's all remote so I get to have dinner with Vic and Jess every night."

"No more Master of the Universe for you," Donny

said as he blew air into his straw, causing chocolate to overflow.

Louie chuckled, saying, "That lifestyle was sucking the life out of me. I just didn't know it."

The waitress brought out their food, and the brothers spent a few quiet minutes chewing their burgers.

"And you?" Josh asked Donny. "How's the teaching going?"

"It's great," Donny said, dousing his fries with ketchup. "I never thought I'd be a good teacher. But there's a huge demand at these coding schools."

"You gonna stay with it?" Louie asked.

"I'm sure trying. I like getting a steady paycheck too. No more feast-or-famine consulting gigs."

"There's a lot to be said for that," Louie said, before biting into his burger.

"Guess that was one positive from Ana. She planted the idea in the first place."

Louie brushed off a french fry that had fallen onto his lap. "I wonder if they ever found her."

Josh put more ketchup on his burger, saying, "I'm keeping close tabs. A guy I worked with has a buddy on the FBI's cyber task force. He says your hacker may be part of an international crime ring. They'll find her."

"It's taking long enough," Donny said through a mouthful of burger. "Man, I swear I never heard any kind of accent."

"Astute as always," Louie said, pointing a fry at Donny.

"Yeah, well," Donny said, "nothing is ever as it seems."

Josh chuckled. "You should try living in Silicon Valley."

"I thought you would be back in DC by now, defending the homeland," Louie said.

Josh knew he had more work to do before he was ready to leave Sway Inc. for good. Not that he had expected to have the chance to stay on the CHERL project, but it turned out that Jenna had more influence with Andre than Josh had imagined. It helped that Josh provided a detailed assessment of their mother's session, comparing her every utterance with the original diaries. His analysis proved that CHERL's inference engine was extraordinary, which Josh had understood as soon as CHERL launched into her dialogue about blood types. He had painstakingly focused on that portion of her diary. Their mother had never written about their blood types in her diaries. And she had never written anything specifically about Tommy being Donny's father. If Naveen hadn't hacked into Coney Island Hospital's medical records, CHERL never would have made the connection.

When Andre saw Josh's report, the Sway CEO begged him to stay, to finish the work. Over the past six months, after introducing Ulysses S. Grant to the current Secretary of Defense, he and Jenna teamed to develop the next CHERL application, one that could change the trajectory of artificial intelligence for the next millennium. DC would just have to wait.

The brothers ate silently for a few minutes. When they were close to finished, Louie looked up at Donny. "Are you planning to reach out to him?"

Donny slurped the bottom of his milkshake. "I'm going to a conference out West next month. I might stop in."

Josh had checked the national databases and found a Thomas Vitola residing in an assisted-living facility in

LA. They specialized in early-stage dementia. He and Louie had been pushing Donny to find out what he could from his biological father before it was too late.

"My offer stands," Josh said. "I can meet you out there. For support. It's an easy flight from San Francisco."

"Thanks, bro. But if I see him, I have to do it by myself."

Josh checked his watch. "Wow, how'd it get so late? We should get going."

"My flight's not for another three hours," Donny said.

"But mine's in two hours," Josh said, searching for the waitress. "I can't risk it."

Louie smiled. "Lunch is my treat. Boy, it's nice to be able to say that again."

Ten minutes later, they walked outside, where a car was waiting.

"Are you heading back to Jersey?" Donny asked Louie.

"Not yet. I'm gonna walk around here for a while. Who knows if I'll ever be back again?"

The brothers exchanged hugs. Donny and Josh tossed their luggage in the trunk, and when they were in the car, Louie tapped on the window.

"Thanksgiving," Louie said. "My house, right?"

Donny gave a thumbs-up; Josh gave a two-fingered salute. When the car pulled away, Josh glanced back at the diner, he assumed for the last time. It didn't look much different than he remembered from when they were growing up, even if it had been renovated many times over since then. Funny how memories worked. Guess you remember what you want to remember. CHERL could help change all of that. You didn't need to bury the past.

The realization made him think about his mother's

headstone, and he smiled. The headstone that looked down on his mother's final resting place, along with the diaries she had always hoped would be buried with her.

RUTH BRODSKY

BELOVED WIFE, MOTHER, GRANDMOTHER

HER MEMORIES LIVE HERE

A LOOK AT BOOK TWO:
ALTERED PAST

Two brilliant but haunted agents plunge into the dangerous world of 21st century technological warfare.

Alina Petrova's mother died of cancer twenty-five years ago. At least, that's what Alina was always told.

Set to launch her career in artificial intelligence, the brilliant and beautiful software engineer learns the painful truth: her parents were Russian spies when her mother disappeared in America.

Desperate to find her mother, Alina poses as a Sugar Baby in Chicago, seducing CEOs and planting ransomware, where she uncovers clues that lead her closer to the truth. With the help of her parents former handler, Alexi Romanoff, Alina pieces together her mother's covert life as a spy—and ultimately discovers Romanoff's sinister intentions.

Now, as the FBI closes in and danger lurks at every turn, Alina must race against time before the Russian plot plunges the world of artificial intelligence into chaos. Will she uncover the secret of her mother's disappearance? Or will she become the next victim in a deadly game of espionage?

AVAILABLE AUGUST 2024

ACKNOWLEDGMENTS

I would like to thank my writers' workshop coach and editor, Chris Belden; my copy editor, Melissa DeMeo; and, of course, all my friends and fellow writers at the Westport Writers' Workshop.

I would also like to thank Rob Zuckerman, a recovery coach at Connecticut Renaissance, who helped me understand the real-life struggles and origins of gambling addiction; Kevin Clark of Content Evolution for his perspectives on artificial intelligence; Dr. Susan Klugman, for her expertise on blood types and genetics; Dr. Robert Young, for his insights on the use of antidepressants with therapy; and Chris Hall, for his perspectives on the investment banking industry.

And special thanks to my very first beta reader, Shirley Ruckhaus, for her insights, her encouragement, and, of course, her corrections.

Marc Sheinbaum grew up in Sheepshead Bay, Brooklyn. He set out to be a writer from a very young age, but like the characters in his stories, life doesn't always turn out as planned. Instead, Marc spent over thirty-five years in business, working for a variety of American companies. Now retired, he spends his time writing and serving on public and non-profit boards. He and his wife, Hildy, split their time between Westchester County and Westport. *Memories Live Here* is his first novel.

www.ingramcontent.com/pod-product-compliance
Lightning Source LLC
Chambersburg PA
CBHW010727250626
47155CB00011B/3589

* 9 7 8 1 6 8 5 4 9 4 1 4 8 *